Through The Backbone Of Night

THE STORY OF HOW ONE NIGHT CHANGED A
YOUNG TEENAGER'S LIFE FOREVER

Phillip G Asher

All character names in the book are totally fictitious and
all names of places are also fictitious.

DEDICATION

This book is dedicated to Linda and Tyler Joseph.

ACKNOWLEDGMENT

Dr. Carl Sagan's TV broadcast program of the series Cosmos Episode 7 inspired me in developing the title for this novel. A special thanks to the late Dr. Carl Sagan.

PREFACE

This is the story of a young teenager living in a small southern Indiana town during 1965 who had his life changed forever after a frightening experience one night. The physical changes he encountered and how he had to adapt to those changes were not what one would expect. Follow along and see how Phillip Marland had to swear himself to secrecy out of fear of his physical changes and our own CIA along with the general public. See how small-town living continuously challenged his way of life.

The names of the characters mentioned in this book are totally fictitious and in no way refer to any other person.

Table Of Contents

CHAPTER 01

A NERD'S LIFE

My name is Phillip Marland, and I live a few miles outside a small town in Southern Indiana. I am 17 years old and a senior at a small high school—Austiana High School.

After a short night's sleep from staying up late, I got up and looked out the window at the beautiful colored leaves on a large Red Maple tree in our yard that was giving evidence of the approaching season. A light fog was infiltrating the air as the early morning temperature was slowly climbing above 10 deg. C (50 degrees F). The radio alarm clock kicks on at 7 am, louder than usual. The song – "House of the Rising Sun" by the rock group-- *The Animals* boomed out – *There is a house in New Orleans, they call the Rising Sun.* I was looking in the bathroom mirror while the song continued and noticed in the reflection a red bump on the side of my face. I think to myself, "What??? Is that a zit on my face? That's just great, getting ready to go to school with a zit that everyone will notice." It was just coming on, so I dare not try to pop it and possibly make it swollen and stand out even more.

I jump in the shower quickly, brush my teeth and shave. After about 15 minutes, I finished and began to put on my clothes, wearing a blue square patterned short-sleeve button-up shirt and blue jeans. All the boys at school wore blue jeans. Then came the task of combing my hair just right which took more time than showering, shaving, and brushing my teeth combined. The radio still booming, now playing *Oh Pretty Woman* sung by one of the greatest singers of today, Roy Orbison.

I faintly heard my mother yelling, "It's 8 am. You better hurry. Why do you have that music so loud?"

I have a makeshift bedroom room in the basement. I quickly trot up the stairs to the kitchen and pour a glass of orange juice.

Janet, my 15-year-old sister added, "Mom is right, that music is loud, and the songs are lousy."

Just before I gulped the juice down, I replied, "Yes Mom, these songs are cool, and the louder they are, the better they sound."

"OK, when you lose your hearing someday, you will know what caused it."

"If I lose my hearing Mom, I love you too much to blame you."

"Don't be late for school. I need to hurry so I can get to work on time. Do you have your lunch card?"

After giving my mother a quick kiss on the cheeks, "Yes, I'm out of here."

My mother is so special to me. She is trying to raise my younger sister and me by herself. My father died about 4 years ago and it has been tough living. She tries so hard to provide us with our needs. She works at the shoe factory, not hard physically but still demanding.

As I walked out the front door, in our gravel drive was my 1962 hunter-green Chevy Impala. It was a few years old but still had some miles to go. It wasn't souped-up and was a 4-door that was not considered a cool-looking car. However, my finances were limited by working part-time at a local grocery store, so I couldn't afford a newer, fancy car. My mother bought it for me so I would have transportation to work and school. This *Old green machine* as I call it served its purpose for me even though it was not a car to attract the pretty girls at school.

As I turned on the main country road to town, the neighbors had this old mutt of a dog that loved to chase alongside the cars when going down the road. The dog was fenced in so he would run along the fence in the yard which was good because I didn't have to worry about accidentally hitting him. Had to get up to about 35 mph before outrunning him. As soon as the race with the dog was over, I turned on the radio and cranked it up, with the pop group -- Four Seasons singing "Walk Like a Man." That song kind of hit home to me. I'm sort of a nerdish, weakling compared to other boys my age. It is hard for me to "Walk Like a Man." Could get beaten up doing that stuff at my school. I had about 3 miles to drive to reach the high school which was located on the outskirts of town.

I pull into the school parking lot, get out and head for the main front door of the school. The enrollment for grades 9-12 was about 350 students. Most of the students were good kids, but there were a few "bad apples." One was Ray Walls, a first-class bully that liked to give students like me a hard time. He was sort of a Basketball star. He was very athletic. He was about 6 ft. 5 in. in height and had a massive, muscular frame. I only come up to his shoulders. However, he wasn't any teacher's star pupil. He struggled to make good grades. He had a couple of buddies who also gave other students a hard time, especially the more academic students (the Nerds). We are called that constantly by Ray and his buddies. Personally, I think they have (shit for brains). However, if I or my friends called them by that phrase, it could likely be a bruised, beaten-up trip home from school. So, most of us keep our distance, keep our mouths shut, and try not to provoke them.

I got out of the car and locked the car doors and began my walk through the main doors of Austiana High school. Yes, good old AHS. I like the school, but it was limited in its subject selection because of being a small school. The school only offered 2 tracts to choose from, Academic or General which included Ray Walls and his buddies, Ron, Jim, and Billy. So, thankfully, I didn't have very many classes with the (shit for brains) gang. But there were some classes that overlapped like History, Geography, and English. My first class was Geography. The hallways of the school were not very wide, so it was hard to avoid anyone walking in your direction. The lockers in sections of 20 were painted in different colors. Some were bright blue, while others were bright red, green, and yellow. Ironically our school colors were black and White.

As fate would have it, walking down the hallway to the geography room, here comes Ray and his buddies. Ray had a tight black T-shirt on enhancing his muscular stature. His buddies, Ron, Jim, and Billy were wearing white T-shirts plus those black leather jackets with the collars of the jackets turned up. I always referred to them as motorcycle jackets. The ones that had pockets here, there, and everywhere.

He barks in a rather ugly tone, "Well, it's Phil the pill." The other boys chuckle.

I gave a reserved reply, "Hello, Ray."

He answers in a demeaning tone, "Are you coming to the big party Saturday night at Jacob's House."

"Yeah! I plan on being there."

"You know there will be A l c o h o l there," purposely wailing out Alcohol in a stretched-out, emphasizing voice. "There probably won't be any milk to serve you NERDS."

"Hey! I drink a beer sometimes." I began to walk away, then I heard from a distance Ray bellowing loudly down the hallway so others could hear, "We wouldn't want any NERDS passing out from drinking one beer or too much milk." More chuckles spilled out from his bully buddies.

Ray continued, "Why don't you stay home, and the party will be more fun." I kept walking, thinking to myself, "Man, I hate that prick."

I kept walking to room 114 where Geography was taught 1st period. I like the class for 2 reasons. First, I like the subject. Secondly, and most importantly, sitting beside me in the next row over to my left was, in my eyes, the most beautiful girl in the world. Her name was Krystin Adkins. She made my socks roll up and down. Yes, I still wore socks; several boys just wore Tennis Shoes or Penny

Loafers with no Sox. We had assigned seats, so it was a great way to start every day of my senior year at AHS.

The geography instructor was Mister Shields. He began discussing why we have seasons on earth at the middle latitudes. Me being a nerd, I was well-read on the subject. It appeared to be my lucky day. Mr. Shields peers across the classroom and then sets his eyes on me.

"Phillip, can you briefly explain to the class why we have Spring, Summer, Fall, and Winter here in Southern Indiana!" I took about 4-5 seconds and began my explanation.

"Well, Mr. Shields, it is a combination of events happening as the earth revolves around the sun. First, the earth's axial tilt of 23.5 degrees from the earth's sun plane stays pointed in the same direction. This is referred to as parallelism of the axis. This causes the sun's direct rays to gradually migrate north and south of the equator. When the sun's rays are north of the equator, the rays are more direct, and the heating is more intense. Our northern hemisphere gets warmer. Also, this causes our days to be longer; having longer daylight hours and short nights causes the sun to be up longer causing more intense heating to be extended for a longer period. Hence, it is summer. The reverse happens in the winter as the sun's direct rays are in the southern hemisphere causing them to be at a lower angle in the northern hemisphere. In winter, we have short days and long nights. That is why our days are gradually getting shorter currently along with a lower sun through the day as we are in the Autumn season. You must also remember that Spring and Autumn are the results of a gradual change from one solstice condition to the other."

After my explanation, I heard whispering by some students "What is this idiot talking about?" However, I saw Krystin look over at me with a slight grin giving me an impressed look while nodding her head agreeing with my explanation.

"You are correct. Good answer." Added Mr. Shields.

Another good thing about today is it's Friday. I was still looking forward to the party at Jacob's house even though Ray and his goons will probably be there. Jacob is friendly to everyone and has a good personality. He also comes from a well-to-do family and a good education is stressed by his parents. After some other questions directed toward other students, the second-period bell rang which sounded like a loud telephone ring.

My next class was typing. Those old manual typewriters can be rugged when you are trying to build up your speed for those wicked timed writings which was a major part of your grade. The typing instructor would give you a page in the typing book to type out on the typewriter and you would type as many words as you could and as correctly as you could in 2 minutes. I sort of had an advantage in typing for two reasons. First, I have small hands for a boy, and second, I play guitar, so my left-hand fingers are very flexible. In fact, I am the fastest boy typist in class. However, it is still difficult for any boy to get an (A) in typing because there are 3 girls in class that can absolutely fly on those old manual typewriters during timed writings. I always welcomed the challenge to outperform those 3 speedy girls, but they could knock off about 80 words per minute without any errors. We spent most of the class period typing and practicing. Your fastest typists were always in the first seat of each row. So, I was in the first seat of my row along with the three-speed demons.

One of those fast typists was the girl that I was developing a crush for – Krystin. Ms. Lathem, our typing teacher gets out her stopwatch and addresses the class.

"Get paper in your machines and get ready for today's timed writing."

I asserted in a low-tone voice toward Krystin and the other two girls, "Get ready girls, you are going down today."

Krystin, who was one of the speed demons chuckles and whispers, "you always say that before every timed writing."

The contest began and I could tell after a few seconds that I was falling behind from the sound of the carriages returning on their machines. I had never outperformed any of those 3-speed demons all year long. We would turn the papers into the instructor and would find out the next day our result. Today appeared to be no different, I was sure that I was about 10 – 15 words per minute shy of their performance. I knew that I was going to be in 4th place again. It was still fun to take on the challenge. In a competition, if you want to get better, compete often against someone better than you. Even though I couldn't beat them, they helped me to get faster and more accurate with my typing.

Around noon, we have lunch in the school cafeteria. After hearing Mrs. Franklin's lecture, the whole hour on Trigonometry, I was more than ready for lunch. I like math, and she tries hard to make it interesting, but some teachers are just boring. In her defense, how can you make Trig exciting? After Trigonometry class, I hurriedly walked down the hall to the cafeteria to get in line early. In front of me was one of my friends Derek Turner, crippled from getting polio, standing in line. He had to wear braces on his legs. Suddenly, Ron, one of Ray's buddies, with his motorcycle jacket still on, shoves Derek to the side and gets in front of him. Teachers usually watch the lunch line to make sure no one jumps the line in front of others. Where are they when you need them? Derek humbly stepped back and let him in. I hate bullies and I'm sure they are not tops on his list either.

When it was time for me to get my food tray with those little compartments to separate your different servings, the cooks would dip the food all dressed up in their white uniforms and hairnets. Most cooks hadn't missed any meals themselves and were usually overweight and weren't going to win any beauty contest dressed in those hairnets. As I moved down the tray line peering through the glass panel that separated the cooks and food from the students, I would begin my little speech.

"Girls, you are just looking so good today and I hear the food is delicious. Mable are you losing weight?" I was hoping to get hefty servings, especially the desserts. My comments still seemed to pay off as the cooks would just smile at me and give me somewhat larger portions.

As I got my tray, I caught up with Derek Turner who was just ahead of me in the line and offered to carry his tray for him. He had difficulty holding his tray and trying to walk at the same time. With Derek being crippled, the trip to the geek table was a little longer than usual. Most of the goons sat at another table which we had to pass by. I could hear humiliating remarks directed toward Derek and me. Billy, one of the goons screeched, "Hey by the time you two nerds sit and eat your lunch, school will be out." Giggles and laughter followed as we slowly passed by their table. I would usually try to sit where I could easily see Krystin. It was easy to place yourself in the right spot because most students usually sat in about the same place every day. Krystin was already eating at the next table. When I sat down, my view of her was perfect.

Cody Lawson, my best friend sat with us along with DeMar Waas, one of 3 black students in the school. Chit-Chat began among us while I was continuously peering over to the next table toward Krystin's position. I would get an occasional glance from her that appeared to be directed right at me, virtually piercing my heart.

Cody asserted, "Phil, you a-r-e still planning on going to the party tomorrow night, aren't you?"

"Yes, Cody, I am going but I have to work at the grocery store, and I hope I don't have to work too late."

Cody added, "Call me when you are leaving, so we can sync up arriving about the same time."

Derek hinted, "I can't dance, but I would still like to go."

I commented, "Jacob is having this party for any classmate at this school."

That is just the way Jacob Evans was. His family was considerably wealthier than the rest of our families, but Jacob didn't make any distinction. He has always been nice to everyone, and I appreciated him as a friend. His father was an engineer at a large company a few miles away in a larger city. Even though he was a senior, his girlfriend, Angela, was a college freshman at Indiana University. Angela was coming home for the weekend. His parents were going to be out of town and Jacob was throwing the party Saturday night for Angela to see as many of her former classmates as possible.

"Hey, Derek, why don't you and DeMar go and just hang out with Cody and me." I urged.

Cody added, "Then it's affirmative; you guys will be there and hang out with Phil and me."

I added, "Be there at 8 pm. Hey, my friend Bobby McGee and his band are playing at the party." Bobby was a small-framed short person that never ran out of energy. He was like a squirrel scurrying about in a walnut tree. I always liked Bobby because he was always willing to give me advice to help me learn to play guitar.

By now, Ray Walls had sat down with his goons. I didn't see who did it, but someone took their spoon full of mashed potatoes and flipped it toward us, hitting Derek on the shoulder and some even landed in his hair. It really pissed me off. However, these guys were looking for trouble, and if you went over and made an issue out of it, you would be playing into their hands. Cody, DeMar, and

I took our extra napkins and wiped the mashed potato splat off Derek. Krystin saw what had happened; she looked at me and smiled as if to say thank you for helping Derek. Finally, the school bell sounded signaling the time for the afternoon classes. It was Friday, and I was looking forward to the big party tomorrow night. I had to work Saturday at the local grocery store. I stocked shelves and bagged groceries. I need this job to help mom with the bills and also give myself a little extra cash. I made every effort to save some money when I could. Going to college was one of my goals.

CHAPTER 02

THE SATURDAY NIGHT PARTY

It is Saturday afternoon, and I just got off work at the grocery store. I'm in my room chilling out while listening to the radio currently playing a Beatles hit – "A hard day's night." While looking into the bathroom mirror, I could see that the pimple on my face had shrunk down somewhat. I have kept dabbing, rubbing alcohol on it every chance I had. I began getting ready to go to the party that was being hosted at my friend Jacob Evans' house. With his parents being out of town for the night, and as teenagers, we like to take advantage of opportunities like this to possibly be alone with a good-looking girl. It was about 7:00 p.m., Saturday evening when I called my best friend, Cody Lawson, to synchronize our arrival time for the party. After a few rings Cody answers. We were driving separately just in case one or both of us might get lucky.

"Hello!"

I responded with a, "Hey Dude! We are still on for the big party tonight, aren't we?"

Cody answered, "Absolutely, I can't wait. Are you sure there are going to be other girls at this party? Do you think Carrie will be there? Jesus, she takes my breath away."

I replied, "I think she will because I think she is coming with Krystin. She typically hangs with Krystin, and you know my feelings about Krystin."

Cody reasoned, "You need to tell her how you feel Dude! When you see her tonight, just go ahead, and tell her that you would like to kiss her right in the face."

"Man, I need to be more tactful than that. Anyhow Cody! Don't hassle me about this; I will tell her how I feel when the timing is right."

Like most nerds, being around girls makes us nervous. I like Krystin and would cherish the moments to "Go Steady" with her and let her wear my class ring, but I haven't been able to get up the nerve to ask. To make matters worse, Ray Walls seems to be hot for her also, and at times, she seems to be attracted to him. I have always wanted to tell her what a total jerk this guy is. She must know how he is. He thinks that every girl in the school should worship him since he is a star athlete, so in his own way, he is popular in school and treats some of the other kids better than he treats the geeks and nerds.

To confirm our plans, I replied, "I will plan on seeing you there at about 8 - 8:30 p.m."

Cody blurs a loud "Right On" then he hangs up.

I still had some primping to do, putting on one of my better outfits, splashing some of my more expensive men's perfume – namely *Brute* on my face, then working diligently with my hair to try to make it succumb and lay the way I wanted it to lay. Finally, I add the domineering gel to the hair. Now, the hair has no chance of getting out of place. It was just a matter of making it do what I wanted it to do while in the back of my mind I was thinking, what would Krystin want my hairstyle to look like? After giving myself a last 2–3-minute look over, it was about 8:30 p.m. and was clearly time to go.

I trample up the stairs from the basement. The advantage of being in the basement is that it has a walk-out back door, and I like being able to come home at night unnoticed if the circumstance arises. I entered the living room in an almost haphazard, clumsy motion where mom was sitting.

"I am heading out mom," as I approached her with a hug and kiss on the neck.

"Be careful driving, absolutely no drinking, stay abstinent with, you know, the girls, and be home by midnight. Promise me, please! You know, I have been seeing some strange lights in the sky at night on occasion and they don't look like any of our military aircraft."

"I know your rules, and I will be home by midnight."

I didn't say outright that I would keep the rules because it is so difficult for any teen to stick to all those rules at the same time. Come on; we have to be realistic here.

As I put on my jacket and headed out the door, I could feel the chill in the air beginning during these October nights. My heart began racing faster from the thought of getting to see and hopefully, talk to Krystin. In the back of my mind, I was hoping not to say anything goofy or stupid.

I get into the *mean green machine* and begin to say, "Come on baby, start-up, it would be a bad time to let me down now." I turn the ignition key and press the accelerator, and that reliable sound of an engine running begins. The radio immediately comes on rather loudly playing the – Ventures instrumental, *Walk Don't Run*. I learned to play guitar and have learned to play that song. It is a fast song, but I love playing it. Jacob's house is about 5 miles away via some back roads dividing the property lines of several farmers. Most of them raise corn or soybeans. Some farmers were already beginning to harvest their crops. The landscape here in Indiana is pretty, with small undulating, rolling hills. I think the Geologists describe this landscape as a series of cuestas... gently inclined rock layers with different resistances to erosion creating the topography of the gently rolling hills. I travel carefully making sure I don't break the speed limit. It is easy for a policeman to hide out in the little paths that the tractors use to get into the farm fields. A speeding ticket is the last thing in the world that I need.

I could finally see Jacob's house in the distance and noticed that there were several cars parked in his parent's yard. The two-story house is about 200 ft. from the road with a long driveway so he had plenty of room for the several parked cars. Jacob is a top student but not very nerdish. He is well-liked by everyone, and he is nice to the school nerds. I think Jacob is a nerd in disguise because he always takes academic classes and is consistent with getting good grades. It makes sense, his father is an engineer and I'm sure he stresses a good education to Jacob. It's nice that it hasn't rained in a while; the yard may be saved from this nightly escapade of all the cars parked on the property. I am roughly guessing that there are 35 to 40 classmates here. I pull in and park beside the other cars, but still must walk at least a hundred feet to reach the house.

As I walked by the other cars, I saw that Cody was already there. As I get closer, I can hear the music pounding louder as I approach. The band was blasting out – *Louie Louie* by the Kingsmen. Jacob had some large speakers that he had put outside which he had connected to the soundboard of the band playing. The base was so loud that I could feel the rhythmic beats vibrating my body as I walked up the steps onto a porch to enter the doorway. It is a good thing that Jacob's house is located off to itself; the closest neighbor is at least ½ mile away. Most houses located out of town like this are separated by large plots of farmland. We always refer to these areas as the "Boonies." The music was so loud I'm sure his neighbors could still hear the music playing, especially if they were outside. Jacob's house had a large Great Room for a living room, and this is where most of the classmates were, and as I walked in, I noticed they had the couch, chairs, and tables all scooted next to the walls, so a large open area was available for everyone to dance if they wanted to do so. There were around a dozen students in the middle of the room dancing. Within a few seconds, Jacob gives me a light tap on my back.

"Hey man, glad you could make it. Several hot babes around."

I respond, "I've noticed."

Jacob adds, "Look across the room," he begins to chuckle, "Who do you see? Yeah! Krystin. Come on man, you know you want her. Go talk to her."

I sputtered, "Quit badgering me Jacob, I'm waiting for the right moment."

My eyes glanced at her; my heart started pounding so hard I thought that it was getting ready to explode through my chest. I immediately began to lose track of time. Her beauty was taking my breath away.

She was talking to some other girls that typically hang out with her at school. Carrie, the girl that Cody is hot after was in the group. Krystin looked stunning, wearing a short tight red dress exposing at least half of her beautiful thighs. Those black 6-inch heels made her stand out and gave her extra height and made her look soooo sexy. Her long brunette hair dangling down just past her shoulders with some nice large curls made her, in my eyes, the most beautiful person I have ever seen. A neat thing about her is she has always been nice and friendly to everyone, even us nerds, and unfortunately, that bastard Ray Walls. If I just had the nerve to tell her what a prick he was.

While I was looking…. No! Gawking at her, she looked at me and appeared to purposefully smile as if she wanted me to know that she was sending a big, friendly smile to me, and me only. It was hard for me to control my nervousness because I was sure the smile was meant for me. My heart was still pounding. Within seconds Ray Walls entered my field of vision and I noticed him walk over and grab her hand pulling her into the dance area set up in the middle of the room. The band was taking a short break and they were playing some pop songs on records at the time. She first hesitated to go when he grabbed her hand, but as he began to pull her harder, she appeared to reluctantly go with him. There were only 3 other couples dancing.

Ray began dancing from side to side, and then she began swaying those beautiful hips rhythmically, hypnotically back and forth to the song which was so appropriate at the time – *You don't Own Me* – by Leslie Gore. I just hope Ray was listening to the words of the song. Her movements were sexy and captivating. She kept some distance away from Ray 2-3 feet as they were dancing while she was hypnotizing nearly every male there. It seemed that all eyes were on Krystin. My subconscious kicks in, *"When she is finished with this dance, go over and ask her to dance."*

Suddenly, Ray pulls her up to him, putting his hands around her buttocks. She instantly pushes him on his chest to escape, but his size and strength keep her close to him, and it takes her a few seconds to get away. I was fuming inside but didn't have the bravery to rescue her. When she does break away from his grip, she walks off the dance floor. There were various barely audible chuckles across the room. When that happened, I could see the anger set on Ray's face. He was not used to being embarrassed. His face turned a glowing red.... a clashing color with his blondish hair. He begins to storm out of the house. As he does, DeMar is standing in the path of Ray's exit. He gets immediately pushed to the floor, spilling his drink, or beer, or whatever he was holding all over him. My subconscious sets in, *Yea! Ray has left the building*. His hangout friends, Ron and Jim follow him out. Jim yells back at the crowd, "Somebody is going to pay."

The band started playing again. They were a good-sounding band called *The Badds*. They kept playing, one song after another. I looked around and saw that Cody already had Carrie cornered. I moved over to a cooler setting on the floor in the kitchen and grabbed a beer. About that instant, Krystin walked in. It was like God had this planned out for me.

She asked, "Are there any soft drinks still available?"

I responded, "Let's see, this is totally a beer cooler. Here is another cooler." I opened it while thinking, *please let soft drinks be in this cooler!* "Here we are, looks like Coke, Pepsi, and Sprite. What would you like to have Krystin?"

"A Pepsi will be fine."

Feeling so thrilled about getting the opportunity to do something for her and maybe strike up a conversation, I reached down well below the ice and pulled out a very cold Pepsi with the ice slowly gravitating down. I popped the top and handed it to her. I was soooo nervous and was thinking, *now is your chance, start talking you idiot.......say something.*

"Hey, sorry about what happened on the dance floor," I muttered.

She responded, "Oh! You saw what happened too? Duh! I guess everyone did. Ray can be pushy at times. He is kind of a spoiled brat."

I was breathing easier now, "You got that right. Some of my friends don't like him."

Krystin begins to halfway defend his actions, "You just have to get to know him; he can be pretty nice."

I'm thinking, *he has never been nice to any of my friends, or me.* Not wanting to say that directly to her and not dispute her statement, I murmur, "Maybe so."

I nervously asked, "Would you care to dance? I promise not to force you to dance like Ray."

"Yeah! I would like that."

I don't consider myself a good dancer, but I can usually get by without embarrassing my partner. Bobby McGee and his band couldn't have played this song at a better time. As we began to dance, they were singing – *Unchained Melody – by the Righteous Brothers.* This was the perfect song to slow dance to. It has been a top seller and a Jukebox staple. The song started ---*"Oh, my love, my darling, I've hungered for your touch"* -- Every word of the song flowed out so passionately as if I was singing these words to her. It felt good to be dancing with her so close and see someone so beautiful lay her head on my shoulder with her glorious hair touching my face. She seemed so relaxed on my shoulder, but she had to feel my heart pounding so hard, and it wasn't beating to the rhythm of the music. With the passionate slow dancing, it seemed as though this moment needed to last forever. Unfortunately, the song ended so quickly. I'm envisioning, *"Oh no, now she is just going over to be with her other group of girls."* Almost immediately the music starts playing another slow, beautiful song – *Don't let the sun catch you crying—by*

Gerry and the Pacemakers, a British group. Several pop hits were published by British bands. The British Revolution in American rock-and-roll was going strong. I think my pal Bobby who was playing bass guitar in the band saw me with Krystin and purposefully had his band kick off another slow song. He had my back.

"Please don't go," my subconscious was pleading as I extended my hand out to her. She extended her hands out to me, and to my surprise, I stepped close to her and put my arms around her waist while she put her arms on my shoulder and clasped her hands behind the back of my neck while gently rubbing my neck. She felt soooo good. The fragrance of her perfume was heavenly. I eased up closer and put my head next to hers; she slowly put her arms around my back and shoulder and rested her head on my chest, her face ever so close to my cheeks. The fragrance of her perfume totally captivated me. Even though this song was a slow song and perfect for a slow waltz, I wanted it to last an eternity.

My mind was wondering, *"Well, this is it, I not only have a crush on Krystin, but now I think I am falling in love. Come on Phillip, come to your senses, you barely know this girl, you can't fall in love with just a couple of dances.* Maybe not, but dancing to "Unchained Melody" can sure increase the chance of that happening. It sure seemed to be happening.

The song comes to an end. I whispered to her, "Would you like to take a walk outside?" I knew Jacob's parents had some wooded areas behind their house and had some very nice night lighting on some pine trees that surrounded a lake on their property. Their property was always neatly mowed and clean.

Krystin responded, "Yes, I could use some fresh air."

"Did you bring a coat or sweater, tell me where you put it and I'll get it for you. These October nights can get a little chilly."

After she told me where her sweater was, I proceeded to retrieve it. I walked by Cody, and he still seemed to have Carrie cornered in the hallway. As I walked by, he glanced at me and secretly gave me a thumbs-up behind Carrie's back where she couldn't see his gesture. I gave him a quick smile and went on to get the sweater. I wrapped the sweater around her shoulders as we began to walk out of the well-landscaped house. There were a few other couples out walking around, but it gave us a chance to at least be partially alone with each other. We walked toward a line of Bradford pear trees extending about 15 – 20 feet up. The pear trees had nice lighting on alternating trees.

Krystin's face turns toward me, and she begins a friendly chat, "You are in my Chem II class aren't you. That was a neat and detailed answer you gave in Geography class on what causes the seasons. I can tell you are well-read."

I replied, "Yeah, I have seen you in there." I watched her walk into the class every day. I wouldn't miss it. "I think you are in my Calculus class also."

She rolled her eyes, "Yes, of course. I really must work hard in both those classes to keep my grades up.

I chimed in, "Ray Walls is in the Chem II class but not in Calculus."

As she stares out in the darkness, she answers, "He really shouldn't be in Chem II; he struggles in that class and just can't keep up. I have tried to help him with Chem II, but after tonight, he was sort of a jerk; I don't know if I am going to help him anymore."

As I looked straight into her eyes, "I can't blame you. You don't deserve to be treated like that. He gives a lot of my friends a hard time purposefully."

"I have seen him shove your friends around before for no reason. He is showing off in front of his friends, mainly Ron and Jim, but he doesn't realize that he is making an ass out of himself to everyone else."

I stretched my hands out, "I know, and it needs to stop."

I noticed that we had walked a good distance from the house and muttered, "We had better turn around and go back."

She agrees, "Yes, let's head back; it is starting to get late."

I looked at her and smiled, "I want you to know that I have enjoyed being with you. I really like you a lot." I was stammering for the right words to say. "You are bright, intelligent, and nice, and did I say intelligent." Come on Phil don't screw this moment up. "And you are smart too." Damn, I already told her how smart she was. She was looking right at me with an unforgettable friendly grin. Finally, my emotions gave in, "And you are sooo beautiful."

With a bigger-than-life smile, she said, "Why! Thank you."

Just then, she stopped and gave me a short kiss on the lips. I got up enough courage to kiss her back which lasted longer than the first kiss. She did not realize it, but she had just put me in paradise with that kiss. I could feel my socks rolling up and down. We were silent for a couple of minutes. I was thinking *"Come on Phil, ask her out on a date. Hurry before you get back to the party."*

I blurted out, "I know this is a little soon, and I wouldn't blame you for saying no, but would you like to go out next Friday night for dinner and a movie." I nervously awaited an answer of *No!*

She responded, "Yes. That sounds like fun. I would like that."

My heart was pounding again. *I have a date with Krystin Adkins. I can't believe it. I must be dreaming; this is too good to be true.*

I nodded, "Great! I will pick you up at 6:00 if that is OK and we can have dinner then go to the outside movie theater. You decide where you would like to eat." The town is so small that her choices are narrowed to about 3 different restaurants.

We began our slow walk back and she took her hand and grabbed mine. I gave her a gentle squeeze with my hand and looked at her and smiled. After we make it back to the house, Krystin gives me a kiss before she goes in the front door of the house, then goes over to her friends and tells them that she is going home. That kiss sent me to heaven and back. The time is running at about 11:30 pm now. Krystin and her friends leave while I hang around with Cody and Jacob for a while. I drank a couple more beers and proceeded to tell Cody and Jacob my future plans with Krystin.

Cody reminds me, "You know that Ray Walls thinks that Krystin is his girl, and he will be on the warpath after you."

Jacob asserted, "He's right man, Ray will pound on you hard. I like you and I don't want to see that happen."

Most of the school thinks that Krystin belongs to him, except Krystin. But Ray thinks that if he can keep everyone away from her, she will eventually become his girl. My father once told me, "Sometimes, a man has to fight for what he wants." Me being a geek, I feel that the odds are against me. However, Krystin is so scrumptious; in my mind, she is worth the risk. My subconscious starts yammering again. *I may pay dear from a Ray Walls beating after school. Maybe he won't find out. Oh! He'll find out, he has too many snitches. Most students are afraid not to tell him. If someone knew something that he should know and they didn't tell him, that person would be on his shit list. Yes, Phillip, you get to worry about this all week.*

Another friend of mine, Derek Turner, overheard our conversation, hobbles over on crutches and wants to put his two cents of advice in. Derek is very likable. He is witty and funny, a joy to be around.

Derek commenced, "Phil, are you crazy, you are a friend of mine, but if Ray finds out, it is going to break my heart to see him pound you unmercifully and hand your ass over to you cooked and well done. Ray left tonight mad. Don't you realize that is what will happen to you! The next time my parents ask how is that nice young man, Phillip doing, I will have to tell them he is DEAD."

I tried to put them at ease, along with putting myself at ease. "You guys are getting worked up for nothing. You just have to know Ray. Besides, it may not work out with Krystin and me anyway.

Jacob replies with wide-open eyes, "He is a prick; he is bigger, stronger, and mean. You are a good-looking dude right now, like the rest of us, but he will turn you into a scarred, ugly creature only if you are lucky to survive. As Derek said, we may have to tell our parents that you died trying to get away while falling in love."

I bounced back, "Relax, I got this."

"No, you don't man, you don't have this," fearfully bellowed Cody.

During this time, I had sucked down another beer. I have had about 3 beers total. I am not used to drinking this much and driving home. I was feeling a little woozy. "Hey guys, it's already almost midnight; I promised my mother I would be home by midnight. I had better get home, or my mom will kick my ass." I was slowly walking to the front door to depart.

Cody expressed with his eyebrows scrunched inward, "Maybe you will get used to having your ass kicked before Ray gets hold of you next week unless he finds out early, maybe Monday morning at school if Krystin tells her friends."

"See you guys' Monday at school," as I looked back smiling at my friends one last time.

I couldn't bring myself to tell Krystin not to say anything about our date. I was afraid that she would think I was a coward. *I am a coward; I just don't want her to know it.*

Still feeling woozy, I left the house and slowly walked to the car. I was now beginning to worry about getting home without getting stopped by the police.... 3 beers......I would be dead meat. Mom would kill me. I made up my mind to drive slower on the way home. As I was approaching the car, I looked up at all the pinpoints of light in the sky. Being out away from all the lights in town, I could see so many more stars. I get my keys out, unlock the car door, rather dizzily slide into the seat, and grab the steering wheel for balance. I start the car as it has religiously started since I bought it. I begin the slow drive home.

CHAPTER 03

THE INCIDENT DURING THE BACKBONE OF NIGHT

While driving down the road trying carefully to get home, there were no other cars on the road. I looked in the rear-view mirror and saw no headlights behind me, and my headlights were the only ones shining down the road in front of me. This was a good thing because there were no police behind me or heading towards me. The dried, brown corn stalks were 6 ft high on both sides of the road, some even higher. Now the only worry was hoping that there was not one hidden behind some of these corn stalks. I was also worried about a deer running in front of me. They are thick out on these country roads. You don't have to be going very fast, and if you hit a deer with your car, you could do some expensive damage to your car. As I continued to drive along, I encountered this horrible smell, a skunk. They are also thick out here, and it must be mating time. I don't know what female skunk would be attracted to that odor, but it happens. Science says that even humans put out pheromones.

Being a couple of weeks from Halloween, it was quiet driving but also sort of spooky. Being farther out of town, I glanced up at the clear sky and I felt like I could see thousands more stars in the sky. As I drove along, I was thinking about Krystin and how pretty and sexy she looked tonight. I turned on my overhead light in the car and glanced at my watch. It was about 10 minutes past midnight. I was passing by some fields that had already been harvested by the farmers and only corn stubble was left on the ground. Suddenly, I noticed the sky turn a reddish hue toward the south, which was the direction I was heading. Then suddenly, I saw this fireball blazing toward me in my direction as it became visible from behind some distant trees. "*What the hell is that?*" I suddenly stopped the car, opened the door, and got out of the car to get a better look at the fireball. I could feel the heat from the fireball as it passed me. Amazingly, it appeared to not have much noise. I thought that it would have been like a jet plane getting ready to land. The whole town would be able to hear it. It had created an atmospheric pressure wave that knocked me to the ground. As the flaming ball went past me, it only appeared to be about 50 ft. from the ground. The next instant came this sudden explosion. The ground shook, and I could see the explosion blaze rising into the air. My mind was racing, "My God, something has crashed over in this open field. It must have been a small plane or something, but the fireball seemed too big for that. Was it something military? I must go over and see if I can help someone that may be injured."

The crash was only about a quarter of a mile from where I stood. I turned the car off, grabbed my keys out of the ignition, and grabbed an old minor's flashlight that was attached to a stretchable band that fit around my head that I had stored in the dashboard of the car. I turned on the light after putting the band around my head and began running over corn stubble toward the crash. As I got closer, I began swerving around pieces of flaming debris along with some corn stubble burning. As I came upon the crash, the object had dug a trench into the ground at least ninety feet in length, around 40 feet wide, and about 6 feet deep and getting deeper as I approached the wreckage. At the end of the deepening trench was this round depression in the ground that was created by the impact of the crash. This depression was 10 to 15 feet deep. The crashed object looked like a mangled spherical mess, but I could tell that it was no plane or helicopter. *"What in the hell is this?"* The distorted mass appeared to be about 20 feet tall, 40 feet wide and 50 feet long. The heat from the smoldering metal was intense. My adrenalin had also kicked in and I was determined to try to save someone if I could. The flames from the fire began dying down and were gradually turning into a smoldering mass of misshaped metal. I saw an opening and began to walk in; the heat was still intense. I kept the flashlight beam in front of me. There were pieces of strewn metal poles and pipes crisscrossed in front of me. The smoldering smoke made it difficult to see but only a few feet ahead of me. I also kept coughing and gasping for air. I took my jacket off to try to remove the hot debris in front of me because it was too hot to handle with bare hands.

I noticed strange writing on some of the debris as I shoved it out of the way. *This must have been something from a foreign country.* I have seen foreign writing before, but never anything like this. It was a series of straight lines, curves, and dots intertwined.

As I walked a few feet farther, I could see some blue, orange, and red blinking lights on an unusual-looking instrument panel. Then I abruptly heard a moaning sound coming from behind a partially downed wall. I shined the light over in that direction and began to move toward the dark opening behind the leaning wall. I slowly peeked around the corner of the wall and, *oh my God, what is this thing? I'm no Einstein, but I'm pretty sure this is an alien.* Total fear came over me as I became petrified. I didn't know whether to run or just stand there and pee my pants. The moaning was legitimate; he was hurt badly. He appeared to be bleeding and the color of the blood was reddish-blue blood. The alien appeared to be shaped similar to we humans....2 legs, 2 arms, and a head attached to this torso. Its skin was a light grey color, pretty much the same color that you hear about on all these alien abduction TV shows. The surface of its skin appeared reptile-like. A lot of the stories depict aliens with big eyes and elongated bodies with thin arms and legs. This alien was filled out like someone who works out all the time to have bulging muscles. It was sitting on the floor of the wrecked ship with its back against the wall and had a pipe penetrating through its side. The alien was bleeding freely from the wound. As I looked closer, its blood appeared to be close to the same color as ours, red. But it still had that bluish hue to it. I thought aliens had green blood. Part of its left lower leg was severed off and bleeding rapidly. There was no hair on its head, and the eyes were elliptical with both sides of its face protruding downward similar to the skin of a bulldog's facial skin. The nose was similar to ours but much flatter. I could tell that its arms were longer than mine, and its hands were considerably larger. There were 6 fingers of which 4 appeared to be about 6 inches in length with at least 1-inch-thick fingernails that were more like claws than our typical fingernails. The first and last fingers were more thumb-like.

As I shined the light on the thing, it turned its head and looked up at me, and began another moaning sound. It appeared to be dying from the bad wounds. I removed my jacket, folded it and pulled his head toward me to put my jacket behind his head.

I tried to speak, "What can I do to help you?" *Phil you idiot, this creature probably can't understand English. However, if you could save this thing, you would be famous. You would be the first person to find and see an alien. That thought horrifies me also; I could only imagine the experiments that would be performed on it. At the same time, I was afraid even though it was severely wounded may feel threatened and attack me.*

It reached out its hand to me as if I should take him or her, I didn't know what gender by the hand and pull him out, but there was no way after observing closely, the pipe had penetrated through its side and protruding out the back of the creature, and into another wall. It was trapped there. Its hand was also bleeding that deep red-bluish hue blood. I reached for the 2-thumb 4-fingered right hand with my left hand. When I did, it began to grasp my forearm, squeezing my arm hard. It began to pull me closer as I began struggling to move back and get away. *What is it doing? I am trying to help it.* "Let me go", I screamed. My heart was beating fast and uncontrollably. Then suddenly, the two thumbnails dug into the skin of my left forearm penetrating my skin while the hand was bleeding profusely. I yelled out in pain. Then it took its other hand in which it was holding an injection needle that was not visible for me to see at the time, and the creature stabbed me in the leg in my upper right thigh. I was frantically trying to pull away.

As the creature injected the substance within the needle into me, the pain was excruciating. It felt as though someone was trying to cram a hard metal ball in a small opening in my thigh. I pulled away from the creature with the needle still in my thigh. I pulled the needle out as I was falling over debris scattered on the floor of the vehicle. As I got my bearings and began to get up, I looked back at the creature, and it was amazingly waving its right arm at me as if waving goodbye. Then I noticed the creature grab a cubic-like box laying nearby. It appeared to be about 6 inches in dimension and was black in color. Then the creature pressed one side of the box, and I saw some strange colored stick-like lights along with half-crescent lights start pulsing on and off in a very rhythmic fashion.....like clockwork. As some lights came on, others went off. Also, they were gradually going out completely. Then the creature waved forward 3-4 times hurriedly at me as if he was telling me to *go and leave, get out quickly*. I assumed the creature was male, but I didn't really know for sure. It had me in his grip earlier and probably could have killed me, but I could sense that he didn't want to kill me.

I quickly reasoned that this cube with the weird flashing lights disappearing in numbers must be some type of explosive device and the countdown had begun. I quickly grabbed my jacket from behind his head. I figured the creature was not about to be captured by us humans to be experimented on. I began to run out of the crashed vessel jumping over crossed bars and pipes and other rubble. Once outside, I kept running letting the light over my forehead be my guide. My right thigh was pulsing in pain. It felt like it was about to explode. I was running as hard as I could not to look back. It was difficult to move very fast running through a corn field that had already been harvested and only the corn stubble was left, along with me limping because of my injured thigh.

"Run Phil, run as you have never run before," I blurted to myself. I began to pray, "Lord help me; I'm not ready to die. Keep me safe from whatever that alien put inside me." Within 20-30 seconds, I heard this high pitch-searing sound. It was so high pitch that it was hurting my ears. I turned and looked, and it was unbelievable what I saw. At first, what was left of the spaceship was exploding out with a brilliant hot white color, then almost instantly it began to implode inward. Except for the high-pitched siren-like sound, the implosive sound appeared to be muffled. With the implosion, its force pulled me toward it so hard it knocked me down. I could see corn stubble bouncing across the ground toward the implosion. After about 3-4 seconds, it was all over but a trail of white smoke plummeted up into the air. By now, I have dirt all over me from lying flat on the ground. I had dirt in my mouth from being scooted along the ground toward the implosion. My shirt and pants were dirty. How am I going to explain that to mom? I get up reminding myself that my leg is throbbing. When I looked back toward the crash, there was nothing there but the linear crater that was created. As I

hobbled back toward the car while enduring excruciating pain still throbbing in my upper right thigh, my mind was racing frantically trying to process everything that had happened.

I began reasoning, *No one will believe me if I tell them what I saw. They will say I'm crazy. But I have this shot of something in my body from the needle. I'm scared, but I'm also afraid to say anything to anyone. What if I turn into an alien myself, looking like that poor bastard that just died? Then I would be the one that would be experimented on. Believe me, I don't want any of that. My classmates would be calling me a freak. I think it is best that I say nothing to anyone, not even mom. Time and the Lord are the only friends I have currently.*

I get back to the car, and by now I can hear distant sirens coming from police cars and maybe fire trucks. The sound is getting louder, closer. Someone other than me must have heard or seen something. I quickly started the car to remove myself from the location of the crash. I don't want to answer any questions. About a mile down the road, I get to make a right turn heading west on another road to get home. I just wanted to get off the main road of the crash site. I can't believe this has happened. What about Krystin, If I look like that Alien, she definitely wouldn't have anything to do with me. My leg is still throbbing, and I am so scared.

I finally made it home. The first thing I do is take off my jacket, shirt, and dirty jeans and throw them in the back of the closet. Not in the clothes hamper. My plan is to wash them myself when mom is at work. I am sweating profusely as I get into bed. When I took off my pants, I could see parts of my right thigh bulging in a rhythmic fashion – like a heart beating. The pain seemed to have subsided some. I am so scared and don't know what to expect tomorrow morning when I wake up. That is if I wake up. Again, I began quietly praying, "Lord, you know that I have always tried to do the right thing all my life. Please don't let whatever stuff that alien put in me do harm to me. Please hear my prayer, Amen." By now total exhaustion has set in. I still have to work Sunday afternoon at the grocery store from 1 – 6 pm. I quickly fell into a deep sleep.

SUNDAY

Sunday morning arrives; it is about 10 am as I was just waking up from a deep sleep and a horrible nightmare involving me witnessing an alien spacecraft crash. This dream was so real I feel like I lived the incident. As I got up, I look down at my right thigh, which was still sore, and saw a circular bruise about 3 inches in diameter where the needle shot penetrated my skin. I opened my closet door and saw my muddy clothes. Now I realize that it was not a nightmare. This really happened. Both of my thighs seemed somewhat larger and more muscular. Except for the sore thigh, I really feel pretty good. In fact, I feel great. I have not felt this good in a long time. I walk to the bathroom mirror to see if any other changes were occurring. My heart was beating fast again because I was afraid to look at my face. Amazingly, there were no noticeable changes to my face. I noticed that my arms were thicker and appeared to be more muscular like my legs and even my calves. My chest and shoulders seemed to be larger and wider. I knew then that somehow, my body does seem to be changing. However, it seems to be for the best. For now, it appears that I am slowly changing from a weak nerd to a muscular "beach body." When I looked closer into the mirror at my face, it seemed that very small changes were also happening to my face. My eyes seemed to be slightly larger and slightly elongated. My nostrils seemed to be slightly larger. Overall, I still looked the same, but if one looks very closely, you can see the ever-so-slight changes. This concerns me, even though I seem to actually be better looking. In the mirror, I could even tell I seemed to be slightly taller. This change I can measure. I had places marked on my doorway facing showing my height over the past 10 years. I was currently about 5 ft. 9 in. tall. When I measured my height this morning, I was 5 ft. 11 in. tall. How can this be? It must have been that shot. How am I going to explain these changes to anyone? All the changes are hard to see except for the height change. Hey! A good explanation is that I'm still growing. I have seen other students grow 3-4 inches through summer. But this was overnight. Could raise some eyebrows, especially mom.

As I trot up the stairs from the basement to get some breakfast, I am asserting to myself, "don't say anything about last night."

My sister Janet began heckling, "How was your party last night, did you make love to Krystin?"

Mother quickly added, "Janet, stop that kind of talk. I won't have that in this house."

I ranted, "Janet, get a life, will you."

"How did your evening go?" mom uttered.

"Things seemed to have gone well," I mumbled sleepily as I opened the refrigerator door to get out the milk.

Mom replied, "Phillip, you are still growing a little taller. If you keep this up, you may be over 6 ft. tall. I heard on the radio this morning that an asteroid may have landed in one of the farm fields not too far from here. You know there seem to be times that I occasionally see strange lights over this area in Southern Indiana. I wonder if we are in one of those asteroid zones."

Now, she had my attention. "Mom, we are not in one of those zones. Meteoroids as they are called, are rare, but they do hit the earth once in a blue moon. Most burn up in the atmosphere, but some can be large enough to not burn up all the way and hit the ground. Then it becomes a meteorite," I explained. That seemed to settle her curiosity.

As for me, I now know that people know about the crash, but they think it was a meteorite. That implosion apparently left no evidence of a spaceship crashing. I pour myself a larger than usual bowl of corn flakes. I added plenty of milk and began eating. I stare at the clock and see that it is about 11:15 am. I need to be at the grocery store by noon which is when they open up. I stock shelves on Sunday, and I have the canned vegetable aisle to keep the shelves stocked. It is sort of hard work for a weaker person like me, but I need the money. Some of those cases of canned goods can be pretty heavy. After I gulp down the cereal, I brush my teeth and head out the door to the *mean green machine*. Before I got into the car to leave, we have this big Oak tree in our yard with a low-hanging limb that is about 4 inches in diameter and can easily hold my weight. I use it all the time to do chin-ups. That is where one pulls his entire body up to where his chin is above the limb. I was pretty good at doing about 4-5 but that was about it. This morning, I jumped up and grabbed the limb, and began my chin-ups. They seemed amazingly easy to do. I knocked off at least 20 as fast as I could while realizing I needed to stop and get to work. Something has definitely happened to me because I feel so much stronger.

I arrive at work with about 10 minutes to spare. I got my timecard and clocked in. As I began walking down my aisle, at the end of the aisle I could see several cases stacked on the floor to be opened and stocked on the shelves. My body was still tingly, but I felt great. In fact, I felt fantastic. My right thigh wasn't hurting anymore. So, I began lifting the cases and putting them in place to be opened up where that particular vegetable was located down the aisle. I noticed that the cases seemed to be very light. I'm pondering, "What? These cases seem much lighter than they usually do. I feel much stronger." As I began opening the cases, I noticed that I was stocking the shelves at a much faster pace than ever before. When I grabbed the cans, I was grabbing them stronger and more accurately. I could tell that something was going on with my body strength. Also, I noticed that I was much quicker at doing things than ever before. All of my senses seemed to be heightened. My hearing, my sense of smell, and even my eyesight all appeared to be more sensitive. It must have been that shot in the thigh that I received. I kept telling myself, "All this will probably go away in a day or two. But for now, it is taking some getting used to."

A lady was walking down my aisle with a shopping cart. I was at least 50 feet from her and began smelling her perfume. This is so unbelievable. A few minutes later, a scruffy-looking man walked down my aisle with his son who appeared to be about 10-11 years old. He sat down a Coke bottle in my aisle and continued walking toward me with the boy.

"Great," I muttered, "I need to go pick that bottle up and throw it in the trash." I walked by him, picked it up, and held it in my hand. He saw me pick it up, turned around, and went on down the aisle. He began mouthing off to the boy. Even though he was a good distance away, I could hear every word he was saying. Almost every other word was a curse word. Suddenly, I saw him slap the boy on the side of his head, then slapped him again across the face, this time knocking the boy down.

He stared at me and blurted, "What are you looking at?"

I turned my head and said, "Nothing." I couldn't afford to possibly lose my job. I grew so angry at that asshole that it was hard to not confront him. When he turned the corner to go down another aisle, I was still gripping his Coke bottle. Suddenly, I broke the bottle with my bare hand. When it shattered, I ended up with several little cuts inside the palm of my hand. I went to the restroom to stop the bleeding. I noticed that my blood, even though was red, was a darker red with a bluish hue. JUST LIKE THE ALIEN'S BLOOD. Now I'm even more worried. When I got to the restroom, the bleeding had nearly stopped, and I could see the cuts virtually closing themselves up. The wounds were healing before my very eyes. Within another minute, I couldn't tell I had been injured.

While in the restroom, I decided to go into one of the stalls for some privacy, to pee. I know my thigh had a large bruise where the injection penetrated last night. I decided to check it out and see if it was still black and blue. I pulled my pants down below my thigh, and that wound was healed up. I don't think it is my imagination, but my thighs seemed larger and more muscular than early this morning. I still feel great, and I feel stronger than ever before in my lifetime. I just didn't know whether to be scared or elated.

When I returned to my aisle, there were 4 cases of green beans stacked on top of each other each case weighing about 40-50 pounds. I began to be in a daring mood, "I wonder if I can pick up all 4 cases." I knew that normally there was no way I could pick them up. I went over to the cases, squatted down, and wrapped my hands and arms around the bottom case. I began to lift all 4 cases with ease. This was amazing. I put them back down to not attract any attention, but I was too late. A young man was walking up the aisle and saw everything. As he walked by, he stated, "Man, you are strong. You must lift weights all the time."

I nodded, "Yes, I do," hoping that the answer would satisfy him. It must have satisfied him because he walked on by.

There is no doubt about it; that stuff in that syringe has done something to my body and I seem to have extra senses and even extra power. As I continued to stock the canned goods on the shelves, I noticed that when I focused,

I could hear people talking in the other aisles of the store. My hearing had increased tremendously. It seems as though everything that has happened to me has definitely been for the best. I can't wait until I get off work. I want to do some experimentation regarding my strength and extra senses.

This incident has also brought up other questions. *Is this something that is temporary and will be going away? Are there any negative effects that may set in that I don't know about? Why would an alien give me that shot to cause this and what was its motive for doing so? What was in that shot? Is it something that is not of this world? Will it eventually cause me to die at a young age, like getting cancer as a teenager and ultimately knowing the outcome? Should I go see a doctor, have some X-rays, and have a blood test? I know my blood is different. What about the rapid healing of the cut wounds when I broke the Coke bottle?* So many questions to which I don't have answers.

I know that I need to see a doctor, but I'm afraid to do so. I don't want to be in the hospital while they study and experiment on me after I tell them how it happened. No one would probably believe my story anyhow. But If I'm this kind of different from other people, they would want to know why and that would require research and possibly experiments. For now, I think I'm just going to lay low. Nothing is bothering me physically. I'm not in any pain. In fact, I feel absolutely super.

It's about an hour before quitting time and I was called up to help bag the groceries in one of the check-out lines. There were three check-out lines and all three were backed up with several people in each line waiting to be checked out. I began bagging the groceries at a pretty fast pace. To me, it was like slow motion. I could do this much faster. Even this brings up another question. I have to be careful not to be too noticeable such as my speed of bagging groceries. I am realizing that what is normally slow for me is a very fast speed for other people. I really must concentrate on controlling these extra senses and powers or I may fortuitously give myself away and people will find out that I am different. I want to keep this secret. I think that is in my best interest.

Finally, quitting time arrives and it is 6 pm. I punched my timecard and left the store and headed to the *mean green machine*. I began the trip home which was only about 10 minutes. My mind was tossing around all those questions about my physical changes. I had to drive down the road where the crash had occurred. As I drove by, there were 5-6 cars parked along the road and I noticed several people out there investigating what they thought was a meteorite trench dug out in that farm field. The dark scorching of the ground was obvious. There were also a couple of police cars and a fire truck parked at the site. I thought this might be a good time to stop and take a look. I pulled my car to the side of the road, got out of the car, and started walking to the trench. The Sheriff was present, who happens to be Ray Walls' Father. His name was Paul. I could only get so close because some scientists from IU had the area roped off.

I did walk up to the Sheriff and asked, "Paul, what happened here?"

"Looks like a meteorite hit the earth last night," as he removed his hat and scratched his head. "I guess we were lucky it didn't land in the forest, and this corn field had already been harvested or we could have had a wildfire started."

I replied, "Yeah! I suppose you are right. Did they find any part of the meteorite left over that didn't burn up?"

"They haven't found anything yet, just a pile of white ash at the very bottom of the trench. Scientists are taking some samples of the ash to analyze what type of meteorite it was. What surprised me was that no one heard any loud noise. This should have made a loud explosion with a trench this deep."

I nodded, "Yeah, someone should have heard something."

While Paul was still scratching his head, "It is perplexing to me that no one knows anything. Willie Willis said he was walking down the road when he saw the fireball coming in. He said it was a spaceship."

"Willie was walking down this road when this occurred?"

Paul added, "Yeah, but he also said that the alien pilot was waving to him. I'm sure he had a few too many drinks. He said that he saw you stop your car and go into the crashed spacecraft. They don't call him the town drunk for nothing."

I wanted to ease the sheriff's thoughts, "I never stopped, and I didn't see anything, sheriff. I've always heard that about Willie, and you can't believe everything he says."

I'm thinking, *Man, I could give you a ton of information, but you wouldn't believe me.* I really wanted to say to Paul – your son has turned into a prick in school and bullies some of the other kids. Anyhow, Paul would be the first to turn me into the government and military if he found out that I was changed from this incident. Phillip, just keep your mouth shut.

I uttered, "Good luck with all this Paul," as I slowly walked away and headed back to my car. When I pulled into the driveway, it was approaching dark. I jumped and grabbed the low-hanging limb on our big Oak tree. I started the chin-ups. Immediately, I felt so much lighter. I was doing one after another. I was doing a complete chin-up about every 2 seconds. After a couple of minutes, I quit counting after I had reached 50 chin-ups and was still going. It still seemed effortless to do. Just another testament to my increased astonishing strength. I let go of the limb and landed on the ground. I still felt like I had extra energy to spare. The neighbor's dog started barking at me. I went over to the fence and stepped out to the edge of the road. There was no one coming down the road.

I jeered at the dog, "Are you ready to chase me, you mangy mutt? Get ready, Go." I started running down the road while the dog started running along with me barking wildly. When I picked up speed, I was easily outrunning the dog. I had to be running at least 40 mph. I wasn't even running at full speed. I was surprised even more than the dog. Again, it seems like I have superhuman strength. I am still afraid of what may happen if anyone finds out about me. I must keep this little secret to myself. Tomorrow starts another week of school. I have a date with Krystin Friday night, going out to eat and then to the outside movie park.

As soon as I enter the house Janet declared, "Phil, that was a meteorite that landed in old man Willoughby's corn field. The Police, the Sherriff, the Fire Department, and even Scientists from IU and also scientists from Cornell University were there. Anyhow, why would they be there?"

"Well Janet, Cornell is home to Professor Frank Drake. In 1960, he used a radio telescope in West Virginia to listen for signals coming from space. Scientists have been scanning the heavens for (techno signatures) ever since. I don't know why they would be there. It was just a meteorite that hit the earth."

I turned and looked at my sister. "Someone must have called them up for some reason. They would like to get evidence of aliens, but they are going to be disappointed."

I grabbed a snack and blazed down the stairs to the basement to call Cody. The phone rings 3-4 times before he picks up.

"Hello!" Cody Blurred.

"Hey Cody, what is up?"

"Phil, did you see that meteorite hit the earth late last night after we left the party."

"I left the party before you did, but no, I didn't see anything."

"Yeah. I left about 30 minutes after you did. On the way home, I saw from a distance the obvious red and blue lights on the police cars and fire trucks, and a white plume of smoke was still rising from whatever was left smoldering. Did they find anything?"

"I haven't heard any more than you, Cody."

"We should have heard an explosion or something. That thing left a deep trench in old man Willoughby's farm field."

"I know, we should have heard something, but I heard nothing."

Cody chimed in, "Regarding the party; I had a great time. Carrie and I made out for several minutes after the party."

"Good for you. I know you both really care for each other."

"How did it go with Krystin? I saw you both leave the house, and you were gone for quite a while. Did you get to make out?"

"You are beginning to be a nosy body, Cody. If you must know, she did kiss me."

"Man, if Ray finds out you kissed her, you may be dead meat."

"I didn't kiss her. She kissed me, and we were alone."

"Right on! You sly devil," Cody echoed.

"I need to get some studying done before school tomorrow. This Chemistry and Calculus are kicking my butt."

"Quit taking all those hard courses all the time," Cody persisted.

"I would like to go to college someday so these courses will help me to get admitted into a university. I will see you tomorrow at school."

"OK man, hope Ray doesn't work you over first."

Now that I have these secret advantages, I boasted, "Chill out; nothing is going to happen."

MONDAY – ANOTHER SCHOOL DAY

The alarm goes off at about 7 am for me and I am a slow mover at first. I get up and the first thing I want to do is check out my body to see if any more changes have occurred. I have never seen my biceps as noticeable as they are now. My vision seems to be very acute. My thigh no longer hurts, and my thigh and calf muscles seem to be more noticeable. After a good night's sleep, I actually feel great.

After going through my morning routine of showering, shaving, and brushing my teeth, I move up the basement stairs to the kitchen by taking around 8 stair steps at a time. I reach the top in less than 2 seconds. I was just testing my agility but again, I need to keep this from my mom and most definitely from my mouthy-tell-all sister.

As soon as I enter the kitchen, mom while still yawning and reaching for some dishes began chatting, "How did you sleep, my favorite son."

"I slept ok," I blurted while reaching into the refrigerator to get milk for cereal. I felt very hungry, so I got a larger-than-average bowel for my cereal. I filled the large serving bowl full and poured some milk in and began eating.

Mom added, "Phil that is a big bowl of cereal that has a lot more carbs and sugars than you need. You keep eating like that and you will start gaining weight. Soon you will have more chins than a Chinese phonebook."

"I'm hungry."

"Ok, just don't overeat like that all the time."

Janet being a sophomore at school muttered in a bamboozled tone, "This geometry is driving me crazy. Phil, you make good grades. How do you study something when you don't even understand what is going on?"

I was already tired of her complaining about school all the time. I necessitated as I was crunching a mouth full of cereal, "Janet, subjects like geometry require vigilance. You can't let up on it. You can't allow yourself to get behind. If you do, you have just entered that dreaded room of not understanding what the teacher is trying to teach. Trust me, that hour of geometry can be an eternity and you will feel like the class is never going to end along with getting farther behind. Spend less time on the phone with your friends and more time studying."

Mom reiterated, "He's right Janet, you tend to get lazy when it comes to studying. I wish you had better study habits along with better grades like your brother."

I stopped momentarily crunching my cereal while still having my mouth full and sent Janet a big smile. She leered back at me and crossed her eyes while looking at me.

Like a tattletale, I murmured, "See how she is looking at me, mom. That is what I get for trying to give that numb skull advice."

Mom added, "Now Phillip, she is your sister and I know in your heart you want her to be successful."

I jeered, "She needs to quit acting like a dork; if you act like one, you end up being one. End of story."

"Phillip, you need to help her with her tough subjects."

"I will; all she has to do is ask."

Janet blurted, "Let's change the subject to something else and get away from discussing my study habits."

Changing the subject, I asked mom, "Did they ever find out any more information about the meteorite crash." I was probing to see what everyone knew about it.

Mom stated, "They just think it was a meteorite that hit the earth just like you said."

I made a faint sound with a sigh of relief even though I was still worried and concerned.

She added, "According to some of the people that I work with, the sheriff is still perplexed as to what happened and still can't believe that no one saw or heard anything."

I finished my cereal and gave mom a hug and kiss on the cheek. "I better get to school." Normally, Janet would ride with me but there were some girls on the school bus in her grade and that bus ride appeared to be their gossip time. I'm glad she rides the school bus because at times, she can be annoying.

As I grabbed my jacket, I walked to the *mean green machine*. As I walked under the big oak limb, it was calling my name. *Come on Phil, how many chin-ups can you do.* I took on the challenge and within a couple of minutes, ended up doing 60 straight chin-ups with no problem at all. My only conclusion was that I am definitely much stronger because of that injection from that Alien. I wish I could have done something to have helped it, but the wounds were too serious. I thought that maybe the Alien could have healed its wounds like my cuts healed up when I broke that coke bottle at work, but they were probably too serious, and it had lost too much blood.

I got into the car and begin driving to school while passing by several trees whose leaves were changing color resulting from the decreasing sunlight and the autumnal season that by now was established. The morning temperatures were in the mid-forty-degree range. The sunlight just glistened off the red and yellow maple trees that were growing along the roadside. I eased into one of the parking spots in the school parking lot. As I was walking toward the front door of the school, I saw Krystin well ahead of me walking in. I was reminded of our date this Friday night at the football game. I began thinking to myself; *I hope she hasn't told anyone about our date. It would only be a matter of time that either Ray or one of his goons, Ron, Jim, or Billy, would find out. If they do, I might as well accept this fact and get ready to face it.*

I began walking down the crowded hallway and passed Mr. Clover, our high school principal dressed in a dark blue suit, white shirt, and red necktie. He could easily have the appearance of running for president of the United

States. As he passed by me, he stopped, put his hand on my shoulder, and spoke.

"Still keeping your grades up, Phillip?"

"I'm giving it my best shot, sir."

"You have been doing well; just don't let up," he added.

I asked him, "Did you hear about that meteorite that hit on old man Willoughby's property Saturday night?"

"Yes, I did. They even had some Scientists from IU and Cornell University examining the crater. As far as I know, they just concluded it was just a meteorite. But I have heard others in the community about seeing strange glowing lights at night and I have seen some myself that did appear to have strange movements."

"What type of strange movements Mr. Clover?"

"Well one night just a few weeks ago, I saw a set of lights moving along which I first concluded was just a jet plane. Then it appeared to stop and started moving sideways. I thought that it must have been a helicopter. We are only about 50 miles from that military base, Camp Atterbury. Other than that, I haven't thought too much about it. Anyhow Phillip, I would like to see you get into college, and keeping up the grades is a must. Our school here is mostly a farming community and we don't get to send many students on to higher education. The more students that we can send to college will make our school system look better in the public's eyes. However, Academic scholarships are hard to come by. A good athlete has a better chance of a college scholarship than a good academic student. Most universities give out academic scholarships, but they are scarce."

I smiled, "Yeah, I'm sure you are correct regarding the public's image of our school. I want you to know Mr. Clover that I feel like I have learned a lot going to this high school. I know I have no other school to make a comparison, but I feel like the more intensive subjects such as Trigonometry, Chemistry, and Physics have been demanding enough that those teachers are preparing us. A student can get a good education if they want it. The responsibility is on the student to learn. I heard this old saying once, **even a bad teacher can't keep a good student from learning. A good student will learn in spite of a poor teacher.**"

"Where did you hear that, or did you read it from some book."

"Honestly, Mr. Clover I can't recall where I came upon that saying. I have sort of used it as my motto."

"That is a good saying Phillip; I will have to remember that one," as he began to walk away from me and continue down the hallway. A few seconds later as I was heading to my 1st-period Geography class, Jim, one of Ray Walls' goons purposefully bumped into my left shoulder. He didn't stop my forward movement, but our collision instantly knocked him back 2-3 feet.

He growled, "Get out of my way nerd."

I dropped my books on the floor and grabbed him by his motorcycle jacket with both hands, pulling him close to me. Then I lifted his entire body up 3-4 inches off the floor where his eyes were level with mine. Then with a piercing stare, "Let me tell you something, you little dumbass, things are starting to change around here. You had better understand that." Then I slowly lowered him to the floor, brushed the wrinkles out of that hideous jacket, picked my books up, and walked on. I could tell that Jim was shocked that I would even have the nerve to challenge him. I could also tell that he had a moment of fear himself. I'm sure he won't be bumping into me again without his buddies being with him.

Bobby McGee, the bass player, and Derek, the one stricken with polio saw everything. Bobby walked over and commented, "Man, he must have really pissed you off. Good for you. I don't like any of those guys either but they know I'll fight them if I have to, so they don't push me around as they do you, DeMar, Derek, and Aaron. I may lose the fight, but they know I will get my share of punches in on them. They want to bully those students that they know won't fight back. That is how they can bully without taking any chances of getting hurt."

I asserted to Bobby, "I'm tired of it and I'm not taking any more of their crap so watch out; the fur is about to fly."

"Good for you; a punch in the nose may hurt awhile, but being humiliated can last much longer."

I gallantly maintained, "You probably notice Bobby that I have been working out and I am becoming stronger. My fear of those goons is dwindling. I know that I may have a day of recollection with them, but I am planning on preparing for that day."

Bobby added, "Don't worry about it; you will be fine."

As I walked into my 1st-period class I chanted, "See you at Lunch."

Jim's close friend, Billy, is in the geography class. As he walked in, I was receiving a nasty stare. He walked down the aisle where I was sitting and He commented to me, "You had better watch out; Jim is pissed at you."

I firmly stared him in the eyes and burst out, "Oooh, I'm scared."

Billy added, "You had better be scared."

By that time, Krystin was walking into the class, so my staring was diverted from Billy toward Krystin. However, I was still talking to Billy and leered, "Well Billy, I'm not scared. You can also tell your little mangy friend that he had better think twice before he decides to purposefully bump into me again. I'll snap him in half like a pencil. Be sure he gets my message."

Billy walked on by and headed toward the back of the class and slammed his books on his desk harder than normal. By that time, Mr. Shields had entered the class and the geography lesson for Monday morning was beginning. Krystin's seat was beside me in the next row.

Just before Mr. Shields began his lesson, I quickly whispered to her, "Looking forward to Friday evening."

With a big smile, she softly remarked, "Me too."

My second-period class was typing. Today, when the timed writing exercise began, my senses heightened. I didn't know it at the time, but I outpaced the speed typists including Krystin. I knew I was typing much faster so I slowed down some toward the end hoping not to make the improvement in typing speed so noticeable that it would catch the attention of Ms. Lathem. My next class was Phys. Ed., Trig, then lunch. Phys. Ed. was going to be an interesting class since I seem to have these extra powers and strengths. Again, I was going to have to be careful not to draw too much attention. My PE instructor was Mr. Bartlett who was also the basketball coach. Most of the time, we would choose teams and play basketball. Two of the boys in my PE class had played basketball the previous year and were planning on going out for the team again this year. I had previously figured that I was probably out of my league when it came to playing basketball for the school team. But now I was having second thoughts. Typically, I wouldn't try very hard in PE class because I just considered myself too weak, or to be more specific, not physical enough to compete. Occasionally, Mr. Bartlett would watch us play probably scouting for potential players that could help the team that was not on the team.

To start class, Mr. Bartlett threw out 3-4 basketballs and we would choose teams. We had the main gym floor along with two others when the bleachers were pulled back. It was easy for us to have 3 games going at once. The class had about 40 boys taking PE, so there were always about 5-10 that would just shoot around on the side goals. Normally, I was not a very good shot but this morning, those goals looked like huge baskets to me. I grabbed a basketball and began shooting. Swish! One basket after another. After I made about 6 in a row from various spots on the floor, I realized that my senses were keened up and it was easy for me to judge my arc with the basketball and hit the baskets easily. What was this marvelous stuff that this Alien had injected into my body? I also realized that I need to purposefully miss a few and not draw too much attention to the sharpshooting.

After about 10 minutes of warming up, we start choosing teams. Two boys in this PE class played on the basketball team last year. Tryouts for this coming year were this Thursday after school. These two boys, Dan, and Stan were pretty good. Ray, the tallest one on the team was not in this class, but Dan and Stan both were about 6 ft. 3 inches tall, still about 4 inches taller than me even though I seemed to be slightly taller myself after the Alien's syringe shot. Mr. Bartlett seemed to be hanging around probably wanting to see if Dan and Stan had improved some from the previous year. Dan and another boy in class, I call him big Al chose up teams. I was one of the last ones chosen because previously, I showed little or no talent relating to basketball skills. Dan and Stan, the two experienced players were on the same team and I'm sure they were assuming an easy victory. Big Al was also about 6 ft. 3 in., but was overweight about 250 lbs. He took up space but couldn't jump. Big Al and Dan shot baskets to see who got the ball first. I was assigned to guard Stan. Dan immediately gives the ball to Stan. He is in front of me at the top of the key dribbling the ball while deciding what move he was going to make on me. All of my senses were turned on and in high gear. To me, it looked as if he was dribbling in slow motion. I could have easily stolen the ball, but I didn't. I stayed in front of him waiting to see his move. He suddenly went to his left and proceeded to go around me toward the basket. Again, it seemed like he was going around me in slow motion. I wanted to let him go around me because I figured he would try to shoot it. I felt like I was moving at a snail's pace. Stan was kind of a 'ball hog' – a player that doesn't pass the ball to teammates very often even if they are wide open. Sure enough, I was correct; he thought he had me well behind him and began to shoot the ball. I leaped from behind him and blocked the shot before the ball even left his hand. He stumbled backward from the force of the block. The ball bounced on the floor once, I grabbed it, held the ball up to shoot and Dan moved over to block my shot. Instead of shooting, I whipped the ball around Dan to big Al. He bobbled the ball and finally got a good grip to shoot. Before Dan could get back to him, big Al was scoring the basket. I gave a quick glance, and the coach was watching impressively.

I could also see that Stan, after the humiliating block from behind, had fire in his eyes and was pissed. So, they started again to try to score on us. Stan was dribbling the ball in front of me again. When my senses are heightened, everything seems to be in slow motion. As he was dribbling, I went around him and hit the ball while he was bouncing the ball in my direction. I quickly turned and headed for the basket straight for Dan. I pulled up short of him and jumped up and shot the ball and made the basket. I figured Dan would not want to leave his feet after the previous quick pass to big Al. He couldn't have blocked my shot anyway. I know that if I got close enough, I could have dunked the ball having both hands on the ball. Me, being only 5' 11", dunking a ball would really get attention. Only a handful of 5'11" tall players across the entire United States can dunk a basketball with both hands. There are some players that can dunk a basketball with one hand, but two-handed takes extra effort. Now Stan is really angry. This next time he doesn't get too close to me. He sees a little daylight and launches a long shot and misses it. It takes a high bounce off the rim while Dan and I are both going for the rebound. We both go up and grab the ball at the same time. I quickly snatched it out of his hands while in mid-air. When I landed back on the floor, I had the ball. I saw one of my teammates wide open in the corner. I bounced it to him with just enough force to get it to him. Stan hustled over just as my teammate was shooting and blocked his shot while knocking the poor boy down as the ball bounced out of bounds. It definitely would have been a foul in a real game.

Our team gets the ball again; the ball is passed to me quickly. Stan runs up and is grabbing and slapping the ball while at the same time grabbing and slapping my arm.

Stan blurs, "Come on Marland, you are mine. I'm going to tear you to pieces."

I asserted, "Quit slapping and grabbing me; that is a foul."

"There are no fouls in this game," he added.

"If you don't stop it, I'm going to hurt you," I assured him.

Stan growled, "Bring it on nerd, you are mine now."

The next instant I quickly punched him in his solar plexus. I punched him so fast that no one could see the punch. He immediately stopped and doubled over as I went around him and easily scored another basket.

After the score, Dan addressed, "What's the matter Stan, can't you guard him."

Stan mumbled, "He punched me."

Dan said, "I didn't see him punch you and I was watching all the time." All the other players chimed in saying no punch was thrown.

Big Al called out, "Stan you were grabbing, slapping, and trying to hold him. If he did punch you, I don't blame him."

By now, the coach had walked onto the floor and added, "Quit crying Stan, you just got your jock handed to you. Phillip, come over here to the scorer's bench; I want to talk to you."

We headed over to the scorer's bench; I sat down as he sat down beside me.

"Phil, I was impressed with your basketball skills. You used to not play with this intensity. Seems like you have changed overnight."

"Well, Mr. Bartlett, I started working out and in time, I have gotten stronger."

"That doesn't explain your quickness and your jumping ability. That block from behind was impressive. And when you stole the ball from Stan, that was so quick that I could hardly see you do it. Stan is one of our better ball handlers. You also seem to have a change of attitude. I heard what you did to one of those punks earlier this morning. You used to let them push you around. I like the idea that you seem to have decided that you are not going to take any more crap off those punks."

Taking advantage of this opportunity, I added, "Mr. Bartlett, your basketball star Ray is one of those bullies. In fact, they hang around with him all the time, probably for extra protection because he is so big and strong."

"Yes, I have heard that more than once and I'm going to have a serious talk with Ray. He is a senior and has a chance for a college scholarship to play basketball. Those punks that he hangs around are nothing but trouble for him. He needs to get his grades up and he needs to be hanging around the very people that he and the others are bullying. I'm sure you and your friends would be willing to help him with his studies. This discussion with him is coming up soon. Now on to other matters. Phil, I want you to go out for the basketball team Thursday after school. After what I observed today, you will not only make the team, but you will also likely be on the starting 5. Stan was a starter last year and you had him totally befuddled today. He will most likely be a starter along with Dan, Ray, and you. I need a good guard that can handle the ball and is quick. You have all those attributes. Also, if you get good grades in school, a basketball scholarship could be coming your way too. Universities like athletes that also have a good GPA."

As I listened to him, I was stunned to hear all the positive comments about me. I began wondering; *this may be my way out. Playing basketball and earning a scholarship. That would save me huge amounts of money. Getting a degree in engineering is looking better all the time.*

With a blissful reply, "Thank you for the information, Mr. Bartlett. I will have to juggle my work schedule, but I plan on being at the gym for the tryouts."

Mr. Bartlett appeared exuberant and urged, "I don't think you will be disappointed, Phil. This will give you a good chance to get to know Ray better. He is not a bad person; he just needs some direction on taking the right path."

Dan and Stan had noticed Bartlett talking to me. The bell was about to ring, and both of the boys came over to me.

Stan softly confessed in an apologetic tone, "Sorry about trying to rough you up during the scrimmage game."

I fretted, "Sorry about the punch to the solar plexus. I know that had to hurt."

Dan added, "So you did punch him. Man, I didn't even see it happen and I was watching you two while Stan was attempting to rough you up. You played impressively today. Our team could use you. We are hoping to win the sectional this year. If we do, it will be our 1st sectional in 25 years. With you on the team, we can do this."

Stan proclaimed, "He is right Phil; we can do this together and pull off this sectional win. It will be a milestone for the school and we will leave our names in the school history book. Try to make the team Thursday."

I added, "The coach wants me to go out for the team; I plan on being there Thursday."

Dan hinted, "I figured that was what he was talking to you about, to try out for the team. With myself Stan, Ray, and you being starters, we can do this. Last year, we always had 1-2 starters that just didn't have the ability to be competitive. You can change that for us. You will root someone out of being a starter, but rightfully so."

"I know, and that sort of bothers me. We better get dressed for the next class, the bell is about to ring, and I don't want to be late." I echoed.

CHAPTER 04

LUNCH AND THE FIGHT

The next class was Trig with Mrs. Franklin. I know that Trig is important but it's easy to get bored spending most of your time using the slide rule. After an hour of the slide rule doing Trig calculations, I was ready for lunch. Finally, the bell rings, and lunch is on. I scurry down the hallway to put away my books in my locker. I caught up with Cody and Derek.

Cody remarked, "I heard about your run-in with Jim the-asshole this morning."

"I'm tired of those guys treating us like down-beaten peasants. Their actions are coming to a halt," was my reply.

"Cool. You have bulked up. Why didn't you tell me you were working out in your spare time? I would have worked out with you. It looks like you have built up like that over the weekend. Man, if I had your build, those guys wouldn't be bothering me either. I thought Ray would have gotten his cast-iron hands on you by now after last Saturday night. I'm sure someone has told him by now."

I asserted to Cody, "I'm not too worried. All those bullies know that if there is a good chance they could get hurt, they think long and hard before they act. I know Derek can't because of his disability. It really pisses me off

65

that they would be so low as to pick on Derek who can't stand up to them. That just shows how cowardly they really are. Everyone else needs to stand up to them."

"I like your change of attitude, but I'm in no hurry," Cody added.

As we entered the cafeteria to get in the lunch line, I noticed that I was getting some nasty stares from all the goons, including Ray. He must have heard about Krystin and me. He may have already heard about our date Friday night. As we were receiving our trays of food, I began the usual praising of the cooks hoping to get more food. The main course today was a bowl of Chili, peanut butter and jelly sandwiches, and apple sauce with the usual half-pint carton of milk. As we began to walk to our table, we had to go past the goon table. Before we began walking by, Aaron who writes for the school paper stopped me and commented about the morning incident. I told Cody and Derek to go ahead of me and I would be there.

Aaron with his new super 8 mm camera hanging on his chest from a strap around his neck asked, "Could I write an article about you in the school paper?"

"No Aaron, I don't think that is a good idea. Tension is still high right now," I replied.

"Please, let me do the article; you appeared to have changed overnight."

I added, "No Aaron, this is not a good idea; for now, end of the request."

I was beginning to be concerned about my little secret. I just had to keep quiet about this. If it was just this little town, I wouldn't be as concerned. My big fear is the United States Government. I have heard horror stories of what researchers have done to animals in their experiments. Imagine what they would do to me, especially the military if they found out about me. It is still in my best interest if I just keep my mouth shut. However, things here at school seem to be turning out great for me.

As I left Aaron's table, Cody and Derek were about 25 feet ahead of me. Cody was carrying Derek's tray. Derek was to the left of Cody walking by the goon table; Ray had his back to me. Suddenly, I saw Ray stick his leg out and purposefully trip Derek. As Derek tried to catch himself, his crutches flew across the floor. Krystin saw what had happened. She immediately hustled over and yelled at Ray as she was helping Derek back to his feet, "How can you sit there and laugh, I saw what you did and I'm going to tell the principal."

Ray commented, "Go ahead; I don't give a shit after dancing with you Saturday night."

Krystin growled unwittingly adding my name, "You are an impossible asshole just like Phillip said."

Ray looked up at her with burning eyes as I came closer. I was so pissed at what he did to Derek that I wasn't even thinking about Krystin's comment. As I got close enough, I pretended to stumble toward Ray and dumped my entire tray on him. He looked like a food garbage can after I had dumped my food on him. Chili was running down from the top of his head and his shirt and pants were soaked with apple sauce and Chili. Spaghetti strands were hanging down his head and shoulders. It was a comical sight, and I could hear laughter throughout the cafeteria.

I quickly said to Ray in a false pretentious apologetic manner, "I'm so sorry Ray, I slipped on something and lost my balance."

He quickly stood up in front of me and yelled, "I gonna beat your ass from one end of this school to the other end."

He was still about 6 inches taller and weighed about 50 pounds more. His eyes were virtually burning with fire inside while his mouth was quivering. Every time I get upset, my senses heighten almost instantly. I added, "Will you accept my apology?"

He glared at me and blurted, "Not a chance, you little roach."

I was only inches from his body when I sassed, "I see then. I saw what you did to Derek you prick. You got just what you deserved."

The other goons couldn't believe I was talking back to him so abruptly. Jim, the one that purposefully bumped into me this morning, grunted, "See Ray, I told you about my run-in with him this morning. He needs to be brought down a couple of notches and put back in his place."

While glaring Ray in the eyes, I madly proclaimed, "It won't ever be you Jim, you little weasel. Okay, Ray, show everyone what a badass you are." I already had my fists doubled up and was ready.

There was total silence in the cafeteria. Suddenly to everyone else but not to me, Ray leaned back his right shoulder and arm and began to give me a haymaker of a punch. To me, he was throwing the punch in slow motion. I easily threw my left arm up to block his punch; then I quickly hit him with my right fist into the solar plexus; my left fist penetrated his stomach, then I threw a right punch above his right eye in the forehead. He simply fell back to the floor holding his stomach. Within a fraction of a second, the fight was over. I'm sure that Ray was going to be sick from the stomach and solar plexus punch. I was caught up in the moment and acted too fast and probably too strong. I should have known better. I could have swept his legs from underneath him and one quick punch to the stomach would have sent the message.

I quickly kneeled down to Ray to help him up but whispered into his ear, "If you hurt any of my friends again, I'm going to hurt you really bad the next time." I noticed a red area on his forehead above his left eye where my punch to the face area landed was beginning to swell. If I had hit him in the nose or mouth, blood would have been everywhere. I purposefully aimed for his forehead. I didn't know at the time, but Aaron filmed the fight with his new super 8 mm camera. Later on, this was going to be a problem.

I could hear other students quibbling, "Phil blocked his punch, then Ray just fell back. Phil didn't even hit him." I realized that the 3 punches that I landed were so quick everyone else did not see it happen.

In just seconds 2-3 teachers ran over who witnessed the confrontation. I knew that we were both going to the office. What would my mother think? I just couldn't stand what happened to Derek. I guess I just snapped.

Ms. Lathem, my typing teacher assured me, "Phillip, I am surprised at you. You don't get into fights. We saw Ray trip Derek to cause him to fall. We already had information about Ray picking on Derek from principal Clover. We would have handled it. Now you are going to have to answer for your actions."

"I apologize Ms. Lathem, but this has been brewing for quite some time. I just snapped after I saw him trip Derek on purpose. Derek wasn't the only one being bullied. Cody, DeMar, Aaron, and myself have all been subjects of Ray, Ron, Jim, and Billy's abuse. Everyone else in this school gets along fine with us. It's just those guys."

"Well Phillip, you have made your presence known," pointed out Ms. Lathem.

As we were walking toward the principal's office, I glimpsed Ray walking ahead of me, still bent over holding his stomach. Suddenly, he stopped and began to vomit. I knew that I had hit him too hard. I need to be very careful about getting caught up in the moment and taking action more than I should. I need to have control of these extra powers. They sat Ray in the principal's office and put me in the assistant principal Gullon's office. I saw coach Bartlett walk into the office area with principal Clover. I could easily hear both of them whispering even though they were in another room. I was very nervous while I was thinking about the worst-case scenario; *there goes my chance to try out for the team. Way to go, Phil; just keep messing up your future plans.*

Clover whispered to Bartlett, "I was just talking to Phillip this morning and we had a nice visit. This is the first incident that I have had regarding his school behavior. He makes good grades and is a good student."

Bartlett added, "I had a talk with Phil myself this morning in PE class. He must have had hidden basketball skills, but they showed up this morning in a scrimmage. He just toyed with Stan. Stan had all kinds of difficulty guarding him."

"Stan is probably your 2nd best player behind Ray. That surprises me," said Mr. Clover.

Bartlett chimed in, "I'm stunned also. I've had Phillip as a student for the last 3 years and watched him on-and-off play basketball. He was always minimal in his athletic skills. It's like it all happened overnight. If he continues to be this good at basketball, I need him on the team so our school can take advantage. He had also told me about Ray and those losers he hangs around and how they had been pushing him and his friends around. I told Phil I was going to have a talk with Ray. Now seems to be the time to have that discussion. I would like to ask you not to suspend them. That will go on their record and be a black mark against both of them. Let me talk to the two boys together."

Clover agreed while loosening up his blue tie, "Go ahead and talk to them, and I will just send them home for the afternoon to cool off."

After I heard them talking, I felt better about my predicament. I saw Bartlett walk into the principal's office where Ray was sitting. Bartlett was wearing a grey T-shirt with a small (A) dyed into the front left shoulder. Only PE coaches didn't have to dress appropriately for class. He began, "Ray, are you OK?"

"I think so coach, he must have hit me with brass knuckles or something. Look at this goose egg on my forehead."

"Some of the teachers and students said they didn't even see him hit you. He blocked your punch and you just fell back to the floor."

"My bruised stomach and this goose egg are on the front of my body. How did I get these if I fell back?"

Bartlett started with his lecture to Ray as he promised me, "Ray, I have been disappointed in some of your actions. Those boys that seem to be hanging around you have been detrimental to you and a bad influence. They are not helping you achieve the goals that you have to complete. You are a senior for God's sake, tripping a crippled boy. Do you know how ugly that looked on you to the other students? You are getting ready to hopefully get a basketball scholarship. They don't want someone that is in trouble all the time. They want someone that is not only a good athlete but someone who can think like an adult and make good decisions. The very students you are bullying are the ones that you need to be friends with. I don't know if you have heard Phil is going to try out for the team. He has improved dramatically as an athlete. He can fill the weaknesses that we had on the team last year. He can help us to win the sectional in basketball this school year. Here you are trying to fight him."

Ray moaned in desperation, "He dumped his food tray on me."

"You had it coming, you pissed him off and he snapped."

Then coach Bartlett gave a big yell, "Phil, come into the principal's office."

As I entered feeling belittled, I immediately noticed Ray glaring toward me as if he had X-ray vision. I sat in a chair on the other side of the room.

Coach Bartlett began his 2nd lecture to Ray and me, "Gentlemen, this nonsense needs to stop. Both of you may be on Austiana's basketball team and will likely have to play together. If that happens, you will learn to depend on each other. Ray, you could use Phil's help right now, especially in your studies. How are those punks, Jimmy and Billy going to help you? You have to know that I am telling the truth. Boys, I talked to Mr. Clover, and he is willing to not do any suspensions if you two boys shake hands and put all this behind us and turn over a new leaf. How about it?"

I stood up and walked over to Ray while he was still sitting, extended my right hand out with my head hanging down, and avowed, "I'm sorry about dumping my tray on you. I will buy you a new shirt. I want us to be friends, not enemies. I have had a belly full of bullying and I'm not going to take it anymore since I have been working out and getting stronger. Again, I apologize to you. Will you please accept it?"

He grabbed my hand, and we shook hands as he added, "Coach is correct about me needing to pick better friends. I need to listen to him because he has my best interest in mind. It is time for me to grow up and act my age. I could sure use your help in some of my studies. I'm beginning to worry about getting into college. I need to take advantage of this year and improve my grades."

"I would be happy to help. I can help in science and math, and Derek can help in English. He is like a walking encyclopedia," I asserted.

It was nearing the end of lunch when Ray and I walked back into the cafeteria. I walked with him to his table and shook hands with him again just so Ron, Jim, and Billy could see our friendly gestures. When they saw us shaking hands, I could tell they were totally surprised.

Arching one eyebrow in disbelief, Jim objected, "Ray, tell me that you haven't made up with that nerd."

Ray uttered, "Yes, Phil and I have put all our differences behind us, and we are friends now. He is going out for the basketball team, and we are going to be teammates playing together to win the sectional this year for the first time in 25 years."

Jim sneered in a negative tone, "Yeah, right."

"That is your problem, Jim. You don't want to see someone else make things better for themselves because you are not doing anything to make things better for you."

Jim whimpered, "Chill out; I was just joking."

I chimed in, "It didn't sound like a joke to me," as everyone else looked on and listened intently.

Jim with an angry look toward me bellows out, "My Dad wants to have a talk with you about this morning."

"Does your dad know that you purposefully bumped into me? You aggravated the whole circumstance. I'm sorry Jim, maybe I need to use simpler words when talking to you. If I messed up that ugly motorcycle jacket, I may have done you a favor. Time to get you a new jacket."

"Funny Phil, you should be a comedian. You going out for the basketball team. Do yourself a favor and save yourself from being embarrassed."

I taunted, "I'll play you anytime as long as I can work it into my schedule. Unlike you, most of us have other things to do." Then I walked away to get with Cody and Derek.

Jim is not used to being addressed like that, especially in front of Ron and Billy. Both of them were hanging on to every word that was said while becoming speechless.

Ray finally coaxed, "Jim, play him a game. I'll referee."

This really put Jim on the spot while his buddies were waiting for his response. He was definitely cornered.

Jim added with a weakened voice, "If he makes the basketball team, then I'll play him one-on-one and beat his ass."

Ray got up from the group's table and walked over to me to relay what Jim had said. At the same time, Ray apologized to Derek as his apology was accepted and Ray shook hands with Derek.

I said, "I'm proud of you Ray, you have had a change of heart."

Ray added, "Phil, you have had a change of attitude, and I like it. I like people that will stand up for themselves."

The bell finally sounded for the afternoon classes. While walking to class I began thinking; *I can't decide if my added abilities have changed my attitude or if I have changed my attitude myself because of my added abilities. I still have a lot of unanswered questions.*

Krystin was slightly ahead of me walking down the hallway; she stopped to let me catch up to walk beside her.

She inquired, "Several students have been talking about you going out for the basketball team. How neat would that be, me being a cheerleader and you playing on the team? I may be putting the cart in front of the horse because I haven't made the cheerleading team yet."

I added, "You have been on the cheer team since you were a freshman. This is your senior year. I would have to say that gives you a big advantage. I would say that you are on the cheer team. I'm the one that has never been on the basketball team and here I am trying out my senior year."

"I was talking to Stan and Dan, and they both agreed that you have increased your athleticism a lot. I have faith in you, Phil. I think we are going to be seeing a lot of each other every game."

I chimed in before I entered my class English class, "I think I will make the team because I've had a change of attitude, I seem to be more assertive, and it appears to be helping me along with working out and getting stronger."

As she was walking on to her class she echoed back, "I like your positive attitude and I also like what you are doing to your physique."

The school day ends, and I scurry down the hallway to exit the school. As I was heading to the car, I saw Ray giving me a friendly wave. I waved back and gave him a thumbs up. I needed to get to work at the grocery store today.

After school, I usually work for about 3 hrs. 2 days a week to get the 20 hours a week that Mr. Mudd wants me to accomplish. However, if I'm to make the basketball team, I won't be able to work weekdays and on some Saturdays, I may have to take off early if there is a Saturday night game. This could be an issue with Mr. Mudd. Maybe I'm getting the (cart before the horse). I haven't made the team yet. Mr. Mudd is a school sports enthusiast. He always buys season tickets to basketball and football games. That may work in my favor.

As I drive to the store, I try to think about how to approach Mr. Mudd. He can be in a foul mood sometimes. I get out of the car and walk into the store. He has an elevated deck in the far-right corner of the store. The deck is about 10 ft. square surrounded by railings and about 5 ft. off the floor. He has his work desk in the middle of it. He likes to be higher to see down all the aisles. At the end of each aisle is a large, elongated mirror angled to reflect the entire aisle toward his desk. I suppose it is to help with shoplifters, and he can keep an eye on the workers. There is a small stairway to enter the deck and his desk or office. As I walk up the steps of the stairs, I could see him sitting there counting money. Without looking up, he inquired, "What do you need Phil."

I muttered, "Mr. Mudd, I am going to try out for the basketball team this year."

"Why Phil, you haven't played on the team before? Why are you interested now?"

I explained nervously, "I just thought it would look good on my extra-curricular activities record for college. The coach talked to me, and he thinks I can make the team. I have been working out lifting weights, and he thinks my athletic skills have improved."

Mudd continued, "I have noticed that you have bulked up almost overnight. The team could use a good strong ball handler. The Johnson boy last year had the ball stolen from him 3-4 times every game. It is tough to have a good win-loss record when that is happening."

I gulped and said, "In order to play, I will have to cut my hours some. Will that be OK with you?"

He then looked up, "I need you as much as possible. I suppose I could cut you back 4-5 hours a week. I definitely need you on Saturday from 8-6 and Sunday from 12-6."

"I will be happy to work those hours unless we have a Saturday game. Then I will need to leave a little early. There are only 3-4 Saturday games for the season until the sectional. All the other games are on Friday night."

Mr. Mudd leaned back in his chair and put both hands behind his head, "I want to talk to Bartlett. If he thinks you can help the team, then I'm all for that. We haven't won a sectional in ages."

I assured him, "This is going to be the year. You just watch."

"You seem to be pretty sure of yourself, Phil. I like that a person has a positive attitude. I'll talk to Bartlett and let you know. It is time for you to get your hours in this evening."

I will get about 3 hours of work this evening. I must remember about those mirrors angled towards Mr. Mudd's desk. Sunday, I picked up those 4 cases of green beans. I don't need to let him see me do those things. I need this job to help with expenses. I also noticed today that schoolwork seemed very easy. My reading speed has picked up at least 3 times faster than I normally read, and Chemistry has even been easier. Could my brain be developing along with the other senses? I still have a lot of questions and I feel like I need to get another opinion from someone or get checked by a doctor. I could be slowly dying and not even know it. Maybe my heart can't handle all these changes with time such as better vision, hearing, smell, strength, and body mass building muscle tissue. However, that shot has made different than everyone else in the school. I'm not afraid of anyone in the school but I am afraid of someone finding out how I got this way.

An hour has passed while stocking the shelves in a speedy manner but not too noticeable. I looked down my aisle and saw Jim's Dad, Orville Smith walking down the aisle toward me. I figured that Jim must have told his dad about me grabbing him and lifting him up into the air. Orville is about the biggest dumb redneck in town. I have redneck family roots also, but I am also a nerd. I must be a redneck nerd. As he walked up to me, I was standing on a step stool stocking one of the upper shelves.

With noisy breathing and a red face with his legs widened, Orville demanded in a threatening tone, "Step down, want to talk to youuu bout Jim."

With anxiety beginning to set in and a churning stomach along with all my senses being heightened immediately, I meekly murmured, "What do you need to talk about?"

With an abrasive voice and not very good redneck English he berated, "What's this I heer about you running into my son and almost flattened him to the ground and then grab him by his nice jacket and picking him up off the floor. When you set him back down to the floor, you called him a 'dumbass'."

I explained, "First of all, your son purposefully bumped into me and then had the gall to say, 'watch where you are going nerd'. Because he had been bullying me and my friends, that is when I grabbed him and picked him up off the floor several inches. I called him a dumbass while he was still suspended in the air, not when I put him down. Your son needs to get his story straight. I apologize for that, I lost my cool, but it was time he needed to be taught a lesson. No more bullying is coming via him or his friends."

Orville looking confused, "What in the hell does via mean."

"It means (by way of). Let me put it into redneck terms for you. No more bullying by way of Jim. I know he doesn't like me. I wish that wasn't the way it is, but because of his actions, I'm beginning to dislike him."

"You thank you are so smart don't you twerp."

"I do alright."

Orville growled, "He said that you started the whole thang."

I humbly added, "3 other students saw him that morning, and he instigated it. That's my story and I'm sticking to it. Hey, that would make a good country song for someone to write and sing -- *That's my story and I'm sticking to it.*"

"You are gitting on my nerves boy," Orville snarled.

"I'm sorry Orville, I don't intend to," I added, but deep down I didn't care if I was getting on his nerves.

"If you touch my boy again, I'm going to hurt you."

I very nicely insisted, "That is up to Jim. I have no more quarrels with Jim. But if he pushes me or any of my friends around again, I'm going to be pushing him. Please give him that message."

This time Orville gets closer to my face, "you don't know who you are talking to. You got a lot of guts boy. You know what happens to people like you, they get gutted."

As I inched closer to his face, by now I could smell his horrible breath and easily see his green teeth, "Are you threatening me?"

Orville added, "You take it however you want to."

I informed him, "You heard what I said too."

Orville began, "You sure have changed. You used to run from trouble like all the other geeks, which brings up another question. Willie Willis told me that the night of the fireball, he was walking down the road. He said it was some kind of a spaceship. He saw you drive by, and when it crashed, he saw you get out and go into the wreckage. Then he said he saw you come running out shortly after that and you were yelling in pain. When the spaceship exploded, you ran back to the car and drove off. There is something going on with you and that spaceship. Did you go into the wreck of the spaceship?"

I quickly added, "Willie is the town drunk. No, I didn't go near the meteorite. That is what it was determined to be – a piece of space rock that fell to earth, no aliens. Did Willie tell you that the alien pilot waved at him before he crashed. That is what he told the sheriff. Who are you going to believe?

Orville was still trying to piece together what happened to be in his favor, "Its jest funny that when this happened, you have changed somehow. I can't put my finger on it, but I'm going to find out what really happened."

Several minutes had passed during our discussion and Mr. Mudd had seen us talking. He approached Orville and me.

"Is everything OK?" asked Mudd.

Orville began to walk away, "Everything is OK Mr. Mudd; I just needed to have a little talk with your worker."

As Orville slowly walked out of the store, Mudd chimed in, "What was that all about Phil?"

"I had a confrontation with his son at school and Orville came in and threatened me."

Mudd raged, "That bum loser doesn't need to be threatening my workers here at the store. If he comes in and threatens you again, you immediately come up and get me."

"Thanks Mr. Mudd; I appreciate your support."

My work evening finally ended. I clocked out and headed to the *mean green machine*. As I started to get in the car, I found a note written sticking in between my windshield wipers. The note was in poor handwriting with redneck flare and was from Orville. It read:

"When I git home, Jim is going to answer to me for letting you get the best of him. He is going to git an ass beating from me. He needs to git even wit you. If he doesn't beat your ass, I'm going to." Signed—Orville.

Now I'm pissed at that goofy bastard. This is what happens a lot of the time. When kids become bullies, one or both of their parents encourage it, usually their dad. Some fathers have the philosophy: (My son needs to be able to take care of himself in this world and sometimes that means standing up for himself. He is not afraid of anybody.) Some young teenagers often carry that philosophy too far, resulting in bullying.

In hindsight, Jim may be forced to act the way he has been treating his classmates. I feel bad that I may have made things worse for him. I have a little surprise for Orville. It wasn't very smart of him to sign it. Look who I'm talking about, Mr. Redneck Dufus whose name is Orville. I'm going to show this letter to the principal, the sheriff, and the town's social services. This will make him even more pissed at me, but they will be aggravating the crap out of him. This may be the best way I can help Jim. I need to talk to him tomorrow at school.

As soon as I got into the house, I called Cody and told him about Jim's Dad. I did not tell my mother. She doesn't need any of my problems to worry about. I read the note to him.

Cody gasped, "No way, dude! He could get into trouble for that."

I commented, "I'm going to show this note to the principal tomorrow and have Ray tell his dad, the county sheriff about the note. It just reminds me that maybe Jim is not a bad person, just like Ray. We made up and we are fine now."

Cody added, "His dad will be pissed at you and may try to hurt you."

"I know; I'll have to be careful and vigilant."

"Dude, just be careful. I will try to be there for you if his dad gets pissy. Not to change the subject, are you going to try out for the basketball team this Thursday?"

"Yeah, I'm going for it. I think I can make the team. That will look good on my resume to enter college. Social activities – Basketball, senior year."

Cody bragged, "I think you will make the team too. You have really bulked up. Heck, you are probably the strongest guy on the team. When I heard how you caused Stan, who is one of the best players on the team, to leave his jock strap hanging on the rim, that convinced me that you are in."

"It would be nice to graduate with some kind of legacy like winning the first sectional in 25 years."

"Dude, that would be awesome."

Looking up at the clock I reminded Cody, "I've got some studying to do for tomorrow. I'll see you then. Bye."

I really didn't have too much studying to do because I was performing my homework 3-4 times faster than I used to. I decided to take a little break before bedtime and trotted up the stairs to watch a little TV. Mom was sitting on the couch watching an episode of a TV show called Columbo which starred an actor named Peter Falk. He played the role of this private investigator that was so annoying and pesky to the murder suspects.

"What's happening mom?" I uttered in a relaxed, peaceful manner while sitting down beside her on the couch.

"Janet told me about your fight today. I'm glad you didn't get hurt. What were you thinking? You could have been expelled from school and that would not look good for someone planning on going to college."

"I know, but luckily Mr. Bartlett saved me and Ray. He convinced the principal that we would be playing basketball together and we have a chance to win the sectional."

She added, "Are you going out for the team?"

"Yes, I intend to do so."

"When are tryouts?"

"This Thursday after school."

"Mr. Bartlett must have a lot of faith in you since you haven't made the team yet." She chimed in.

"I will make the team and if I do so, it will look good on my college resume."

"What about your work hours?"

"I will lose a few hours, but I can still work on weekends. I have talked to Mr. Mudd about it, and I think he will work with me."

"Ok Phil, I hope you know what you are doing."

"I'm going to bed mom and hopefully, get a good night's sleep and be ready for school Tuesday." As I headed down the basement stairs to my cellar dweller abode, I was having mixed feelings about Jim. I can't help but think that his dad has instilled Jim's bullish attitude. I am going to try to talk to him tomorrow.

TUESDAY – ANOTHER SCHOOL DAY

The alarm goes off and I begin my morning routine which now includes looking in the mirror closely for any physical changes to my body. This morning, everything looked OK. However, through the night I kept having this tingle feeling around my shoulder blades. I grabbed another mirror and turned my back to the main mirror over my sink to be able to see my back. I did notice a slight reddening around both of my shoulder blades toward the middle of my back. So far, I'm not too concerned but I need to keep an eye on it. I don't want to get paranoid about all that has happened either. After doing the 3 S's (shit, shower, and shave), I head up the stairs to grab a bite of breakfast.

"Good morning mom," I happily chirped.

"Good morning, sweetheart. I was just watching the news and the war in Vietnam is accelerating and the military is intensifying the draft. I'm really worried about you, Phil."

"Not to worry, they are not drafting any college students. So far, if you go to college, you can still get an academic deferment, which is another reason to go to college. I'm having difficulty understanding why our country is even over there fighting that war."

Mom persuaded, "Our country doesn't want other countries to establish a communism-type government."

I added, "What if that is what most of the people of South Vietnam want anyway?"

Mom spoke softly, "I know; who can understand politics?"

I proclaimed, "It's a vicious circle."

Janet finally walked into the kitchen and sat down at the table and blurred out, "You going to be a big basketball star now?"

"I don't know Janet; I would like to play on the team."

"Good luck with that," she added in a defiant manner.

"Thanks for all your encouragement."

In a more grateful tone, Janet looked at me and smiled, "Oh! By the way, thanks for helping me with geometry. You helped make it easier to understand."

"Remember, you just can't let up on it. Any challenging subject, you just have to stay with it almost every night."

"I have a test today; hope I do OK on it. I'm tired of getting D's on exams."

As I got up from the table and headed out the door, "Good luck Janet, make mom and myself proud of you."

Before I got into the *mean green machine,* I jumped up and grabbed the low-hanging limb of the oak tree that I parked my car underneath the tree. Yes, it is chin-up time. I started doing them so easily. As I picked up speed doing about 1 per second, I knocked off 100 and still had energy left. I just wanted to see if I continued to have the strength that I had apparently been blessed with. I let go after 100 chin-ups, get into the car and head to school.

After parking the car, I headed into the doors of the school hoping to run into Jim. I first went into the principal's office and gave Mr. Clover the note that ignorant redneck Orville wrote to me and put on my windshield.

Mr. Clover asked, "Phil, what is this all about?"

"Monday morning, Jim was walking down the hallway and purposefully walked over and bumped into me. He yelled and said, 'get out of my way nerd.' Mr. Clover, you know that I don't cause trouble for anyone in the school, but I've had enough of that group of boys pushing me and my friends around. You know that Derek can't defend his self. Cody, and DeMar won't fight back. I apologize; I just finally snapped. I picked him up off the floor with both hands and asserted to him, "Let me tell you something, you little dumbass, things are starting to change around here. You had better understand that. I then set him back to the floor and brushed off his jacket. He likes to hang around Ray, so I am sure he told Ray what happened. Lunch rolls around and Ray and I get into a fight. Jim's Dad is encouraging him to fight me, and I don't want to fight anyone. I have said what I needed to say to Jim. I think his dad wants him to be a bully. I would like to talk to Jim and see What I could do to help him in that horrible parenting situation. He said that he was going to beat Jim's ass because I supposedly got the best of him."

"Let me bring Jim into my office and talk to him. I may call you out of class also."

"That would be OK; I don't want to put him in a bad relationship with his father."

I left the principal's office; I started walking down the hallway to my 1st period class. I recognized this voice behind me getting closer. I knew it was Ray.

He shouted with an enjoyable tone, "Phil, I want you to meet my new girlfriend. Have you met Amanda? I took her out on a date last night and we really hit it off."

I replied, "Hi Amanda, Nice to meet you. I understand that you are a Junior here at AHS."

Amanda affirmed my statement, "Yes, a Junior. Ray tells me that you are going out for the basketball team and our school has a shot at winning the sectional this year."

While patting Ray on the back I implied, "Well, it's early but that is our intention. It was so nice to meet you Amanda. Ray, may I talk to you later today about something else."

Ray said, "Sure Phil, I'll catch you at lunch or after school."

I gave Ray a personal wink and a thumbs up while nodding toward Amanda as she had begun conversing with another girl at the time.

I didn't know Amanda personally, but she is attractive, and I have heard gossip that she has been promiscuous at times. If that is the case, I need to warn Ray to be careful and at least have protection during any sexual activity. I feel like he has a good opportunity to get a basketball scholarship. I also am overwhelmed with Ray and his change of attitude. I am currently proud of that boy. I still need to talk to Jim.

1st period geography class starts and within 20 minutes into the class, Mr. Clover's voice comes over the intercom, "Mr. Shields, please send Phillip down to my office."

Mr. Shields answered back, "He will be right down."

I left my books on my desk, started to walk out of the classroom when Krystin whispered, "Is everything OK."

I whispered back to her, "Everything is fine; Mr. Clover needs to talk to me about another matter." She still had a worried expression. She looked so beautiful sitting there beside me in a pretty red sweater and grey skirt with a matching grey scarf tied around her neck. Her beautiful hair hanging just past per shoulders.

I left the classroom and while walking down the hallway to the principal's office, I figured that he had Jim in his office and Clover has probably showed Jim that note. I was thinking about how to approach Jim. As I entered the office, I saw Jim sitting there across the desk from Mr. Clover with a black eye. I quickly asked. "Jim, what happened?"

"I got nothing to say to you. You are the reason I got this shiner." snarled Jim.

Mr. Clover started his talk, "Jim, did your dad write that note to Phillip?"

Jim added with a negative attitude, "I guess so; he signed it. Why are you badgering me about it?"

Mr. Clover revealed to Jim, "Your dad could get into trouble doing something like this."

I chimed in, "Jim I'm so sorry that our little incident caused you trouble at home. I certainly had no intentions of that happening. I was just tired of you picking on me and my friends and just wanted to let you know that those days are over."

Jim looking down at the floor, "So my dad could get into trouble. Who cares? I sure don't. In fact, I hate him because he beats my mom all the time. He gave me this black eye because I didn't stand up to you."

Mr. Clover being silent continues to listen and look on intently.

I reiterated, "I am sorry Jim, I feel halfway responsible for causing this riff between you and your dad."

"It's not you Phil; my dad and I don't get along because he treats my mom so badly. He is not my real dad; he is my stepdad. There is one other thing; he found out from big mouth Billy that we are supposed to play a basketball game and he wants to be there to see me kick your ass. If you beat me in the game, I'll get another beating when I get home."

"It was my understanding that if I made the team, we would have that playoff. I haven't made the team yet."

"After listening to some of the other boys in your PE class. You will make the team. It's like you have changed over the weekend. You used to not be able to play ball that good. Also, my dad says that was an alien spacecraft that crashed the other night, and you went in the spacecraft. He said that his friend, Willie Willis was walking down the road that night and saw the whole thing including you entering the crashed spacecraft."

"Did your dad tell you that Willie saw the alien wave at him before it crashed. That's what he told me. Willie is a drunk, and on Saturday night, I'm sure he was drunk. It was nothing but a meteorite. I have changed because I have been lifting weights and working out," I boasted.

"Well dad is convinced that is what happened, and he was somehow going to prove it."

Mr. Clover started laughing at Jim's comments and agreed with me, "Jim, you know how Willie is. He has told more wild stories than anyone else in this entire county. You already have more education than your father. Don't believe those stories."

I added, "If we have to play that game in front of your dad, what would be your outcome if you win the game, or maybe I back out and don't play you at all."

Jim said, "I'm not sure how he will react."

I declared as I extended my hand for a handshake, "If we play, I'm pretty sure you will win the game."

Jim extended his hand, and we shook hands. I gave him a pat on the back.

Clover concluded, "Jim, you can go back to class now, Phil I need to talk to you about something else, so you stay here a couple more minutes."

Jim left the office. I asked, "What did you need to talk to me about Mr. Clover?"

"That was a noble thing you just did for Jim. I won't forget this either. Coach Bartlett told me how much you had improved in your skills since you have gotten stronger. He is convinced we will win the sectional. Needless to say, you have impressed him. There is no way according to coach Bartlett that Jim could beat you in a one-on-one game."

"I think I can stage a victory for Jim to keep his stepdad off his back. You know his stepdad is a few bricks short of a full load, mentally speaking."

Mr. Clover continued, "I will show the sheriff this note and make him aware of Orville Smith. He has been in jail more than once for domestic abuse. Now you can go back to class Phil."

As I left the office, I could hear Clover chuckling to himself and mumbling, "Alien spacecraft, waving at Willie, give me a break."

So far, no one believes Willie and his story. He must have been walking down the road that night because he said that he saw me go into the crashed spacecraft. He could have said anyone's name in town, but he said my name. I went back to class, and I could tell that Krystin was glad to see me because she had a big, relieved smile on her face as I sat down in my seat.

LUNCH TIME

The bell rings and I rush down the hallway to lunch. When I got in the food line, I noticed that Derek was about 3 people ahead of me. I also observed that no one was trying to jump the line in front of us. Word must travel fast. Huh! As I headed down the tray line, I began my usual bragging on the cooks.

I started boasting, "Girls, you all look so pretty today, and you cook this food so well that it wouldn't surprise me if students started fighting over this scrumptious food."

One of the cooks replied, "Mr. Marland, you make remarks like this every time you go through this line, but we still appreciate it."

"It's true girls, it's true," I pleaded.

After receiving my food with somewhat extra helpings, I walked to the lunch table where Krystin was setting.

I asked, "May I sit here beside you Krystin, the queen of the school?"

She answered, "Yes, I would like that."

I had just started eating when Ray and his girlfriend Amanda came to our table and sat across from Krystin and me. I was so glad to see Ray separate himself from the goon table. This was a golden opportunity to talk to Ray about Jim and his redneck dad. I began to tell him what happened as Krystin and Amanda both listened intently.

I began, "Hey Ray, I had the experience of meeting Jim's dad yesterday evening at the grocery store while I was working. He was mad about my incident with Jim that Tuesday morning before classes started. He threatened me and told me he was going to beat Jim's ass because of him not standing up to me. All I did was pick Jim up off the floor and let him know that I, along with my friends wasn't going to take his crap anymore."

Ray added, "I heard about your confrontation with Jim. When you picked him up off the floor, you scared the Be-Jesus out of him. Jim's stepdad is an asshole. He beats on Jim's mom all the time. I'm pretty sure he slaps Jim around too."

Krystin spoke with a cheerful voice, "Ray I'm glad to see you not eating at the loser table. Ron, Jim, and Billy are here to pester the rest of us, and they think they have that right."

"I know, coach told me to get away from those boys —
they're nothing but trouble."

As Ray continued talking, I was thinking, *what was
that marvelous stuff that was injected into my body by
that alien? My life has changed so much. I'm scared that
all this may come to an end. Currently, I'm in a perfect
position in this world. I feel as though I can accomplish
almost anything.*

I butted back in on the conversation, "Jim's stepdad is
expecting to see Jim and I play a game of Basketball, and
I'm sure he wants to revel in Jim's victory over me. I know
I can take him in a game, but that could mean misery for
Jim. I don't want that. I can live with a loss to Jim."

"Coach told me that you have improved a hell-of-a-
lot," Ray added.

Ray kept talking, "Coach told me how you handled
Stan, and he is one of our better players. Jim is not a very
good player. He may make the team, but he will be sitting
on the bench most every game unless we get ahead by 25
or 30 points. Then and only then, he may get to play. That
is why Jim's stepdad doesn't like coach Bartlett. He doesn't
play Jim much. I can't blame the coach; he has to play his
best players. If this one-on-one game comes about, that
would be very admirable of you to throw the game to help
Jim."

"I have told Jim that I was pretty sure he was going to
win the game." I replied while both of our girlfriends and
Ray listened intently.

CHAPTER 05

THE BASKETBALL TEAM AND FRIDAY NIGHT DATE

I'm sitting in the final class of the day, Chemistry, and just received my last exam score. I had a score of 96%. I could have gotten a 100% but I missed a couple of questions on purpose. Hardly anyone gets a 100% in Mr. Sexton's Chemistry class. If someone in class does get 100%, the next exam is always much tougher. This is just a reminder to me that my mind has also developed. I read much faster, don't have to spend much time on homework, and I understand the more difficult concepts much better. Everything about me has improved.

Krystin showed me her score and she scored an 86%. She gave me a soft, sexy whisper, "I may need your help in this class."

"I believe I am understanding Chemistry more. Would love to help such a beautiful girl." I confessed, whispering back to her.

The bell rang and Krystin was on her way to cheerleader tryouts, and I was to be on my way to the basketball tryouts. As we were walking out, she was smoothing her clothing and with a hopeful voice and

97

strong eye contact, she leaned up and kissed me, "Good luck. After everything I have heard, I know you will make the team."

Exhaling while looking up, "Thanks, I will do my best. You have helped to inspire me. I want to be on the floor playing while you are cheering."

Going down the hallway, we headed in different directions. She was going to the school stage where the class plays were performed, and I was heading to the Gym to change clothes and put on my PE clothes. While changing clothes, Dan was walking by and mumbled, "Hey Phil, what are those two long scratches inside your shoulder blades?"

I went to a mirror to see, twisted my head back as far as I could and noticed long red abrasions going down the inside of my shoulder blades, the Scapulas. They both looked like long scratches, but they were definitely red and irritated.

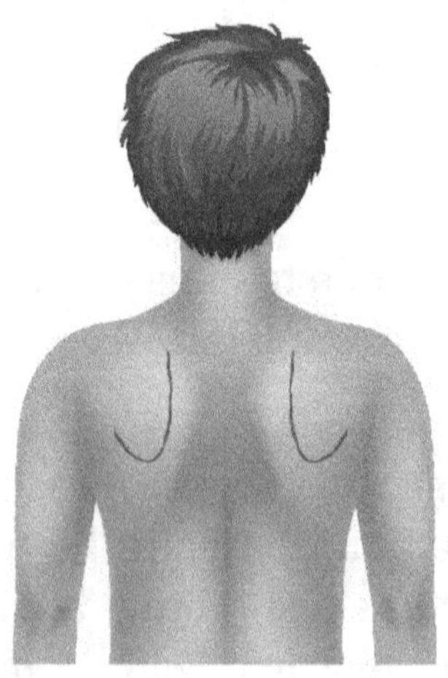

This was very concerning, but for now I had to shrug it off.

"I got into some thorns the other day at home and got scratched up." I replied.

Dan added, "that is just odd; they are both almost mirror images of each other."

Thank goodness, no one else questioned anything. I believe that my transformation is not complete yet. Am I just now starting to turn into the Alien? When I saw the creature, I did not see its back. Just one more thing to worry about. I quickly put on my shirt to cover the scars. They really didn't bother me but was just somewhat itchy.

We scurried from the locker room to the floor to warm up for about 15 minutes. I started shooting the basketball with my senses and abilities already heightened. I shot several long shots occasionally missing one. Little did I know that 22 years later, the 3-point shot would be established in high school basketball in 1987. But the 3-point shot didn't exist in the '60s. The goal still looked huge to me, so it was easy for me to make short baskets. The long shots took a little sharper eye but were still pretty easy to swish. After we shot around for about 15 minutes, coach Bartlett came out and decided to scrimmage a game. He matched his best players from last year which included Stan, Dan, Ray, Nick, and Ron who was one of Jim's friends. Ron was another bully to my friends. No love was lost there. All the other players have come around and grown up somewhat. I may have helped them with that incident with Ray.

Unfortunately for Ron, who was the least talented player on Bartlett's starters, had to guard me. At the same time, I had to guard Ron. It was not going to be a good night for Ron. Bartlett's starters got the ball first after a jump ball and Ray tipped the ball to Stan. He passed the ball to Ron. I immediately guarded him, again not to bring forth too much notice of my abilities, but for Ron it was like a bad dream. Just as soon as he started dribbling the ball, it was as if he was dribbling in slow motion. He stopped and proceeded to make a pass back to Stan. Just as he did, I made a quick lunge and deflected the ball and easily beat him to it. Most of the other players on my team were not very good, but Big Al was on my team. His size made him a decent player.

My experience from PE class, big Al took up space in the middle. It was easy for me to get past Ron and I headed toward Ray who was guarding big Al. When Ray switched off big Al and lunged to guard me, I quickly shoveled the ball to big Al. I knew not to shovel him the ball too quickly because he didn't have good hands. Within a second, I was dribbling the ball and made the bounce pass to big Al. He turned toward the basket to shoot, but he missed; Ray leaps up around the rim and grabs the ball. I leaped up a little higher, got my right hand on the ball. Even though Ray was the strongest person on the team, I was so much stronger than him and easily snatched the ball from him before we landed back on the floor. By the time Ray turned around, I was already back up into the air shooting a beautiful shot and swishing the basket.

It only took about 10 minutes for Bartlett to see that he wanted me with the starting team. Bartlett interrupted the game, "Ron, you and Phil switch teams.

I replied, "Thanks coach I would cherish the opportunity to play with those guys." I was going to get to play with Ray, Dan, Stan, and Nick. I know that I could get such beautiful passes to them. The rest of the tryout was like clockwork. We scored every time on the other boys. If someone shot and missed, either Ray, Dan, Stan, or me rebounded the ball and played until we scored. I took it upon myself to help rebound. A couple of the rebounds forced me to get high into the air, slightly above the rim. Often times I passed the ball to Ray where he scored easily. The other boys trying out for the team had no one that could even come close to guarding Ray or myself. I didn't want to outscore Ray, but I played a close second. Ray finished with 25 points. I scored 20, 8 of those were long shots, just showing off. I made every basket I shot. I wanted to secure my place on the team.

Ron was hoping to be a starter this year and his dad was looking forward to him playing. To make the team, I had to take someone's place. It was going to have to be Ron. Ron would probably make the team, but he was not going to be a starter. He would probably get to play some to relieve the starters. In small towns, every parent thinks their son or daughter, whatever the sport, is a superstar. I knew Ron's dad, who is a friend of Orville was going to be pissed at me like Orville was. Jim would make the team also but would probably not play much.

After the tryouts, I knew that I had made enemies, but I also had just made 4 friends. Everyone had the same goal, and that was to win the sectional. Our school's nemesis was the Scottsville Warriors. Their school is more than double our enrollment. We haven't beaten them in 13 years.

As we were heading to the locker room, Ray, Dan, and Stan all ran over to congratulate me.

Ray bellowed out, "Phil, you looked great out there. I'm really excited about this year. I just hope no one gets hurt. I just loved those tipped passes to me. You made it easy for me to score."

Stan quickly added, "We are going to win a lot of games this year,"

I quickly reminded them, "I haven't made the team yet."

Dan asserted, "Oh, you have made the team. Bartlett is no dummy. If you don't, his head in the sand."

"If I make the team, I think we will have a fun year."

I then received several pats on the back along with one dejected and dirty look. Coach Bartlett will post the team roster outside his office Friday morning.

Heading home from the tryouts, I felt good about getting on the team. I am concerned about the 2 red linear marks around my shoulder blades. They seem to be getting a deeper red and a little more irritating. When I arrived home, I called Cody.

"Hey Cody, Phil here; what did you think of the tryouts?"

Cody replied, "You made the team for sure, Phil. You were the best one on the floor tonight. Ray looked great because of your great passing to him. I just hope I made the team. Remember, I didn't make the team last year, but I practiced a lot in off-season and have improved."

"I did notice that you showed improvement tonight. You played better than most of the other guys trying to make the team."

I excitedly added, "It would be so much fun to have both of us on the team. That will show all the goons that even nerds can play basketball. How are things with you and Carrie."

"I really like her," said Cody. "She is pretty, smart, and yes, I want to jump her bones. But I have to keep control because both of us are going to college. I don't want to mess that up."

"I have the same feelings about Krystin. You and I are both sort of in the same boat if you know what I mean."

Cody sighed, "Yeah, I know. It's a cruel world out there when it comes to sexual tensions for boys like us. Not to change the subject, but none of the goons have pestered me lately. That run-in with you and Ray and Jim at school must have done something. I think they are afraid of you."

"Maybe so, but I might add that I have been happy with Ray's change of attitude. I think the coach gave him a good talk and told him to quit hanging out with losers. That is why he has been sitting with us more during lunch, and you have had to notice that he hasn't been mouthing off to any of us. If you can be of any help to him with his studies, please help him. I think he is on the right track now."

"Sure," Cody calmly added while yawning.

I commanded, "I know we both have some studying to get done. We'll get to school tomorrow, and both our names will be on the list. I have a good feeling about it. Going to hang up and will see you tomorrow, friend."

"Bye, my good friend." Cody avowed.

FRIDAY

The alarm goes off on my radio which I have set to music. The song 'A Hard Day's Night' by the Beatles began to play and seemed appropriate at the time. The lyrics matched my circumstance well. *It's been a hard day's night, and I've been working like a dog; It's been a hard day's night; I should be sleeping like a log.* It was a busy night, going out for the team and all, getting home to get my studies finished. I go through my typical routine and make sure to look at my back and shoulder blades. The areas of irritation seem to be getting slightly wider. I realize I may have to talk to mom about this. I'm still not mentioning the crash. I know our military and I don't want to be a guinea pig for someone to be probing my body. As I hurried up the stairs, the next song on the radio was (Down in the Boondocks) by Billy Joe Royal. It often appears that these songs are telling my life's story. Sometimes that could be a bummer.

I had just opened the refrigerator door when mom spoke. "How did the tryouts go last night?"

"It went OK. I think I have a good shot at making the team." Janet was sitting there rolling her eyes while all the time me knowing that siblings can be spiteful to each other even though they have that deep family love for each other.

She added, "I overheard Ron and Jim, the buttheads talking about how they were going to be starters on the first five this year. If you hope to be one of the starting five, there's no room for all three of you along with Ray, Dan, and Stan. Somebody is going to have to sit on the bench with much less playing time."

"Oooh! Janet has all the answers." I replied.

Mom interrupts, "Cut the squabbling; we don't need any of that this morning."

I finally get up the nerve, "Mom, I want you to look at my back. Something is going on and I'm not sure what it is."

As I faced away from her and lifted my shirt she said, "Let me see."

When she looked at the 2 mirror images of the marks which looked like long irritated scratches, she inquired cluelessly, "I have never seen anything like that before. I need to make a doctor's appointment to see what is going on. People are dying every day of cancer."

"Gee, thanks for the encouragement mom. Will you and Janet not say anything to anyone about this? It is embarrassing to me when I have to shower in front of the other boys in PE. One of the other boys asked about it last night. I told him I had gotten into some thorn bushes."

"I hope you made the team, Phil and enjoy yourself today. In the meantime, I will call Dr. McClain and set up an appointment Saturday. He is a good doctor; if he doesn't know, he knows a lot of specialists. We will get it figured out."

"Thanks mom," I finished my cereal and headed out the door while yelling back to Janet, "Remember Janet, not a word or you will be flunking Geometry."

Except for the minor irritation, I still feel absolutely great. I just hope I can stay this way and get through college, get that degree, and make my mother proud. I need to concentrate on my date tonight with the most beautiful girl in school, Krystin. Even her name drives me insane. As I was driving to school, I saw Willie Willis, the town drunk who told Orville he saw me go into the wrecked spacecraft. I decided to probe him a little to see if he was sober enough to answer any questions. I slowed my car down while no one was traveling opposite of my direction on the road and slowly eased alongside him.

"Hey Willie, what's going on."

"Howdy, Phil." He drunkenly babbled.

"Someone told me you saw that meteor crash the other night."

"I did. But it was no meteor; it was a long cigar-like spaceship. And after it crashed, I saw you go into the crashed ship. Did you see that alien? He waved at me just before he crashed."

"Aw! Come on now, Willie. You had been hitting the sauce pretty heavy. I was not there, and you didn't see any aliens either. It was just a meteorite."

I was hoping to convince him that he was too drunk to know what happened and to divert attention away from me.

He blasted back. "I know what I saw. I bet you saw that alien too. You just don't want to admit it. They have done something to your brain. You're brainwashed."

As I spun off in my car waving I yelled back, "Take care, Willie."

When I got to school, I ran in the door and scurried down the hallway to the gym where Bartlett's office was. As promised, there was a list of the students that made the team. The first five boys were listed first, then down the page after a couple of line breaks was the rest of the team. I saw my name in the first five list. I was elated. I saw that Cody, my friend made the team also. Jim and Ron made the team but was farther down the list. Jim and Ron were both standing by Bartlett's office door when I walked up. I could see the dirty looks. At the same time, Ray and Stan walked up and both congratulated me.

Ray confirmed, "See Phil, we are on our way to a sectional. You are just what this team needed."

Jim and Ron were not enjoying his statement. I said, "Thanks Ray, it should be a fun year."

Cody ran up to me and added, "You and Jim have to play a one-on-one. He said if you made the team he would play you. Isn't that right Jim?" Jim was only a few feet away.

He commented, "It looks that way unless Phil wants to back out."

Cody barked, "He is not going to back out. Have you seen him play lately? Well, I have, and he is like lightning. Scores with ease and jumps like a deer. He is not afraid to mix it up. He is tougher than nails. I wouldn't want to be in your shoes."

Just then I told Cody to cool it. I left to go to my first-period class to see Krystin. I'm sure she made the cheerleading squad. When I got to class, she ran up and gave me a quick kiss while hugging me.

"I saw where you made the team and looks as if you will be one of starting five players. That is super. I made the cheerleading squad also."

I commented, "That is great. It will be hard for me to play the way I should because I won't be able to keep my eyes off you. I am looking forward to our date tonight." Just then the 1st-period bell rang for classes to start. "We had better get into our seats."

The rest of the day went well. The first basketball practice went very well. I could tell that Bartlett was impressed with my accurate passing to Ray, Dan, Stan, and Nick. Nick was only a sophomore but was quick and played rugged. His shooting would get better as he got older and more experience. Nick knew his role on the team. He knew to only take short jump shots or layups. I made all four of them look good and they knew that they could play better offensively as long I was feeding them the ball. After practice, I had to get home in a hurry to get ready for my dinner date with Krystin. While rushing home in the mean green machine, I was thinking about where we will go for dinner. Tough decision even though I only had 3 choices of restaurants in town unless I travel 25 miles to Jasperville. We have a local eatery, Bill's Café. Then we have a Jerry's and a Frisch's Big Boy. We also had a popular Park and Eat Drive-In restaurant that was popular with the teenagers. The best thing for me to do is to leave it up to Krystin.

I get home and quickly shower and put on my clothes. I was wearing a light blue short-sleeved shirt with navy blue dress pants. It is cool this time of year; in fact, Halloween is arriving a week from Sunday, but next Wednesday on the 27th, is the big party. Jacob is throwing another Halloween party at his house on the 27th. Krystin and I have already been invited to attend. It is a costume party, so I have to think of a costume to wear without getting too expensive. I grabbed a light gray jacket to throw in the car. I run up the stairs, give my mom a quick kiss and barge out the door to the mean green machine. I have this fear all the time of it not starting, but it proves to be old and reliable. While driving to Krystin's house, my heart starts pounding again. I suppose having a crush or being in love will make your heart do all kinds of things. I also have this pulsating in my stomach and my knees feel weak. I also arrived at her house about 10 minutes early.

I pulled into her driveway and got out of the car. I slowly walk to the front door. I hesitantly ring their doorbell. The door swings open, and there he stands.

Krystin's dad, whom I have never seen before. My heart sinks and I feel like we are having a staring contest. He finally speaks, "Hello, you must be Phil."

I gulped awkwardly, "Uh! Uh! Yes, I am Phil."

"Well, please come in. Krystin is not quite ready yet." As we walked toward the living room couch, Krystin's mom was standing in the middle of the living room. He extended his hand for a handshake and declared, "I'm John Adkins and this is my wife, Sarah." I extended my hand and shook hands with both of them while I said repeating, "So nice to meet you." The nervousness was easing up a bit. I could tell where Krystin got her beauty. Her mom was a knockout for someone middle-aged.

John grinned, "Krystin tells me that you are playing basketball this year. Sarah and I go to all the games since Krystin is a cheerleader. I look forward to seeing you play. I am a friend of coach Bartlett, and he seems to be very impressed with your talent so far."

I squeaked, "Yes sir, I have been working out and it appears to be paying off."

"Krystin also told me that you have a part-time job at the grocery store."

"Yes sir."

"I like that in a person when they are active, and they stay busy."

Sarah asked, "Phil would you like something to drink while waiting?"

"No mam, I am fine." I replied.

I looked back at John and calmingly said, "I need to make some extra money and the grocery store seems to help out in that respect. So, I work when I can. I am planning on going to college hoping to have a better career and outlook on life.

John praised me adding, "Young man, it seems as if you have (all your ducks in a row). It is so important for young people to make appropriate plans. We have tried to instill that in Krystin."

"Thank you sir, I appreciate those comments."

"Oh! One more thing," John added. "I want Krystin home before midnight. Not at midnight, I mean before midnight."

I gulped again, "I will have her here sir before midnight."

Finally, Krystin walked into the room. It felt like an eternity to me. She was dressed so beautifully. She had a pretty peach-colored dress on, and man did she fill it out. I really don't care for skinny girls. Krystin's body make up is, ... Well, slightly pleasantly plump. Mercy, she has a body to die for. Her long brown wavy hair draped just past her shoulders. I was also surprised at her mom and dad letting her wear that peach dress that came about 6 inches above her knees. She couldn't wear that at school, all dresses or skirts have to touch the knees. She walked over to me as I stood up to greet her and she gleefully gave me a quick hug. She grinned, "Hi Phil, glad to see you. You look nice."

"So do you Krystin," I assured her.

"I guess we better get going. I have to have you home before midnight."

She rebelled to John, "Dad, you didn't!"

"I only have one rule, sweetheart." He noted, "And that is it."

We began to walk to the door. As we opened the door to leave, John and Sarah both echoed, "You two have fun and drive safely."

As we were walking to the car I responded to Krystin, "You have nice parents."

"Yes, I love them dearly. Dad can be a little overprotective at times."

"Hey! I don't blame him. If I had a daughter that looked as beautiful as you. I probably wouldn't let her date at all. I know how some of these boys think with lust on their minds."

"Oh, you're silly." She spoke.

"Nevertheless, I don't want to get off on the wrong foot with your dad. I will make every effort to have you home before midnight."

"I don't think he would say anything if we were just a few minutes late."

As we got into the mean green machine, I gave Krystin a serious look, "I would like to keep dating you, so I don't want to take that chance."

"I understand." She added. "I'm going to have to have a little talk with dad. Am I right in saying that your father died a few years ago?"

"Yes, he had a sudden heart attack."

"I am so sorry. Even though I get upset with my father, I can't imagine trying to live without him."

I remarked, "It has been tough living on all of us. My mom does the best she can, but the available extra money has been very limited. That is one of the reasons I work part-time at the grocery store, but it is very little help. I'm sorry about the fact I just don't have much extra money to spend with me trying to get enough to go to college etc. You deserve more than I can afford to spend."

As Krysten stared directly into my eyes with a self-approving stare, "Phil, I'm going out with you not because you have money, but because you are bright, intelligent, well-read, and you have career goals in mind. I need to be with someone that is fun to be around. I need to be with someone that can make me think and laugh. Someone that goes after what he wants. Just like you getting chosen for the basketball team, and from what I'm hearing, you are probably going to be one of the best players on the team. You didn't even play last year. That is quite an accomplishment."

"Thanks."

By now we are heading into town, so I asked, "Where would you like to eat?"

"I like the Park and Eat. We could see a lot of our friends there, but I think I would like to go into a restaurant and sit down just you and me, and no one else bothering us. Bill's Café is a little cheaper in prices, so let's go there."

"Are you sure? We could do Jerry's if you want."

"No, you are saving up for college; you don't have a father; Bill's café will be just fine."

She began to scoot across the seat and pressed up against me with her arm draping over my shoulder. My knees got weak, and my heart started pounding harder. Because of her being so close and pressing up against me, I began to get a rise (you know where). I quickly had to get my mind off of that rise. I stammered, "Y-Y-You are too nice. Bill's it is. They do make up a good, dressed hamburger with fries and coleslaw."

"That sounds good to me. I like a lot of ketchup on my fries." She added.

"So do I."

We reach our destination, we get out of the car and walk in. Cody's girlfriend, Carrie, is working there and seating people.

I gleefully chirp, "Hi Carrie, how are you tonight?"

She replied, "I'm doing OK. Some of us have to work, you know."

I assured her, "Tell me about it."

"It's good to see you, Krysten. Will it just be the two of you?"

Krystin replied, "Good to see you Carrie and yes, it will be just the two of us."

Carrie and Krysten were walking ahead of me, and they didn't know it, but my hearing was much more enabled than they knew. I could hear Carrie whisper to

Krysten, "He is a nice boy, a good catch for you. You know him and Cody are best friends. They share a lot of their information with each other."

Krysten whispered back, "I know that Cody and Phil hang out at school every chance they get. Yes, I like him. I'm not saying yet, but he could be the one for me."

I was pleased to hear their whispering comments.

Carrie addressed the both of us, "Is this booth OK?"

I said, "This is fine." We were sitting by a nice window where we could see the courthouse across the street. In front of it was a beautiful maple tree that was showing the yellow fall colors of its leaves. The sun was setting and was showing a golden-glistening light on the changing maple tree.

After a few minutes, an older waitress came and took our order. We both ordered the dressed hamburger with fries and 2 Pepsi soft drinks. We had a nearly full Heinz ketchup bottle on the table. While we were waiting for the food, Krysten asked me a surprising question.

"Phil, that took a lot of nerve Monday at school to stand up to Ray. I have been meaning to ask you what happened during that scuffle. I couldn't help but notice that it appeared to me that he was getting ready to punch you, you blocked it extremely fast, and then he just fell back to the floor. I didn't see you lay a finger on him. I saw your body make a couple of very quick jerks. And that was it. He had a big red place on his forehead, and he was holding his stomach before he vomited later. Did you hit him?"

"Krystin, I was so nervous that I quickly punched him in the stomach, and it must have been a lucky punch. You know that I have been working out and my strength has increased and out of fear, I guess I punched him too hard. I felt really bad about that. I don't know how he got that red bump on his forehead."

"That is admirable of you, but you shouldn't feel bad. He was getting ready to hit you hard in the face. He is big enough and strong enough that he could have broken your facial bones."

"Well, we made up in the principal's office and we are friends now. He is as happy as anyone that I am on the team this year. He knows I can get the ball to him; he can score easier and get more points."

"That's typical of Ray, anyone stands up to him, become his friend." Krystin noted.

"I think he has really changed this time. He is not giving any of my friends a hard time. He is concentrating on getting a basketball scholarship. He has been contacting Derek and Cody and myself for extra help on his courses. He knows he needs to get his grades up."

Krystin spoke, "He seems to have found a new girlfriend in Amanda. Ray was promiscuous and was expecting me to be that way. I wasn't about to be that way for him. It just wasn't going to work between us. That is OK because now I have found you." She reached over and took my hand into hers.

"What a sweet thing to say," I calmly uttered as my heart started pounding again and my socks began to roll up and down with excitement.

Our food finally arrived. The hamburgers were dressed with lettuce, tomato, Mayonnaise, and onion. The French fries were thicker than the average fries.

While we were eating, I chimed in, "After we eat, how about catching the 2nd feature movie at the drive-in theater? We may be late for the first one."

"What is showing tonight?" Krystin inquired.

"The first feature is the new James Bond movie (Goldfinger). I think the second one is a mystery comedy (A shot in the Dark). I think it is about this bumbling inspector Jacques Clouseau played by Peter Sellers. Elke Sommer is also in the movie. She is really pretty, but she has nothing on you."

"Stop it Phil, you are embarrassing me."

"I can only describe what I see, and my vision is very good. I have the most beautiful girl in the school; let me rephrase that, in this entire state of Indiana sitting across from me. Right now, I feel lucky to be here across from you."

"You know the right things to say. You have probably practiced saying things that girls like to hear."

"No Krystin, I am being honest with you. If I didn't believe that you were the most beautiful girl in the state of Indiana, I wouldn't have said it."

As we were finishing our sandwiches and fries. It was turning into a perfect evening until........until the worst was getting ready to happen. We were just getting ready to leave when Ron's dad, Willard, and Jim's dad, Orville walked up to our Booth. Ron was hoping to start on the team this year but that got ditched because of me. Jim wasn't good enough to ever start but both boys made the team. My friend Cody, who is not the most athletic person, is still better than Ron and Jim combined.

Orville the redneck, leaned over the table toward me and abruptly barked, "Well lookey heer Willard, this is the boy that went into the crashed spacecraft and visited the alien. Where are you two love birds heading? To Mars?" He chuckles showing his green unbrushed teeth.

I calmly replied, "You have been talking to Willie, the town drunk. It was a meteorite that landed and there was no alien on that piece of rock that plunged to earth and exploded. We are going to catch the 2nd feature of the movies at the drive-in."

Willard rudely interrupted, "If you hadn't gone out for the team, my boy Ron would have started on the team."

I looked at Willard and spoke, "I have just as much right to go out for the team as anyone else." Krystin had a concerned look while listening.

Willard added with a louder voice, "He has played basketball for four years. This is the first year you have tried out for the team. How are you going to help the team?"

I was beginning to get irritated, "If you want to be a starter, you have to improve enough to make that position. Bartlett is going to play his best players. Maybe you need to talk to Bartlett."

"I already have." Willard interrupted. "Bartlett pissed me off. He said that you could outplay both our boys at the same time. I'd like to see that."

Orville interjected with his green teeth showing, "You and Jim are supposed to have a game, a one-on-one match. He is waiting to kick your ass."

"I didn't agree to that, and my time is too valuable to waste on you, so tell Jim that I'm not playing him."

Orville abrasively added, "What's the matter boy, are you too sceered to play him."

I think these guys are getting on my nerves, so I added a little redneck dialogue, "Tell Jim I'm too sceered to play him. That should settle the dispute."

Orville bristled up again, "Did that alien look like you."

Krysten interjected, "Sir, there was no alien. It was jus......." Before she could get her sentence completed, he leaned over the booth farther toward her and growled, "You mind your own business missy."

She leaned back in fear. Now I am really pissed. I jumped up quickly took my hand and easily pushed him away from her. I gritted my teeth and spoke softly in his ear so Krystin couldn't hear me and only Orville could hear me, "You leave her out of this, or I'll snap you like a twig."

Orville stepped back and berated, "You have gotten awful brave since you went into that spaceship. I think you need to be brought down a few notches." By now, other people in the restaurant were looking on. The restaurant owner, Bill Wilson, came over and asked, "Is everything OK here."

I added, "Everything is OK sir; sorry for the disturbance." Even the manager knew that Orville could be loud at times.

The manager gently took Orville's arm and added, "If you are finished Orville, you should go."

Orville shouted, "Git yer dam hands off me, you some-bitch."

The manager implied, "Hang on Orville, I don't want any more problems, but you need to leave this young couple alone. When you walked over to their booth, that is when things seemed to escalate."

Orville backed away from the manager and he and Willard started to exit the restaurant. Orville looked back at me and said, "This is not over boy, we'll meet again sometime, and you will not like our next meeting."

The manager apologized to us, "Sorry about him; he usually drinks a few too many beers when he is in here to eat. We have had issues with him before."

Krystin added, "That man is crazy, and he scares me."

I took her hand while showing embarrassment and asserted, "Don't worry Krystin, I'm not going to let him or anything else hurt you. I promise you that."

While leaving the restaurant and walking to the car, Krystin inquired, "Do you want to tell me what that was all about?"

"Last Monday morning, Jim was walking down the hallway and purposely bumped into me. He yelled at me and said, "Get out of my way, nerd." He has been that way for the last 2 years bullying my friends and me. After working out and building some strength, I decided I have had enough. I guess adrenaline shot through me and I took both hands and grabbed his jacket and actually picked him up off the floor and basically told him things were going to change around the school. I shouldn't have but I did call him a Dumbass. Then I sat him back down to the floor gently and brushed the wrinkles out of his jacket."

Krystin started laughing before I got the story finished. She admiringly suggested, "He must have really been surprised."

"It was funny afterwards Krystin; he had this look of fear that I can't describe. Then later on, he told Ray about it. At the time, Ray was their go-to guy if someone confronted them. I'm referring to Ron, Jim, and Billy, Ray's followers at the time. Then at lunch, when Ray purposely tripped Derek, a cripple, mind you, I went into an immediate rage. That is when I dumped my food tray on Ray."

Krysten interrupted, "Yes, I saw all that. I yelled at Ray and was so upset. I don't know what you did but you certainly got Ray's attention."

"Well, Ray and I are friends now. Jim must have gone home and told his dad, Orville. So, Orville is pissed at me.

To make matters more complicated, Willie Willis, the town drunk, told Orville that he saw me go into the supposedly crashed spaceship. Orville thinks the alien has somehow transformed me."

"You did bulk up extremely fast. It was like Saturday, you were the nerd, and by Monday, you looked like the professional wrestler, Dick-the-Bruiser. I could see where he might be skeptical."

I knew where Krystin was going with this, so I needed to plant more information and formulated to her, "I had been working out several weeks before that weekend. I just wore loose shirts and pants to not show my muscle build-up until they started to make a difference in my appearance. Anyhow, there was no spaceship. It was just a burning rock. You know how goofy and crazy some of these town folks can be. Now, Ron's dad Willard is mad at me because he thinks Ron would have started on the team."

Krystin chimed in, "That's just too bad. Ron was the weakest player on the team last year. I can't tell you how many times he either threw the ball away, got it stolen from him, or whoever he was guarding just took him under the basket and muscled in a score on him. To top it all off, he was not a good shooter himself."

"I know, even Cody, one of my best friends, made the team and he can outplay Jim or Ron."

We finally made it to the drive-in. It had already turned dark. The first movie was near the end. While planning ahead, I found us a parking spot that wasn't close to any other cars. The closest car was about 4-5 parking spots away. I reached back to roll the back window down a little way on my side of the car to hang the speaker on the inside of the car. Then I rolled the window back up. Turned the volume up but not very loud. Krystin scooted across the seat and pressed herself right next to me. I could feel her left thigh pressing against mine. I put my right arm over her shoulder while she partially parked her head on my right shoulder. My breathing began to deepen. She was making my socks roll up and down again. How can I fight against this desire to explore further with our bodies? I was telling myself, *just cool off Phil.* It would be nice to have a bucket of cold water poured over me right now.

The first movie finally ended. On top of the giant outside screen, they had 4 very bright large spotlights that came on. They lit up the entire parking area. They even lit up the inside of the car. This lasted for about 20 minutes. It is like an intermission so people can go to the food building and get snacks before the final movie starts.

Krystin and I continued to make small talk until the 2nd movie began to start. The spotlights go off and we have only the light from the projector being reflected into the car. It was dark enough that no one could see inside the car unless they were standing right next to the car. Even then, they would have to press up against the window of the car. Drive-ins have always been the perfect place for heavy necking.

As the movie started, I could tell that neither of us had any intention of watching the movie. Krysten scooted back over to her side of the car seat and suggested, "Scoot over here next to me so you don't have that steering wheel in the way."

I did, and as soon as I put my arm around her again, she planted a big kiss right on my lips. She began to sit sideways and put her right leg over my lap. My breathing was getting deeper and so was her breathing getting deeper. For the rest of the night, we continued to grope each other. At one point, she straddled my lap and sat on my lap facing me. I know she had to feel the excitement between my legs. Thankfully, neither one of us carried things too far. No clothes were removed. We only had heavy petting. For an hour and a half, she was driving me insane. I can see why some people go too far because it is torture to your body and emotions and since my senses are heightened, for me, it was brutal to have such a beautiful girl romping all over me.

Finally, the show ended, the torture ended as she sat back in her seat and the bright spotlights perched on top of the screen came on. I scooted back behind the steering wheel still breathing deeply, trying to settle down. We decided to stay parked for a while to let the other cars leave and not have to sit and wait.

Krystin remarked, "You are a great kisser. You had me aroused. However, thank you for not trying to remove any of my clothing. I really appreciate that. Other boys I have dated try instantly to remove my clothing. I wouldn't let them and that was usually the last date. Not that they wouldn't ask me again; I just wouldn't go out with them anymore."

"Well Krystin, I don't mind telling you that with your great kissing and beautiful firm body, it was absolutely torture for me. I'm just now settling down from this wonderful but brutal emotion. I have too much respect for you to do something like remove your clothing and maybe carry things too far without your permission. We have to think about our future plans."

"You are so right, Phil. Why can't other guys see that? I know we could take precautions and probably still have safe sex. But it is still not the same. This is what sets you apart from most other guys."

I finally started the car up to leave the drive-in. As we were heading back home, it was about 11:30 pm, I knew I didn't have long but I had time to get her dropped off at home before midnight. She scooted over next to me again, pressing her firm body against mine.

I smiled and whispered, "You are killing me here."

She chuckled and said, "You are just going to have to get used to it."

I pulled into her driveway, I got out of the car and walked her to the front door of her house. We still had about 15 minutes, but I wanted to get her home a little early. Her porch light was on. I put my arms around her and gave her a quick kiss.

I asserted, "I better let you get in your house and honor your dad's demand."

She whispered back to me, "Yeah! I'm going to have to talk to him."

"Don't upset the apple cart, please. I have to work tomorrow and Sunday. I will see you Monday morning. Would you like for me to stop by and pick you up."

"That would be great; I could have dad or mom pick me up after cheerleading."

"Deal! See you Monday morning before school."

"Phil, be careful going home. I don't trust those two guys. They are nuts."

"Oh, I would love another evening with you next Saturday night. Yes, I'm asking you out for another date."

"I accept. I don't think I have anything going on."

I added, "I also would like for you to go with me to Jacob's house Wednesday night. He is throwing a Halloween party."

She gleefully chirped, "I'll get my studies done early so I can go with you Wednesday night."

As I left and started home, I didn't say anything to Krystin about my Dr. appointment tomorrow. I had left it up to mom to call Mr. Mudd at the grocery store to let him know about my appointment and I would have to come to work late. The places behind my shoulder blades still itch, but not as much as they did the day before. Anyhow, I still need to be secretive about all this unless my life may be at stake. I have heard too many stories about our secret intelligence in this country. I know what they do to some of the animals for research. If they found someone like me, they would be doing all kinds of experimentation on me. All those stories about the Roswell, New Mexico crash in 1947 are still going around, and there are several stories about all the experimentations done on the aliens. I don't know if it is true, but I'm not taking any chances. I do know how sneaky our CIA can be to get any advantage on other countries even if it means sacrificing a human life.

I think these places between my shoulder blades are the result of that alien material that was injected into me. It will be interesting to see what the Doctor says. My appointment is at 8:15 am tomorrow morning. I will be getting up earlier.

<u>CHAPTER 06</u>

THE TRANSFORMATION AND FINALLY THE TRUTH

The radio alarm went off and the music started blasting and "A Taste of Honey" by Herb Alpert and the Tijuana Brass were playing. I had set the alarm for 6:30 am. Mom was already up fixing breakfast. The bacon aroma infiltrated the air all the way down in the basement of my place of hanging out. It immediately made me want to hurry up and go upstairs to eat. After brushing my teeth, I quickly do the 3 S's (Shit, Shower, and Shave). I pick up a hand mirror and while standing in front of the bathroom mirror, I take a quick look at the two elongated marks on my back. They appear to have created little skin flaps over the reddened areas. The skin flaps seemed to cover up the openings that stretched down my shoulder blades. Hopefully, I can find out more about this without arousing too much attention. Maybe it's nothing.

After eating breakfast, mom and I hurried to see Dr. McClain, the local town doctor. Our appointment was set for 8:30 am. About 10 minutes later, I was called back to one of the rooms in the Doctor's office. I told mom to stay in the waiting room even though she wanted to come back with me. Dr. McClain came in and said, "Hello Mr. Marland, what seems to be the problem?"

I spoke nervously, "Well Dr., I have had these two elongated places form along the inside of my shoulder blades. I'm concerned about what may be causing it."

"Take off your shirt," the Dr. added, "let's take a look at your back. Oh yes, I see them. I don't know what that is. Can you breathe and move around, OK?"

"Except for a little itching which seems to have subsided in the last couple of days, I feel fine. In fact, I feel great."

Dr. McClain implied, "You appeared to have bulked up a lot since I saw you last time."

"I have been working out a lot and have made the basketball team which has added more exercise to my schedule."

As he put his stethoscope in his ears, "Let me listen to your heart." After a couple of minutes, he added, "Your heart sounds very strong. You definitely have developed an athlete's body. Keep up the good work. I'm going to check on something. I'll be right back."

About 10 minutes passed and McClain came back into the room and informed me, "I made a call to a specialist over in Jasperville. It is about 25 miles west of here on Highway 64. His name is Dr. Spear. I think he has dealt with this before. He wants to see you today. He told me to tell you not to be alarmed, it's nothing serious, but he wants to talk to you ASAP about it. So, if it is OK with your mom you need to drive over there."

I replied anxiously, "Is everything OK?"

"Yes, everything is fine. He just needs to inform you about what is going on."

"Will you talk to my mom; she will get all wild and crazy if she thinks something is wrong."

"Sure, "I'll talk to her and put her at ease."

"Thanks, Doc."

I put my shirt back on and met mom in the lobby area. McClain is briefing her on the situation. She looked at me and started to get teary-eyed.

"Relax mom, everything is fine," I boasted.

McClain added, "Your son has one of the strongest heartbeats I've ever heard. It was like a base drum banging in there." He looked at me and said, "Listening to your heart through this stethoscope, it was hurting my ears, it was so loud."

Mom uttered to Dr. McClain, "Thank you, doctor. We will drive straight over to Jasperville. Dr. Spear is his name, right?"

"Yes, his office is on the north side of the courthouse square. He has a big sign in his window."

Mom and I got into the car and rushed to Jasperville. I wanted to hurry and get all this done so I could get to work. I didn't want Mr. Mudd to get mad at me. Due to some farmers doing their harvest of corn and soybeans and even pumpkins, their tractors pulling the fresh harvest to market slowed us down some. It took us about 40 minutes to get there. We entered the office waiting room.

Dr. Spear came out of his office wearing a neatly pressed white lab coat that extended to his knees. He was slightly grey-headed and was very clean-cut and distinguished-looking.

He nodded, "Hello, I assume you are the Marlands that have driven from McClain's office. He is a good friend of mine. You are Shirley, his mother I hope."

Mom weakly nodded, "Yes, I am. Is everything OK, doctor?"

Dr. Spear affirmed, "Yes, everything is fine, Shirley. You have nothing at all to worry about. I want to see Phillip in my office first, just him and myself. Don't be alarmed but we may be awhile. Phil, please come with me to my back office."

I followed him down his hallway while his neatly pressed lab coat floated in the air behind him on both sides as if a large white bird was about to go into flight. When we got into his office which appeared to be quite advanced in medical equipment, he nodded, "You had better sit down."

Little did I know that I was about to be overwhelmed with the truth of what was going on. He began pacing across the room back and forth while talking, "Here it goes. You let me know if I'm incorrect. First of all, you must keep yourself sworn to secrecy. Can you promise me that?"

"Yes," I meekly uttered.

"A week ago, last night, there was something that occurred over in your town. I think you know what I am talking about. Am I correct?"

"Yes," I added with another faint weak voice.

"There was a spaceship that crashed that had an alien inside. First of all, don't worry. What you tell me will be our little secret. Be honest with me, did you go into the spaceship before it imploded and removed any evidence of its existence?"

I was hesitant to say anything at first; then I saw him pull out a syringe that looked just like the one the alien shot me with. Then I gave in.

"Yes, there was an alien there; he was dying."

"Did he inject something like this into you?" as he showed me up close the syringe filled with the shiny silvery liquid that was moving around in the syringe."

I said, "Yes, he did. It has scared me to death."

"Well Phillip, we have something in common because I have had a couple of these put into my body."

"Doctor what does that stuff do?"

"I'm going to explain; hold on to your seat because this is going to be overwhelming to you. You have probably noticed your body has changed somewhat."

"Yes, my body has changed," I eagerly nodded.

Dr. Spear kept talking, "This has actually been a good thing. You probably feel great. This syringe is filled with what the aliens refer to as nanobots and alien blood. These are microscopic robots that circulate in your bloodstream, and they actually repair damaged cells. You have probably noticed that your blood is a deeper red with a blue hue to it. That is because your blood is super rich in oxygen thanks to the nanobots and the alien blood cells which can hold considerably more oxygen than our blood cells. This helps enhance everything in your body. It enhances all your senses. I'm sure you have noticed that you are considerably stronger and are very fast in your actions if you need to be. I have another very important question to ask you. You have not been showing off to anyone, have you?"

I spouted, "This is unbelievable. Everything you have just said has happened to me. I have been so scared of the CIA that I have not been flaunting my abilities. I was afraid that if our CIA found out, they would be using me to experiment on. I did go out for the basketball team, and I used my abilities just enough not to draw attention and make the team. When the boys are playing, it's like they are moving in slow motion. I could easily steal any ball, intercept any pass, and block any shot if I'm close to that person. It didn't take me long to realize that I have far greater abilities than anyone else on the team or in the whole school for that matter. Something else happened that night also. There was one other person that saw the crash that night and he swore he saw me go into the crashed spaceship. However, he is the town drunk. No one believes what he said. But he told another person in which I have had a confrontation. He believes the town drunk's story and he said he was going to prove that I was affected in some way by the alien. But so far, he doesn't have anything on me."

"You need to keep it that way, Phil. You must be secretive. Don't worry about the CIA. They already know that some of these aliens exist. They know that some humans like you and I have our blood mixed with theirs along with the nanobots. The CIA doesn't want the general public to know. They don't want a worldwide panic."

This is a project between the CIA and the aliens. The aliens were able to create a special coating on the nanobots to prevent our antibodies from trying to attack the nanobots. You know how antibodies attack a virus in our bodies.

Dr. Spear removed his lab coat and his shirt and tie to show me his marks on his shoulder blades. His muscular physique was awesome.

He commented, "Do you recognize these?"

"Yeah! That is why I'm here. I showed my mother and we both were concerned about the marks."

He commanded, "Remove your shirt while I talk to you about these."

I proceeded to remove my shirt and stand with my back to him while he observed my marks.

As he breathed softly, "This is probably the only other transformation you will have. Everything else has already happened. You may not believe this, but these are the beginnings of gills forming and attaching to your lungs. I have talked to several of these aliens. Yes, they do exist, and one of their home stations is close by. That is why people have been seeing strange lights for the last few years. One of the reasons they picked this area is: not a lot of population, Karst topography – several underground caves. There have been some caves on private property, and they are off-limits to anyone else. The CIA and our government see to it. There are several of these alien stations around the world in very sparsely populated areas."

I asked, "Where are they from?"

"I got this information from one of the aliens. Our technology, in time, will be able to recognize other planets orbiting other stars. Currently, our astronomers can't detect that. However, contrary to popular belief, our scientists will, in a few decades, find out that the solar system of planets is not unique in the Milky Way galaxy or even in the universe. The aliens have the technology and advancement in science and know that there are hundreds, even thousands of other solar systems in our Milky Way Galaxy alone that have planets orbiting around them. Most of the planets are just too small to be seen by our telescopes, even our Radio Telescopes. These aliens are from a planet orbiting a star in the Constellation Libra. They refer to the star as Gliese. Our scientists haven't discovered it yet, but someday they will. The head alien told me that it is 20 light years from earth. It takes about 2 weeks for their ships to get here."

"How can they travel that fast?" I replied.

"They are far more advanced than us by at least 5,000 years and our world leaders know that. They have developed a unique metal that is much stronger than any metal we have, and it is still flexible. So, while in space, when they hit a small piece of rock going faster than the speed of light, it just bounces off their ship. A rock hitting our rocket capsules at just 40,000 mph would puncture our ship and most likely end the mission. We, humans are trying to learn as much as we can about their advanced technology. Here on earth, every country is racing to see who can gain the advantage over the others. Fortunately, the aliens know how we humans are. They are very stingy with their technology secrets."

By now, I had dozens of questions to ask. I added, "What is the deal with these gills? Are you and I turning into some type of aquatic species?

"Their planet is about 80% water and only 20% land. Through their evolution, some live in water and some live on land. A large number have both habitats. They are interested in merging their bodies with ours. Our life expectancy is about 70 years. Theirs is about the same, maybe a little longer. They have found out that by merging our bodies and merging our blood, with the slow aging process, the aliens and our CIA estimate that we can live 150 – 200 plus years. By the way, that is why your blood, like mine, is a deep dark red with a blue hue. My gills are fully developed. Yours will be in just a few days. I want to alert you about this ahead of time. If you are in a situation where you are underwater, freshwater, or salt water and under for a prolonged period of time, you may first feel like you are drowning. If it wasn't for your new gills, you would be drowning. But your gills will kick in and start taking oxygen out of the water in your gills and within a few seconds, you will start breathing underwater. I have already experienced this. At first it is horrifying; you will be fighting to get air. It takes a few seconds for the transformation. Then you will start breathing through the back of your gills. The reverse is true when you come out of the water to breathe the air. You will feel like you are suffocating at first. This gives you and me a whole new world to explore. To make a long story short, you was in the wrong place at the right time. The alien had no intention of crashing. When you went in the crashed ship, you must have shown kindness and compassion. That is when he gave you the shot from the syringe."

My jaw dropped, "I'm speechless. I have all kinds of questions. Why couldn't he repair himself? How long have they been on earth?"

"Whoa, one question at a time. His body was damaged too severely for it to repair itself. He had too many cuts and was bleeding profusely in too many areas of his body. I'm sure he knew he was dying. You and I are the same way..... we can heal up small cuts quickly, but we can't survive major wounds where we bleed out too fast."

I commented, "When I saw him with a big metal pipe penetrating all the way through the body, bleeding profusely, I knelt down beside him and held his hand. He had some device that caused everything to implode. It was a small cubical black box that had flashing weird lights that were slowly going off completely. I figured that it must have been some detonating device. So, I left hurriedly from the crash site. Within about 25 seconds is when the implosion happened."

Spear continued, "It was a detonating device with a timer. He could have detonated it instantly and killed you. He chose not to. I received my shot and became part of the alien family 10 years ago. I am 67 years old now but as you can tell, I only look about 30 – 35 years old. So, as it appears right now, you are one of the lucky ones. You trying to keep secret about it was the right thing to do but for the wrong reason. The CIA is not your enemy, but the general public is. If people found out that we were part alien, there would be mass hysteria along with some crazy people trying to kill us."

"How did they find out about earth?"

"We have been sending radio signals out for years and in 1939, the first TV broadcast was sent out. All those waves travel through space."

I asked, "What about the CIA? Will they be watching over me?"

"You may or may not have noticed a couple of new faces in town. They are watching over you, but they don't want anyone else to know about you and your condition. They want you to live a normal life. You can use your abilities within limitations, and you appear to have been doing that."

"I was using the abilities while playing on the basketball team."

"That's fine but be careful not to expose your very advanced abilities."

"I was in a fight the other day and was scared because the other boy was so much bigger than me; I reacted too fast. I blocked his punch and hit him twice so quick that no one saw it."

"That is the kind of things you have to be careful about. Don't expose your abilities. Did he know you had hit him?"

"Oh yeah. We are friends now and we are the two best players on the team. He is not super-intelligent either, so I think I'm Ok with him. I want to be good enough to get a college scholarship."

"Let him be the best player on the team and you be the second best. You won't have to worry about a scholarship. You will get one; just keep your grades up. That should be easy because of your enhanced mental abilities. Your college won't cost you anything. Our government will take care of your college finances. Just keep your abilities hidden from the general public. You must do that. When you are playing basketball, for instance, I know everyone appears to be moving in slow motion. You have to learn to move in slow motion also, but if you need to, move a little faster. Even your mind is quicker and faster. Your grades should be easy to keep up with much less effort."

"I have already noticed that too Dr. Spear. The other night I had to read about 50 pages in this big literature book. I read them in about 2-3 minutes and understood everything. Math and Physics seem to be so much easier to understand. If I don't turn all the way physically into one of those beings, and I still think they are ugly, I think I will be happy."

"If it is any consolation, they think we are ugly," added Dr. Spear as he began to chuckle. "Phil, I'm going to give you my home phone number. You already have my office number. Call me anytime that you feel the need, my office during the day, and my home at nights and on weekends. With your permission, I want to give you another shot of the nanobots and another shot of the alien blood."

"Thank you, Dr. Spear. I really appreciate that. I have so many questions so don't be surprised if I call you."

"That will be fine Phil, especially at night when I will have the time to talk to you. There are only 2 other people that I know that are like us in all of southern Indiana. I stay in contact with them also. By the way, one of the top aliens wants to meet you. That was his brother that crashed, and he wants to thank you for your compassion. Everything was recorded, even after the crash. The recording was sent to their receiver until the implosion occurred. You were on video that night. I saw the video, that is why I knew that you were caring and showed compassion. Also, aliens like people that have these types of personalities. Had you been like some of your classmates, the bullies, etc., you probably would have already been eliminated. They definitely don't want someone to have the powers and abuse them. That is not going to happen."

I blurred a meek "Wow. I saw that alien die from a bad wound, so I am assuming we are not invincible."

"No, we can be killed in an accident, but small wounds heal up pretty fast on us. We just do not want to have a large gash wound where we quickly bleed to death. We also need to stay away from doctors that don't know about us. We don't need any hospital drawing our blood and looking at it under a microscope. From now on, you need to see me. I need to be your family doctor. The CIA has a secret hospital should we ever need one.

I will go out and tell your mom that you are fine. The overlapping flap will make the marks on your back very faint and hard to see unless someone is looking closely at them. I'm going to tell your mom this story and it is a good one to tell other people if someone questions you. I am going to say that when babies are in the early fetus stage, there is a short period of time when the baby develops pharyngeal pouches. In fish, these develop into gills, but in humans our DNA causes them to develop our eustachian tube, middle ear, and tonsils. On rare occasions, some humans can have small slits that are basically scars between the shoulder blades. This last statement is false but gives a decent explanation to most people if they ask. The pharyngeal pouches are true which is just another testament to evolution. Overall, we humans probably did emerge from the sea."

That explanation was OK with me. Dr. Spear walked out ahead of me and began giving my mom the (nothing to worry about story). After I put my shirt on, I followed him out. I could tell mom was breathing a sigh of relief.

As I walked up to mom, I commented, "See mom, I told you there was nothing to worry about."

Dr. Spear added, "Make sure you bring him back to see me and not any other doctor. This is a unique case and I have treated these before. I do want to keep a close observation of him. Right now, those scars between his scapulars are benign."

"What are scapulars?" mom asked.

"That is his shoulder blades." Replied Dr. Spear.

We left the office; I dropped mom off at home then went on to work. The day at the grocery went well with no unexpected visitors this time. Krystin did go with her mom grocery shopping, and she hung around my stock aisle for a few minutes. I'm glad that she tries to be with me. That is a good sign that she at least likes me. I have asked if I could come over later this evening. She said yes, she would like that. I told her I would arrive about at 7 pm.

At the end of the day, just as soon as I came home from work, I got a surprising phone call from another one of my friends, Aaron. Aaron helps with the school newspaper and is a film/camera man buff. He is also overweight, weighing about 300 pounds. He has been another that has taken abuse at school because of his size. My only concern about his weight is that it is just not healthy. Other than that, I don't care that he is heavy. He is still smart, has a pleasing personality, and is fun to talk to. It was about 6:30 pm when the phone rang. I picked up the phone, "Hello."

"Phil this is Aaron, can you come over to my place, I have something to show you. I think this is important for you to see."

Aaron only lived about a mile from my house. I confirmed, "I'll be over in about 10 minutes."

As soon as I hung up the phone, I picked it up to call Krystin. Her phone rang a couple of times.

"Hello," Krystin's mom Sarah answered.

"Hi Mrs. Adkins, this is Phil. May I speak to Krystin?"

"Sure," she replied.

I could hear her calling Krystin's name out and saying, "Phil wants to talk to you." I heard a distant OK, and after a few seconds, she picked up the phone.

"Hello, Phil," Krystin spoke with a soft voice.

"Hey Krystin, I may be a few minutes late arriving at your house. Aaron just called me and said that he had something that he wanted me to see. He thought it was important. So, I will stop by his house first and then be on over. It should be only a few minutes."

Krystin asked, "Is everything OK?"

"Everything is fine." I replied.

"I'm still spooked after that ordeal with Orville and his buddy in the restaurant the other night." Krystin remarked intently.

"I know, and I am still so sorry you had to witness that. If there is a next time, I have enough witnesses that I will call the police on him. I will see you in a little while."

"Call me when you leave Aaron's house."

"I will; I can't wait to see the most beautiful girl in school."

She barked, "Stop it, will you? See you after a while."

I ran up the stairs and told mom that I was going over to Aaron's house for a little while. She Ok's my going with a firm reply, "I want you back home by 10 pm."

"I should be back before that," I assured her.

I got in the mean green machine and drove to Aaron's house. I walked up to the front door and rang the doorbell. His mother answered the door, "You must be Phillip. Aaron is downstairs in the basement." She pointed to the stairs.

Their house was somewhat junky. As I walked down the stairs, I had to watch my step because there were several steps that had books and papers piled up. When I reached the bottom step, I saw Aaron sitting at this machine called a film scanning machine. It is a machine that you can see each frame of the movie. The typical movie runs at 24 frames per second. Aaron had a Super 8 mm film camera that had just come out this year, 1965. The 8 mm films typically run at 16 or 18 frames pe second. The basement looked like some type of early movie-producing studio. There was very little lighting in his basement. He had a table lamp nearby where he was working. The rest of the basement, except for the dim glowing of the one lamp, was dark.

"Hey Aaron, what is going on?" I speculated about what was so important.

"Phil, I wanted to show you this. That Monday that you and Ray got into a fight, you didn't know it, but I filmed it on my Super 8 mm Camera, shooting at 18 frames/second. Boy, I was glad to see Ray go down. I couldn't stand that prick at the time."

"Well, Ray and I had a come-to-Jesus' meeting," I proclaimed as I gave Aaron a big smile. "He is different now and not the bully he was."

Aaron added while still looking perplexed, "You are right; he has been nicer even to me. Well, back to why I wanted you to see this film of your fight."

As soon as Aaron said that, I immediately began thinking, Uh Oh. I know what he has found out.

Aaron continued, "Phil, this machine breaks down a movie frame by frame. No one, not even me saw you hit Ray. I got curious and wondered why Ray just fell back. When I started to watch this film frame by frame, this is what I saw."

As he scrolled the film frame by frame to the point where Ray threw his punch which took 8-10 frames, then another 5 frames for the punch to be blocked, then he had this one frame where there was a blur of my right arm punch to Ray's stomach, and my left arm, also very blurry, hit him in the forehead. He repeated this frame 3-4 times for me to get a good look at them.

Aaron marveled in a low tone, "Dude, maybe a professional boxer but no human is that quick. You hit him three times in 1/18 of a second."

"Maybe you had a faulty film or maybe your movie camera locked up for a couple of seconds," I argued hoping he would buy the explanation.

"I don't think so, Phil. With several students watching, no one saw you hit him, and with Ray who is known to be a bad ass, just falling back to the floor with a big goose egg on his forehead raises a lot of questions."

"Aaron, has anyone else seen this?"

"No, I just noticed it before I called you."

"You are my buddy; can I count on you to keep this as our little secret. I would love for you to give me the film and I would buy you another movie film to replace this."

"Phil, you are one of my best friends too. I have other important school movie clips on this film. Will it be ok with you if I just cut out these 18 – 20 frames, give them to you and I'll splice the rest back together."

I gave a sigh of relief, "Thank you buddy, I really appreciate it. I have had trouble with Jim's dad, Orville. If he got his hands on this, he could create numerous problems for me."

"Oh!" Aaron looked up at me from his chair, "Jim saw me shooting that movie that day. I think Jim said something to his dad about me shooting the movie of you and Ray fighting."

"What?" I barked with a surprised look.

"Orville saw me the other day at the hardware store and asked me about it. You know Orville can be mean. He sort of demanded that I give him that movie."

"It would be a big favor to me if you cut out those 18-20 frames, splice it back together, and if he gets his panties all in a wad, just give it to him. He will just have the crucial second missing in the film. Tell him your camera is messed up. Then you would be off the hook."

"That sounds like a good idea; I don't want to get you in trouble with him either."

"You don't have any more copies of this anywhere else, do you?"

"No, this is it," said Aaron as he began cutting out the fast action stuff and spliced the rest of the movie back together. After he finished, he gave me the small 8 mm strip of movie which was about 3 inches long that had incriminating evidence.

"Aaron," I grinned, "You are a life saver. I am scared of Orville; he is a dangerous person."

We watched the spliced movie and when the fight came on his little movie screen, Ray was just beginning to throw his punch, then the screen went blank for about a second; when the movie began again, he was just falling to the floor.

"This is perfect," I asserted. "Now if he gets nasty with you, just give it to him."

"Why does he want this movie anyway?" asked Aaron.

"Thanks to the town drunk Willie Willis when that meteor crashed the other night, just after our party at Jacob's house. Willie was walking down the road, probably all shit-faced drunk, he claimed it was an alien space craft that crashed, and he claimed that he saw me go into the wreckage and come out a couple of minutes later running for my life."

Aaron rolled his eyes, "Oh! Please. I wish I had a dollar for every person around here who claims to have seen a spaceship or an alien."

"I know, go figure." I added. "To top it all off, Orville Smith believes him, and he is trying to prove that I have turned into an alien. Thank you for this film segment. This should keep Orville from getting all bent out of shape. Orville and Ron's dad Willard are mad because I kept Ron from being a starter on the team this year. Orville has his head in the sand because Jim was never going to be a starter. Ron would have been questionable to start even if I hadn't gone out for the team."

As I was rolling the 8 mm slice of film and putting it into my left front jeans pocket, Aaron inquired, "Phil, you have beefed up fast, and your ability to play basketball seems to have developed over night. I could see where a redneck like Orville could easily believe all that garbage. Aliens! Please! Send us the wizard of Oz so he can give Orville a brain. He needs one."

"Hey, I have to get Krystin's house. Thank you so much, friend. I am hoping this will avoid trouble for me and you."

Aaron added, "Don't worry Phil, you have taken up for me before at school when I was being bullied. I got your back. Krystin's house huh! I see something more than just friends going on here."

I slowly made my way up his cluttered basement stairs. I asked Aaron's mom if I could use her phone to call Krystin briefly.

She said, "Go ahead."

I dialed her number, and the phone rang only once. She picked it up immediately. "Hello, is this you Phil?"

"Yes, it is me, and I'll be there in a few." I confirmed.

She said, "Be careful."

When I got back to the car. I breathed a big deep breath and mellowed a whispering, "Whew." I just hope he doesn't have another copy somewhere. I am looking forward to the Halloween party Wednesday at Jacob's house. I'm taking Krystin to the party. Jacob wants us all to dress up in costumes. It is not required, but he would like that. Since Krystin's mom is a nurse, she will probably dress up as a nurse. She could take my blood pressure anytime she wanted to, and she would always find my blood pressure high as long as she was around. She would swear that I have hypertension.

As I am driving over to see Krystin, I am trying to take in all that has happened today. All this information that Dr. Spear gave me is mind-boggling. Aliens living among us in secret, and to think that he is like me and has been for quite a while. Spear said that the transformations that have occurred are about over regarding physical changes. I hope he is right.

I finally get to Krystin's and walk up to the front door, push the doorbell and a faint Chime echoes through the house. The front door opens and its Krystin.

"Glad you could make it over to see me." She said as she was dressed in tight shorts that almost seemed too small for her. Her blouse was short and tight also which exposed her boobs.

"Is your mom and dad home?" I uttered while thinking what is this beautiful scantily clad girl trying to do to me?

She added, "They are upstairs getting ready for bed."

"Are they ok with you being down here with me?"

"They let me go to the movies with you Phil; I suppose they feel that you here at my house is safer than being out somewhere else."

"I would have to agree with them."

She hugged me and whispered into my ear while giving me small, interrupted kisses on my neck, "You had me so hot last night," (kiss on the neck) "you were driving me crazy while we were at the movies." (Two kisses on the neck).

"You drove me insane; I had to get home and take a cold shower. That is what you did to me. And now, you are doing it again by wearing this provocative outfit and caressing my neck. Shame on you."

"I like it that I turn you on. It tells me that you care for me and you like the way I look."

"You got that right young lady." I agreed with her pulsing out a weak voice as we both sauntered to the sofa.

The living room is a large room with the sofa sitting against the wall. There was a lamp that was sitting on a coffee table beside the couch. Other than the one lamp, the only other light that was on was an overhead florescent light on over the kitchen sink. The TV was on with the sound turned down low. The Ed Sullivan show was on at the time, and I could hear the music of the Byrds performing *Mr. Tambourine Man.* She sat down on the couch to the right where the lamp was. I sat down beside her.

Krystin asked, "How is everything with Aaron? He is quite the film buff."

"Oh! He had a question to ask me about a movie he shot when I got into that fight with Ray. I watched the movie, and you know how no one saw me hit Ray."

"I know; I didn't see you hit him either. That still puzzles me."

"Well maybe I just flinched, and it scared him so bad he just fell back."

"I don't think so, not Ray."

"Well, when I watched the movie, there was a blank 1-2 seconds in the movie right when I was supposed to have hit Ray. When it came back on, he was falling to the floor."

"That is strange Phil, for it to quit working at that second."

"I have no explanation except for Aaron's Super 8 mm camera getting jammed or something. That is what I told him. Ever since, Ray has been a different person. He has been nice to me and all my friends."

"I have noticed that too. Ray and his new girlfriend, Amanda, are like peanut butter and chocolate. They are all over each other in the hallways. I could only guess how they may be acting if they were here, alone, like us," Krystin whispered as she reached up and turned off the lamp. Then she got up from the sofa and walked over and turned off the TV.

The only light that was on was the fluorescent light in the kitchen. It was almost totally dark in the living room. When she came back to the sofa, she straddled me and was sitting on my lap. Our bodies were pressed so close as if only one body. The kissing and heavy petting began. I was still somewhat nervous for fear of her dad or mom sneaking down the stairs and catching us.

"Krystin, you are making me so hot; you are killing me."

She insisted, "You are doing the same thing to me."

While breathing heavily, "Krystin, we are both planning on further education; we can't let this go any farther."

"There are a lot of things we can do without having intercourse."

"Yes, this is true, but you are so beautiful; I'm not sure my body could take this punishment of ecstasy that you are giving me."

I could feel my lap beginning to get wet as she was gyrating over me in a circular and back and forth motion. My heart was beating so hard and fast she had to feel it because I could feel hers beating just as fast.

I whispered, "I don't think I can take this anymore; you are going to cause me to have an accident."

She proceeded to take things a step further. She wasn't letting up. "Lay down on the sofa for me."

When I did, she immediately laid on top of me. This is virtually a cardinal sin when you have been aroused this much. For the next 30 minutes, I thought my heart was going to explode. She finally got up from laying on top of me. We sat back up.

Once I came to my senses, "You are going with me Wednesday night over to Jacob's house for the Halloween party, aren't you?"

"Are you asking me out on another date?"

"Yes, I am. Maybe I was assuming too much too soon."

"Yes, I'll go with you. There is no one else I would rather be with than you. You should know that by now."

"I would like to ask you something?" as I reached and pulled off my high school class ring. I couldn't afford to purchase one with a gemstone set to put in it. So, the ring ended up being solid 14-carat gold. It cost me $20.75. I proceeded to complete my question, "Will you wear my ring and be my steady." Even in the darkness, I could see her eyes light up and a big smile came over her.

"I would love to Phil; will you take my ring and be my steady. I even have a chain here for you to put it on and wear around your neck since you probably can't get it on your finger." She got up and pulled out the side table drawer and retrieved a chain that appeared to be about 18-24 inches long. She put the chain through her ring and proceeded to put it around my neck. "I will probably need some angora fabric to wrap through your ring to make it fit. By Monday, I will be wearing it."

I gave her a big smile and suggested, "I better get home, I have to work tomorrow."

She said, "I don't want to let go of you, but I know I have to turn you loose."

"What Halloween costume are you planning on wearing?" I asked.

"I'll probably go as a nurse. It will be easy for me since my mother is a nurse."

"It will be hard for me to go as a shoe since my mom works at the shoe factory."

She chuckled, "You're silly."

"I'll have to come up with something else."

Krystin insisted, "Hey! My dad has an old Dracula costume in the closet that he hasn't worn in years at Halloween parties. I'll bet he wouldn't mind you borrowing it."

"That would be great and take one thing off my to-do list."

"Don't leave yet, I'll get it for you, and you can see if it will fit ok. It should; you and dad are about the same size, except you are more muscular which makes me want to ravish your body."

She went up the stairs to retrieve the costume. After a couple of minutes, she came down the stairs with the costume all neatly pressed in a box.

"Are you sure he won't mind?" I asked.

"I know he won't; once I ask him, it is a done deal."

"Be sure to thank him for me."

I grabbed her passionately and gave her a passionate kiss as she decided to French kiss me back. She knew what to do to get me sexually aroused. I knew I had to get home before she caused me to cream my jeans in front of her. How embarrassing would that be? As I was walking out the front door I stated, "I will pick you up for school on Monday."

She said, "Good night. See you Monday morning."

I scurried out to the mean green machine with her dad's costume in a box under my arm and began my drive home. It was a little after 10 pm so I knew that I wasn't going to be too late from mom's deadline time for me to be home. As soon as I arrived home, I hustled down the basement stairs to my humble residence. I began to lay down but was interrupted by a phone call.

"Hello!" I answered.

"Phil, this is your best pal Cody."

"Hey Cody, what's happening?"

"I had not talked to you in a while. I called earlier and you were not home. Your mom said that you had better be home by 10 pm. Were you visiting your hot girlfriend, Krystin?"

"Yeah, I was over there for a while. How are things with you and Carrie?"

"I was over there last night. We are really hitting it off. She loves to kiss me all over," insisted Cody.

"So, you two are getting into the serious kissy-face huggy-pie stuff. Krystin and I are doing great together. We are doing some very serious kissy-face huggy-pie stuff ourselves."

"Hey Phil, it is all I can do to keep from ravishing her body."

"I know all about that feeling Cody. Trust me, at times it's torture."

Cody paused a few seconds on the phone then began, "Friday, at school, I saw that schmuck, Jim and his dweeb buddy Ron pushing Aaron around. I overheard them talking to Aaron demanding some type of film. They were not being very nice to him, and it sounded like they were giving him a deadline to give them the film and Aaron said he had nothing to ...."

I intervened in Cody's statement, "I think I know what film they are looking for. Aaron happened to film the fight I had with Ray. I had just seen the film tonight before I went to Krystin's. It is funny; you know how everyone said they didn't see me hit Ray. Someone had to have seen that because I hit him in the forehead. It feels like time stood still for everyone except Ray and me. Even Aaron's film, for some reason, went blank for about a second right when I was punching Ray. So, Aaron's film didn't even catch it. What is up with that? Also, why are some people so bent on seeing that?"

Cody added, "I think it happened so fast, maybe faster than the eye can see, and it has aroused curiosity in some, along with the apparent fast changes that have come over you. You realize that you look as if you have been lifting weights for years and your physique appears to have changed over the weekend."

"I know, and I can't explain it. I have been lifting weights for about 4 months now, and I went weeks with the same weakling appearance. Then, like you said Cody, over the weekend, I mushroomed out with muscles." I knew I was lying about the 4 months of working out, but I had to come up with something.

"Hey Cody, I have to work tomorrow so better get some shut-eye. If you see those two goons bother Aaron again, let me know."

Cody finalized, "See you Monday at school my friend. Looking forward to the party Wednesday night. Don't forget the big game Friday night with our most intense rivals. We haven't beaten them in 13 years, but I think our team is much better with you playing basketball with us. You and Ray will be unstoppable."

"I hope so; see you Monday," then I hang up the phone.

I am wondering if I should call Dr. Spear about all this. I don't want to let all this talk of the film get into the wrong hands. I have also been thinking about Dr. Spear wanting me to meet the main alien. Maybe compassion is universal. Man, that is powerful. The possibility of any life form having compassion as an emotion throughout the universe. I know that even humans don't always use compassion, but the emotion is within us. I think I will call Dr. Spear tomorrow night and let him know what is going on about this talk of the film.

SUNDAY

Sunday is the only day I get to sleep in, which means that I am not going to church with mom. I don't go to work until noon on Sunday and they close at 6 pm. That still gives me 6 hours of work time for the week since I can't work through the week because of basketball practice. My next question is: Why am I working at all? Based on Dr. Spears' comments, I will get a college scholarship from the federal government. However, once I find out for sure, I probably will still work to help mom out with some of our bills, etc. I just hope Spear is right about the scholarship.

Sunday at work went well. I clocked out and headed home. As soon as I got home, I ate a cold dinner quick and headed down to the basement of my dwelling. I like it down here because I can be alone and no one bothers me, namely Janet. I sort of told her that this basement is off-limits to her. She probably ignores that statement and I have no idea about her coming down here and rummaging through my stuff when I'm not here.

I keep a little notebook of phone numbers hidden down here on top of one of the floor joists that is part of the ceiling of the basement. It is rather dark where my notebook is and nearly impossible to see. I usually have to feel for it to get it down for use. I just have to not let Janet see me getting it down. I trust mom; she wouldn't look for it anyhow. I get Spear's number and begin dialing. It is Sunday night and I'm a little nervous about calling a doctor on Sunday night. Within a few seconds, I could hear the ringtone through my phone. I hear a click and on the other end of the line is a female voice answering......

"Dr. Spear's residence."

"This is Phillip Marland. Is Dr. Spear available?"

"For you, yes, he is. He told me to always take your call if possible. Hold on for a few."

After a few seconds passed, "Hello Phillip, Dr. Spear here. What can I do for you?"

"I felt as though I needed to call you about the fight I had at school that we had talked about."

"Is there a problem with that incident?"

"I hope not but could be. It just so happened that during the fight, one of my friends was a movie buff and worked for the school newspaper. He had just purchased one of those super 8 mm film cameras that was recently developed. He filmed the fight. He is a good friend and he called me up about the filming of the fight. He got curious about no one seeing the punches. He has this movie editing machine where you can crank it as fast or slow as you want to go, and you can look at each individual frame. He had a frame where both my arms were just a blur. He is pretty smart, and he knows his super 8 mm clocks at about 18 frames per second. Aaron is his name, and he knows that I hit that boy twice in 1/18 second."

"This could be a problem, Phil."

"I talked him into splicing out about 8-10 frames of the film. I have the piece of film. I feel that he knows something is going on in regard to all that has happened, but he is loyal to me. I came to his rescue during a couple of bullying events, and he has been thankful for that. The problem is this other student's father wants the film. His father is the one that doesn't like me and has called me an alien before. This guy is also a 100% dysfunctional redneck and pretty stupid. He tells me that he is going to prove that I went into the crashed spacecraft and came out part alien."

Spear commented, "He's eating dream sickles there. That implosion removed all evidence of any alien craft. The only people that know are people like me and a few military and science experts that are sworn to secrecy by the CIA. However, people like the boys' father can still be an annoying part of your life. This guy could be dangerous because he may try to kill you. So be careful of him."

"I'm very vigil of his presence. I have had a couple of confrontations with him already. One confrontation was when I was with my girlfriend."

"Does she know about your transformation?"

"No, but I am concerned that sooner or later she will find out. This brings up another question for me to ask. If I stay with Krystin and we later on get married, how is my transformation going to affect our having children?"

"Good question Phil, I know of two other people like us that have had children, and everything was fine except the parents had to be aware of the extra powers the child would have. Young children sometimes don't understand their circumstances. They don't understand that they need to keep these extra abilities suppressed."

"Yeah, I see where that could be a challenge."

"Phil, can you drive over to my house this Tuesday evening?"

"Yes, would you tell me the reason you want me to come over."

"Sure, first of all you need another shot of the nanobots and some of their blood. This shot should last you for the next 4 years. As the aliens come to earth and go back to their home planet, they keep humans that are merged with their blood supplied with the nanobots and their blood. The next thing I want to do is to take you to one of their sites. One of the reasons the aliens picked out this region of southern Indiana was because of the number of caves in the area. They made a pact with this farmer who owns about 550 acres of ground and there is a large cavern on his property. The CIA is involved also, and they have built a large barn-like structure over this cavern. The government pays this farmer handsomely to keep quiet and keep plenty of NO TRESPASSING signs posted on his property. There are CIA agents all around the perimeter of his property. If you remember, the head honcho at this facility is a brother of the one that you tried to help in the crash. He wants to thank you for showing compassion to his brother at his moment of death."

"Dr. Spear I would love to meet an actual alien. Can we communicate?"

"Sure, they have developed a machine that interprets our language for them, and the same machine interprets their language for us. You will be able to talk to him."

"I have so many questions to ask him Dr. Spear. It is he isn't it? Do they have males and females like us?"

"Amazingly Phil, they do have males and females. They have actually given birth to young aliens here on earth. There are a few females at this establishment I'm taking you to see. Anokmar is a male species. This makes you wonder if evolution is close to being universal, also. I'm sure the planetary circumstances play a big role in evolution. Also, we must remember that their planet according to them is 6 billion years old. Ours is only 4.5 billion years old. They have about 1.5 billion years of evolution over us assuming that their evolution started about the same time period of planetary development."

"When do you want me over to see you Tuesday."

"Be here by 7 pm if possible."

"OK, I will see you then. Thank you, Dr. Spear, you have been so helpful informing me about what is going on and how to deal with these changes that have been occurring."

"You are welcome, Phil; I'm just glad that it was someone like you that came upon the crash and showed compassion to Anokmar's brother. That is the name of the head honcho – Anokmar. Anokmar didn't want you harmed, and he kept the CIA from intervening and possibly eliminating you."

The next thing I hear is the faint click of hanging up. I have so much to think about. I jumped into bed, but it will take me awhile to get to sleep with all this information I'm having to deal with.

<u>CHAPTER 07</u>
VISIT WITH ANOKMAR, THE HALLOWEEN PARTY

MONDAY

I am a little nervous about Dr. Spear's offer regarding me meeting a true alien. A life form that is not of this earth but living among us. On the flip side of that, what an opportunity that is for me. As I was driving to pick up Krystin and then head to school, my mind kept churning over and over on how to approach this Anokmar – the head honcho of this alien site. I pulled into Krystin's driveway, and she was out on her porch waiting for me.

As soon as she entered the car, she leaned over with a kiss and then with a smile she beamed, "This is a busy week for both of us. We have the Halloween party Wednesday night and the big county rivalry basketball game Friday night. We haven't beaten this team in 13 years."

I chimed in with a return smile, "I have this feeling that we are going to beat them this year. I will try my best. I just hope the rest of the team plays well. I'm not worried about Ray, he will hold his own, but we need good performance from everyone else."

"Phil, if you are right about this, this will top off our graduation year, beating the county rivals."

As we pulled into the parking lot of the school, we walked in with Ray and his girlfriend, Amanda.

"Looking forward to the party Wednesday night and especially the big basketball game Friday night," said Ray.

I added, "I know, if we can pull this off Friday night, we will be the first to defeat Scottsville not only in our high school careers, but it will be the first time in 13 years."

"I know," said Ray with a smile and excitement.

Ray added, "This will help me a lot with my possible basketball scholarship, especially if we do well in the sectional."

I chimed in, "You are going to be fine this year with your basketball scholarship. Remember, you are going to have me out on the floor feeding the ball to you when you get open."

While giving me a thumbs up, Ray graciously put his arm around my neck and said, "I know Phil, you have been awesome this week in practice. Scottsville, you belong to us this year."

I replied, "That's the right attitude, pal."

As we entered the school doors, Ray and Amanda had to go their separate ways. Krystin and I were heading down to 1st-period Geography class. We had about 5 minutes before the bell rang and as we turned the hallway corner, I noticed that Jim and Ron had Aaron pinned up against the locker. I overhead them demanding the movie. I told Krystin, "Wait here."

As soon as they saw me, they let Aaron go. Aaron continued to look on but thankfully didn't have his movie camera in case things got messy.

I blurred out to both Jim and Ron, "Are we going to have to have another (Come to Jesus meeting)?"

Jim barked out loud, "This doesn't pertain to you."

"I think it does; you want a film that Aaron has of the fight because your dumbass dad wants the film for some reason."

"You know what the reason is," Jim added. "Dad is going to deal with you himself."

I got close to Jim's face and assured, "I don't give a rat's ass about your dad. If he keeps on, I'm going to be dealing with him. If I see you boys pestering Aaron again, it's going to get really ugly for you because I'm going to hurt both of you, and it won't be pretty. Jim, you may be too stupid to know it, but I did you a favor by not playing you one-on-one in front of your dad because I thought he might beat you and slap you around. Apparently, you don't even appreciate when someone is trying to help you."

Jim with a meek voice replied, "What makes you think you can even beat me?"

"I know I can beat you; I would even spot you 12 points and still beat you to 24 points. You can't even outplay Nick, and he is just a sophomore. If you are not convinced from watching us practice every night, challenge me to a one-on-one game."

I figured that this Orville is pretty dense mentally. There is an old cliché – give a man enough rope, he will hang himself. If I piss him off enough to do something stupid, then I may get enough against him that the sheriff may arrest him. However, I would regret that regarding the rest of his family. Who knows, they may be thrilled to get rid of him for a while. I know he smacks Jim around, so he probably beats his wife also.

When I walked across the hall back to Krystin she asked, "What film are they talking about?"

"It's a long story. I'll have to tell you about it when we have time. The bell is about to ring; we need to scoot along."

I couldn't wait until 2nd-period typing class. This is the day that Phil Marland will win the timed writing exercise. Along with my other abilities, my mind has developed, and I can read so much faster. My fingers can move across those typing keys much faster. This is also where I have to be careful. I have mom's old typing machine in the basement and the other night I easily was typing 160 words per minute. I cannot go in there and show off like that. I just need to barely beat the 3 speed demons of which one is Krystin. I also cannot be coming in typing and winning the timed writings every morning. Just once in a while will keep those 3 girls on their toes. I have to keep the comments that Dr. Spear made to me about not blatantly showing my abilities. I have to keep these abilities concealed. It's just like he said, I need to keep these abilities hidden from the general public. Currently, there is a dumbass redneck and a town drunk that think I'm half alien. So far, everyone else thinks I'm a cool guy.

First-period Geography went well. We had an exam and I aced it. My reading abilities have improved dramatically. I can read several pages per minute now and remember almost everything. It just keeps getting better. Now the time has come for 2nd period typing and the timed writing exercise.

Mrs. Lathem gets out her stopwatch and says, "Get a sheet of paper in your typewriters and get ready."

I continued my routine speaking softly, "Ok girls, you are going down today."

After a few seconds, Mrs. Lathem with a louder than usual voice, "Begin."

I took off like a jack Rabbit running from a fox. After about 30 seconds, I realized that I needed to slow down and not be too obvious. When the 2-minute timed writing was over, I heard "Stop." When she says stop, you had better stop. If someone keeps typing for just 2-3 seconds longer, you receive a big red F on your timed writing. I felt good about my position. Have to wait now until tomorrow to see the results.

Basketball practice after school went great. I keep feeding Ray, Dan, and Stan the basketball when they get open along with scoring myself at will. We should be ready for the big county championship game Friday night. Bartlett has been on the other three boys about feeding me the ball when the opportunity arrives. It seems like we have a good balance. The other starter is only a sophomore, Nick Barger. He is going to be a very good player by the time he is a senior. He is very quick and fast.

That probably makes Nick and me 2 of the quickest guards in Indiana.

TUESDAY

I am excited about this day, especially 2nd period typing. During the beginning of typing class, Mrs. Lathem caught me at the classroom door as I was walking in. "Phil, you were the top student on yesterday's timed writing. You typed 112 words per minute with only 1 mistake. I have never had any boy type that fast, and only 1 girl a few years ago at another school timed out at 108 words per minute. Do you think that you can keep this up?"

"I was lucky Mrs. Lathem; I think I just had a good day. I may never get that speed again. Not that I won't try. I put my heart into those timed writings and want to beat those 3 girls."

"They have been beating you down all semester. So, this has been a welcome change, plus it will put extra pressure on them to perform well knowing that you are lurking to outdo them."

As soon as class started, Mrs. Lathem blurred out, "We have a new first place in yesterday's timed writing, Phil Marland."

The speed demons including Krystin's jaws dropped, displaying unexpected surprise.

Krystin asked, "How did you reach that speed?"

"I just had a lucky day. You girls have beaten me all semester long. It probably won't happen again."

After basketball practice, I had to get home and travel to Jasperville. I still had mixed feelings about this meeting. My mind was loaded with questions that I wanted to ask. Dr. Spear had already filled me in on some things. I have this feeling that I am going to be totally amazed.

I finally arrived at Dr. Spear's residence. He was coming out the door of his house just as I was getting out of my car.

Spear insisted, "Get in my car Phil; I will drive."

Spear had a beautiful red 1965 Ford Mustang. As for me, I was traveling in luxury. As soon as I sat down in the passenger's side front seat, which was a beautiful white leather, I chimed in, "Nice car."

"Thanks, I like it."

"How far do we have to go?"

"We will go about 25 miles east of Jasperville toward the eastern escarpment of the Crawford Uplands and the Mitchell karst plain section of Indiana. We will be just a few miles outside Mitchen, Indiana."

"By the way, I came upon 2 school kids threatening my friend Aaron today at school wanting the film he took of me during the school fight. They were trying to scare it out of him and just give them the film. I stepped in and told the boys to leave him alone or they would have to deal with me. Aaron would not give them the film on his own. He thinks too much of me, but I am alarmed about the boys' dads."

"You keep me informed on that Phil; I don't want the wrong people finding out about things they don't need to know. We'll have the CIA step in if we have to."

"Thanks Dr. Spear; it is comforting to know that someone has my back."

It was very dark on the country roads that we were traveling on. We had made 5 or 6 different turns on different country Roads. We finally arrived at an old 2-story farmhouse. When we pulled in, off in the distance behind the house on a gravel road was a little shack by the gravel driveway. The shack was at least .25 mi. from the old farmhouse and a good ½ mile from the main blacktop country road. As we pulled up, these 2 gentlemen came out of the old shack that had electricity running to it. There was a gate by the shack that had to be opened. One of the gentlemen approached the car window on the driver's side. The other person stayed back behind the gate holding a rifle that appeared to be an AK47. As the 1st gentleman reached the car, he said, "No one is allowed back here." Then Dr. Spear showed him what appeared to be a special badge. Then the gentleman that was actually dressed in a suit and tie replied, "Oh! I didn't recognize you Dr. Spear. Who do you have with you?"

"This is Phillip Marland." Then Spear commanded, "Give me your driver's license to show him."

I reached into my back pocket, brought out my billfold, and retrieved my driver's license to give Spear. He took it and handed it to the gentleman. The gentleman then took a flashlight and shined it into my face. Then he turned the light on the driver's license. He said, "Wait here."

Then he went into the shack and after a couple of minutes came back out to the car, handed me my license back, then he motioned to the other gentleman behind the gate to open it and let us pass through.

As we drove past the shack, ahead of us by about 50 feet was a thick patch of forest trees. The gravel road was the only clear spot in the forest; the rest of the forest was an almost impassable thicket of trees and brush. We traveled another ½ mile into the forest and finally we came upon this large clearing. In the middle of the clearing was this large barn-like structure with several army men surrounding the structure. All of them were carrying AK47 rifles. We pulled up, got out of the car, and began walking to the front of the building which had a large white barn-like sliding door. The door appeared to be about 35 ft. wide and at least 20 feet tall. I hear one of the army men yell, "Open up." Then you could hear the large door that appeared to be hanging from some heavy-duty rollers rolling along a large metal track. The door only opened about 10 feet, a large enough opening for Spear and me to walk through.

When we walked past the main door, I saw in front of me about 30 feet away this large steel floor platform that was square-like and appeared to be at least 50 feet wide. Then I looked up at the roof and saw that the roof appeared to be attached to several metal beams. This made it look as if the roof of the barn may open outward. I followed Spear over toward the corner of the building where there was located a set of stairs. We walked down about 4 flights of stairs, dropping down at least 40 ft. from the platform. When we reached the bottom of the stairs, another door opened up and to my amazement, I realized that we must be in a large cavern that was lit with electricity. I could see several large stalactites hanging from the ceiling surrounding the large square platform that I saw when first entering the barn. The platform had several metal beams attached to it. The beams appeared to be attached to this large hydraulic engine. The platform is apparently a receiving and launch pad.

As we walked down another flight of stairs, there was this large room that had been carved out by the carbonic acid dissolving the limestone over thousands of years. The stalagmites had been removed and the floor had been leveled. The room was full of electronic instruments and TV screens which appeared to be displaying words and numbers over black screens. The words/numbers on some TVs were green while others were white. These must be computers that I've always heard about. However, I thought that computers used by the military had these punch cards that had to run through the computers. I don't remember any TV screens displaying the data and electrified typewriters entering the data. Then I realized that the aliens must have developed these computers. I saw several humans mixed in with the aliens walking about and several were sitting at these computers. I also noticed these billfold-like plastic cartridges that were being put into an opening leading into the main compartment of the computer. Other cartridges were being pulled out of the openings. Everyone and everything seemed to be very busy.

As we were walking into the busy area Dr. Spear noted, "See the large spacecraft over to the side of this large room.

When they need to lift off, the large square platform above us will sink down to this level of the cavern. They will maneuver the spacecraft onto the platform and the platform will rise up to the ceiling of the barn. The roof will open up and the spacecraft will take off. Somehow they run very quietly. On occasion, no lights at all. Other times they will be lit up and then flicker off. That is why you have heard so many stories of flickering lights in the sky just disappearing."

"This is amazing, Dr. Spear." I responded.

As we walked up to this one alien, he stood up and appeared to be about 7 feet tall. He had gray reptile-like skin. Dr. Spear said, "They have a machine that interprets our language and then it responds back to us in English what they say."

Dr. Spear continued, "Phil, I would like for you to meet Anokmar. He is the brother of the one that died in the crash. Had it not been for Anokmar letting the CIA know not to eliminate you but to spare you, you probably wouldn't be here tonight."

Anokmar extended his 4 finger 2 thumb hand out to me and grabbed my arm just above my wrist and began shaking my hand and lower arm. Spear suggested, "Take his lower arm and hold it while shaking hands. This is their method of shaking hands."

I did so and with a feeble voice, "It is an honor to meet you. Thank you for sparing my life."

After about 5 seconds, the interpreting machine began making unusual noises as Anokmar listened intently. Then he started making some unusual noises and after about 5 seconds the machine began speaking English.

Via the machine, *"It is a pleasure to meet you, Phil. I saw how compassionate you were to my brother in his dying moments. He wanted to give you some advantages over others, and he decided to give you the shot of nanobots along with his blood. By your human standards, I suppose that makes us related. That is when I told the CIA to spare you. My brother wanted you to live or he would have detonated the implosive device immediately. He wanted to give you time to get away from the implosion. I wanted to thank you for making my brother's last moments compassionate. Luckily for us, you seem to be the very type of person that we want for this experiment of merging humans into our species and hopefully get the positive results we want. So far, it has been a success. We just haven't been doing this very long. So, long term by your human years, we are not sure. We and humans involved think we can extend the life expectancy of both species by 100 or more years."*

I smiled and added, "Where are you from?"

"We came from a red dwarf star in the constellation Libra that your humans have not discovered yet. Currently, they don't have the technology, but within 50 – 100 years humans will have the technology unless humans destroy themselves or destroy the earth. Humans have already done severe damage to the earth's atmosphere and water system by emitting various pollutants into the air that are selective absorbers of long-wave radiation of heat. They have also added toxic chemicals to the waterways. Their largest environmental

problem is staring them in the face, but they don't see it. It is overpopulation. The planet simply has too many people. We came to this planet to hopefully help save the planet. We want to have some of our population exist along with your population peacefully while at the same time controlling the overpopulation problem that already exists. This will take several years. We don't want to just kill off humans. But our species is not sure this world would welcome us. There is a lot of evil happening on this planet. We are amazed at the continuous fighting among countries."

"I know what you are saying. Let me ask you a question. You talked about me being compassionate to your brother. Is this some emotion that exists throughout the universe? Is it a universal emotion?"

"We know of several other alien species existing within just 50 light- years from your sun. There appears to be so far, good and evil, throughout the universe. We have encountered very evil species before that were power-hungry and existed at the demise of others. Thank goodness they have not discovered earth yet. Other alien species are more like us. They want peace, but like us, they will fight to protect themselves. Our planet is about 2 billion years older than your planet. Our advancement in technology far supersedes human technology. However, humans have been able to develop the hydrogen bomb along with other nuclear capabilities. We and other species are concerned that there may be a 3rd world war using nuclear weapons. If it comes to that, humans may destroy the earth themselves. If they don't destroy the earth in a nuclear war, there won't be much left anyway.

We, along with some other alien allies will finish the task of destroying the earth. Good must win over evil. This seems to be a universal law."

"Many people here on earth believe in an invisible superpower Deity in which we have different names. The common one for us is (God). Other countries have other names. **Names different cultures ascribe to God include Yahweh, Zeus, Allah, Vishnu, Xavier, and Jah.** Depending on the religion, believers might view a god as a personal being, impersonal force, singular deity or one expression of deity among many. In fact, most of the wars on earth are the result of some religion that was different than some others. Do any species of aliens have a deity belief?"

"What we have observed so far involving the radial distance of 50 light years, we have not come upon any other species that have such belief."

"A lot of people on earth have been unfortunate in their well-being. We have had slavery exist on earth since the beginning of humans along with different societies having an upper- and lower-class system of existence. I suppose this belief of a deity gives those unfortunate people hope."

Anokmar added, *"Hope is an emotion that at least our species has. We hope that humans won't destroy the earth with their nuclear powers. If they do, our species may likely reach the point that – <u>All hope is lost</u>. That is a terrible feeling. I might add Master Phil, you have been asking some great questions."*

"I think you have already answered the question about (hopelessness) which is similar to the emotion of despair. What about love, hate, sadness, revenge, or loyalty."

"I loved my brother when he died; I cried because of his death. But we can't display physical liquid tears from our eyes like humans. One of your favorite pets is a dog. Humans believe that they can cry but they don't just display the physical tears along with their wailing. Love, hate, and revenge tend to be universal emotions. Remember, even the evolution of species is universal. We are all made of the same star stuff. But the smallest environmental difference can play a huge role in evolution. We have compared our DNA with human DNA. We are still about 95% the same DNA. Your scientists will have the technology to make DNA comparisons in a few decades."

Dr. Spear chimed in, "Anokmar, you have given us a lot to think about. Your philosophy is very similar to mine and Phil's. However, there are people around us that would not be welcome to Phil or me because of our changes even though we virtually look the same. Even the various colors of our species' skin have created massive abuse to people throughout the history of our human race. Phil and I both agree with you; this is something that is going to take some time. With the slow addition of people with the right personalities and emotions being part of our race is the best way to blend in."

Anokmar asserted via the interpreting machine, *"Phil, you must be like Dr. Spear. You must be as secretive as possible. Whatever you do, don't let anyone know about us and our location. The CIA is not your enemy. The general public that don't understand is your enemy."*

Dr. Spear added, "Believe me Phil, there a numerous Orville's out there and others similar to him that will feel threatened and will never understand."

I replied, "I know, but it is so hard not to use my special abilities for the greater good."

We both shook hands with Anokmar using their method of handshake, similar to some early American Indian cultures and then left the premises.

Spear reminded me, "When we get back to my house, I'm going to give you that other shot. This one will not hurt you like the first one did. Your skin is very tough now and the nanobots in your body will accept the new nanobots and alien blood easily."

"How often will I need one of these shots?" I asked.

"After tonight about every 4 years. If you quit getting them, your extra abilities may gradually disappear after several years plus your aging process will speed up and be more like humans. We have been given a gift of several abilities along with quicker thinking and reasoning skills. We need to use them best for our human race."

"Thanks Dr. Spear; I view you as my mentor."

"I will be going to the big county championship game Friday night, Phil. You be sure to secretly make us proud."

"I will do my best without being too obvious."

"That's what I'm talking about."

When we reached Spear's residence. I followed him into a back room where he had a refrigerator. He opened the door and pulled out one of 4 syringes. I removed my jacket, rolled my sleeve up, and took the shot in the arm.

Spear added, "Your arm will get sore for a day or two, but after that you will be fine. In fact, you should feel fantastic. I also want to make you aware that your hearing of faint noises will increase considerably. This is one drawback to the shot. I get so tired of hearing people talk that are 30 ft or more away from me. Once in a while, I hear people say things about me. Some things good, but occasional bad remarks. You have to learn to shut out the extra noise. Sometimes, it is not easy. I wish I had given you this shot about 2 weeks before the big game so you could get used to the extra quickness and strength that you will develop very quickly."

I chimed in, "Those little nanobots must work pretty fast."

"Absolutely, be sure to go out somewhere alone and test your strength and quickness so you can get used to using them properly before the game."

As I was walking toward his front door to leave, "I will, Dr. Spear."

I got into the car and saw him waving bye to me from his front porch. I waved back and began my drive home while being reminded of the gift that had been given to me for just being compassionate. This needs to be a lesson for everyone; being compassionate to someone will always bear a gift. It may likely not be the gift I have been given, but one should get the gift of caring and being helpful knowing that they have been a part of that.

I have another problem that is going to surface. Sooner or later, Krystin is going to find out about my condition, or I am going to have to tell her. If we stay together, I can't keep this secret from her forever. When she finds out, how is she going to react? Will she shun me, or will she want to be part of the action? It seems as though for every question I answer, I have 5 new ones come up that I can't answer. Thank goodness for Dr. Spear and now my new friend, and maybe relative, Anokmar.

After about a 30-minute drive, I finally pulled into my driveway in the mean *green machine*. After that 2nd shot Spear gave me, I felt fantastic. Even though it was after 10 pm, I jumped up and grabbed the big tree limb for chin-ups. They were so easy to do. After about 50 chin-ups, I wasn't the least bit tired. I started to climb this big maple tree leaping from limb to limb with precision-like accuracy. Before I knew it, I was a good 50 ft. off the ground. I was running out of limbs that would support me. I started to climb back down. After about a 20-foot descent, I began to wonder if I could just jump down from this current height of about 30 feet. I said to myself, "*here I go.*" I jumped all the way to the ground and landed on my feet with ease. This was great. I realized I needed to get some rest and be ready for school tomorrow. I still had some reading to do but it would only take 10-15 minutes. I had a chapter to read in Chemistry involving acids and bases, another one in Physics involving force and acceleration, and 2 stories to read for English. Tomorrow night is the big Halloween party. I'm going to be going as

Dracula. Krystin is going as a nurse. It would have been neat for Krystin to go as the (Bride of Dracula). With her outfit, she could still be Dracula's nurse. She could be anything she wanted to be as long as she was with me.

As soon as I got into the house, my mom yelled from her bedroom, "Krystin called about 9:00 pm and I told her you weren't here. I told her I would have you call her as soon as you got home. I didn't realize that you would be this late. Good God, it's almost 11 pm."

"Sorry for being late mom. I'll talk to Krystin tomorrow morning when I pick her up. I need to get some studying done."

"OK but be quiet; you know how early I have to get up in the morning."

I knew my reading wouldn't take long. My grades have improved to where I am getting all A's in my subject. I am amazed at my tree climbing which took very little effort. I am already feeling stronger from that 2nd shot. After about 15 minutes of reading and doing my homework, I plop into bed and finally conclude an amazing night.

WEDNESDAY

It is 7 am when the radio alarm clock goes off with the song blasting out – *I Can't Get No Satisfaction – by the Rolling Stones.* -- When I hear the lyrics – Cause I try, and I try, and I try – they seem to be fitting and appropriate in my current life. Regardless of how hard my mother and I try to get ahead, life always slams us down again. I suppose at least half the people of this region fit this category with only a few that have beaten the financial needs of living. I go into the bathroom to do the 3 S's (shit, shower, and shave). I look at my body in the mirror, and I notice that my arm and leg muscles have bulged out more. I also noticed that the top of my head is not visible now unless I hunker over slightly. This calls for a measurement. I measured my height and realized I might be a couple of inches taller. I am near 6' 2" now. I need to use the excuse that I have been working out more preparing for the big game for the extra muscles, but I don't have an answer for the rapid increase in height. None that I could give anyone. When I finished getting ready, making sure I put on a plaid shirt over my t-shirt, I want to be an enigma at school. I don't want to attract too much attention. The door to the basement was closed, and while no one could see me, I decided to make one leap from the bottom of the basement to the top step which was about 12 feet up. Success except for the loud thump when I landed.

As soon as I open the door and enter the kitchen, mom immediately asks, "What was that loud noise?"

"I was running up the stairs and I slipped on one of the steps and caught myself."

"Well, be careful; you could hurt yourself. Phil, I swear you are still growing."

"You feed me well mom. What else can I say?"

"Phil, have you measured your height?"

"Yes, I am approaching around 6'2".

"It seems like just a few days ago, you were only a little taller than me and I'm only about 5'7". You have shot up fast."

"This will help me for the basketball team. Being a little taller gives you an advantage."

Janet was sitting there eating some cereal as she taunted, "Your wife Krystin called twice last night, first about 7:30 pm and then about 9:30 pm."

I asserted, "Why didn't you tell me that she called twice?"

"You should have been home dork to answer your calls. She sounded kind of upset the 2nd time she called. I'm sure she was wondering where you were and what you were up to."

"Thanks for nothing, Janet."

"Hey, it wasn't my day to watch over you, Phil."

"So, this is the thanks I get after helping you in Geometry."

"I didn't know where you had gone. I couldn't help you anyway."

"I guess you are right; sorry for snapping at you."

I finished eating a quick breakfast, a couple pieces of toast with strawberry jelly on them. I kissed mom as always and headed out the door to the *mean green machine.* As I drove to Krystin's house to pick her up, I was wondering how to tell her what I was doing last night when she called. Her calling twice concerns me. When I arrived, I got out of the car to ring the doorbell. Her mother opened the door before I got there and said, "Krystin's friend Margaret picked her up about 15 minutes ago and went on to school. Sorry, you missed her Phil."

I asked Mrs. Adkins, "Is she ok?"

"I think so, but she seemed a little distraught about something," replied Mrs. Adkins.

The only thing I could say was, "Thanks, Mrs. Adkins. I'll get up with her at school."

In my mind, I'm thinking what is going on here? If I didn't know better, she may be mad about something. Come on Phil don't be too hasty to pass judgment. I know that sometimes girls talk, and some girls even make up stuff about us boys. Boys are just as bad at doing the same thing. I should know more when I get to school.

I sped up the car some to buy me a little extra time. While I'm hurrying to school, the song that is playing on my radio was (Love Hurts) by the Everly Brothers. The words were tearing my heart out at this moment. I had the radio on pretty loud --- *Love hurts, Love scars, love wounds, and mars.* This was not the song that I needed to be hearing at this present time. I pulled into the parking lot of the school and hurriedly walked in the front door. Just as soon I enter the main lobby of the school, a young girl in her junior year stops me and begins talking to me. Her name was Janene. I should have told her I was in a hurry and went on, but she kept getting in my way.

Janene boasted, "Hey Phil, I wanted to let you know how impressive it was the other day when you stood up to Ray. That took courage. I like that in someone when they don't let fear get the best of them. Everyone knows that Ray is a bad ass."

As I was trying to walk past her, she kept sliding in front of me regardless of which direction I tried to take. "Thanks Janene, Ray and I have developed a friendship now. If you don't mind, I'm in sort of a hurry."

She kept in front of me and stated, "If you ever need to talk, I'm a good listener."

"Thanks, but I have to go."

As I finally get around her, I look down the hallway and see my friend Cody standing by the lockers. Then I looked farther down the hallway and there was Krystin turning to walk down the hallway to her 1st-period class. She saw Janene talking to me.

As I began my walk to my 1st-period class, Cody yelled at me and motioned me over as if he had something to say to me. I only have about 5 minutes before class starts.

Cody with anticipation grabs me and chants, "I have to tell you."

"Tell me what?"

Cody continues, "Carrie told me that someone told Krystin that they saw you out last night with another girl at the Park-&-Eat drive-in restaurant."

"There is no way I was with another girl. I was at a friend's house in Jasperville."

"I know that, and you know that, but you also know how some of these teeny boppers can make up stuff and lie just to break up a couple that is going steady."

"So that is why Krystin appears to be upset. Who would make up such a story?"

"Hey, my man, you may have been just talking to her. Carrie thinks Janene wants to jump your bones. The best chance she has to do that is to break you and Krystin up. Unfortunately, I think Krystin is falling for lies and gossip. Apparently, Janene told Margaret and Margaret called Krystin and told her what Janene had said. It just ends up being a vicious circle of gossip."

"Now the fog is clearing up. That is why Margaret picked Krystin up this morning."

"Just tell her that you were out of town with a friend and have them vouch for you."

"I wish it was that simple Cody, but it is more complicated than that."

"Oh dude, if she believes those girls, you could be out of options."

"The only thing I can do is to talk to her and just hope that she cares for me enough to trust me. I have to get to class. Thanks for the information, Cody."

"If there is anything I can do – cool cat – let me know."

I hurry down the hallway to 1st-period Geography. Me knowing that Krystin will be sitting beside me in the next row over, I hope I can get her attention enough to meet with her at lunch and tell my side of this story. There were still a couple of minutes before class started. As soon as I walked into the room, Krystin was not even looking up. Instead, she was looking down at her Geography book.

I sat down and whispered, "Krystin, I think you are upset over some gossip that is not true. Please sit with me at lunch and let me explain. At least give me a chance to tell my side of the events last night."

She didn't even acknowledge me. With one last quiet gasp just as Mr. Shields walked in, "This is tearing my heart out." Then class started and she kept focused on the instructor never looking my way.

It was the same thing, ignoring me in the other morning classes. In between the classes during hallway passage, it was worse. Other students kept coming up with statements such as: *What is going on with you and Krystin? Is Krystin mad at you? What did you do to piss off Krystin?* I would continue to reply --- "I'm innocent; I haven't done anything."

Just before lunch, Janene stopped me in between classes. Janene fretted, "I think it is terrible the way she is treating you. You don't deserve to be treated this way. I would treat you differently if I had the chance."

"Janene, did you say anything to anyone about Krystin or me?"

"No Phil, I wouldn't do that."

"Well, I'm trusting that you didn't because it would be a terrible thing to do."

Janene replied, "Phil, I would just like to have the opportunity to be with you."

I headed down the hallway to Trigonometry class, the last class before lunch. Janene was a pretty girl herself but wasn't even close to Krystin's beauty. Janene has been known to spread rumors before. With that 2nd shot, I caught myself virtually reading her mind as she was talking to me. I kept hearing in Janene's mind – *If I can break up Phil and Krystin, I may just have a chance with him.* Mentally realizing what people are thinking is a new experience for me. I need to see if I can read Krystin's mind.

Just as I was ready to walk into the Trig room, Ray and Amanda were walking by and Ray remarked, "Phil get with Amanda and myself for lunch; we have something to tell you that may explain Krystin's actions."

"Thanks Ray; it appears that I will have that option during lunch."

Amanda added, "You won't have to stay but a couple of minutes and you can go sit with Krystin and set things right."

"Thanks to both of you. You are a good guy Ray."

"Hey Phil, I know how much you are helping me in basketball, and a scholarship is looking better all the time thanks to you, and we are going to prove that Friday night. After we beat Scottsville, we will have more college scouts coming to our games giving me and you more exposure. You could be in scholarship territory too you know, especially with your GPA."

I remarked, "See you at lunch."

LUNCH TIME

The bell from Trig class finally rings. It felt as though this class was never going to end. I hustle out of the classroom trailing behind Krystin. I walk somewhat faster, even going into a jog to catch up with her. I finally caught up with her as she was looking straight ahead and continuing to ignore me. I stepped in front of her as my eyes reddened and tears began welling up.

"Krystin, please talk to me. Sit with me at lunch and let me explain. I was not at the Park-&-Eat the other night and I was not with any girl. Please believe me."

Krystin finally gave in and said, "I suppose everyone needs a chance to explain themselves. I'll save a seat for you."

"Thank you, you won't be sorry for giving me a chance to explain."

As we began walking to lunch again I added, "I have to stop by Ray and Amanda's table first; they know something about all this gossip. Then I'll be there."

I let her go ahead of me as I sauntered back. Within seconds Aaron catches up with me. Aaron inquired, "Hey Phil, I heard about the rumors going around. Probably everyone in the school has. Some people can spread nasty rumors fast. I just wanted to let you know that I know you better than that."

"Thanks Aaron, I appreciate that."

Aaron added, "I'm still getting dirty looks from Jim and Ron. They still want that film."

"If push comes to shove, give it to them, but let me know, I'll have another talk with them and this time it won't be pretty."

"If I have to give up the film, I will let you know."

I continued on to get in the lunch line. About that time, I saw that little weasel Ron buck the line in front of Derek again. I walked up past about 6 other students and grabbed Ron by his shirt collar and pulled him out of line while he was wailing, "*What are you doing man, let go, I'm going to tell the teachers.*" I walked him to the back of the line. When I did, about a dozen students began clapping their hands and cheering. Then I got back to my proper place in line while receiving several pats on the back.

Ron yells at me, "You got out of line; you lost your place in line. You need to go to the end of the line." I ignored him and went through the line to receive my food tray. I started the same old routine with the cooks.

"Girls, all of you are just looking so good today. Mable I can tell you are still losing weight." Mable, only about 5'4" was probably approaching 250 lbs. She certainly hadn't missed any meals. I received my tray and began walking down to Ray and Amanda's table. I noticed that Janene was sitting with Amanda. I sat down quickly beside Ray. Ray leaned over and whispered in my ear and said, "Can't talk now; Janene is eating with us."

Just then, Janene spoke to me, "Glad you could eat with us Phil."

"I'm not eating here, Janene, I just had to tell Ray something really quick about basketball practice." Then I got up and proceeded to Krystin's table and sat across from her.

I began my plea, "See Janene sitting over there with Amanda. I think she started the rumor about me being with some other girl."

Krystin apologetically surmised, "Since I have been here at school this morning, I have heard other people say that Janene made it all up about you and some girl. I asked her and she said she didn't know who the girl was. She thought she was from another town.

The question I have to ask you Phil, is if you wasn't with some other girl at the Park-&-Eat, where were you last night. I would just like to know the truth."

I began my story of my whereabouts, "It's not that easy to explain without me being embarrassed."

Krystin looked into my eyes, "Now you are making me suspicious again."

"I don't mean to Krystin, but I had to see a doctor at Jasperville about something."

"You didn't get someone pregnant did you?"

(I knew that I was going to have to tell her something along with making up something.)

"No, no, noooo. Ok, here it goes. I have had this linear skin separation on both sides of my shoulder blades. This doctor from Jasperville is a specialist in this. It is kind of embarrassing, but that is where I was. I didn't get home until after 10 pm."

"He is open at night?"

"No, I had seen him previously about this at his office and I met him at his house. He was born the same way, and we have become friends."

I was telling a little lie there to maybe make things easier. Dr. Spear's markings came on after his shot of alien blood and Nanobots.

"So, this is something that has come on you at birth, said Krystin."

"For him it was, but not for me. It had just come on me just recently, a couple of weeks ago."

"He can vouch for your whereabouts then."

"Yes, but he is a very busy man, and I would hate to ask him to vouch for me. This is why it is difficult."

"Would you be willing to show me your markings as a testament to where you were?"

I knew that it would be coming to this. However, I knew that sooner or later, she would see me with my shirt off. So, she needs to know what it is.

"Yes, if you will just get back with me. Put my class ring back on your finger, angora and all. I have not removed your ring from around my neck. Do you still want to go to the Halloween party with me tonight? Please say yes."

"Yes, I will go with you. Come over tonight after basketball practice. Come early, bring your Halloween costume, and if you show me the markings, then we will see about going steady again. I will be more inclined to believe your side of the story."

"Will your parents be home?"

"Yes, but we will go upstairs to get ready and as you change into your costume, just before you put your top on you can show me. Mom and dad will be downstairs."

"I'm afraid you won't want to be with me if I show you. You may not want to go steady with a freak."

"Nonsense Phil, you should know me better than that."

"I wish it was that easy, Krystin."

"You can tell me anything, Phil."

"Again, I wish it was that easy."

"Ok, if we are going steady, you will eventually see them anyway. But I'm embarrassed."

"Don't be, trust me."

"I'm asking the same thing from you; trust me and don't believe school rumors."

"I know. I realize that you have suddenly become so popular in school. Along with popularity comes rumors. I should have realized that and should have talked to you first. My bad."

"That is all I am asking Krystin, just give me a chance to explain."

Just about then, the bell rang, and school lunch was over. We still had afternoon classes to finish.

As we were getting up, Krystin reminded me, "See you tonight after practice? The party doesn't start until 8 pm. Come a little early so we can get this other problem settled."

"I'll be over about 7 pm."

As we were walking out of the lunchroom, Amanda caught up with Krystin and proclaimed, "Krystin, glad I caught up with you. I just wanted to tell you that Janene would like to break you and Phil up so she could have a chance to jump his bones."

Krystin replied, "That is what I keep hearing."

Amanda added, "She has been known to screw about any boy that would let her. As long as he doesn't go through with it – screwing Janene I mean, don't blame Phil. Be glad you have someone as popular as Phil. You and I are steady with the two most popular boys in school."

Krystin looked at Amanda and said, "I know; I just need a little time to get over the rumors."

Amanda sputtered, "I know it is hard to take when someone says something about your steady that reflects back on you. When you are dating the two most popular boys in school, the rumors go with the territory."

"You are right Amanda; it sometimes puts us in an embarrassing circumstance."

Amanda explained, "I have already heard rumors about my Ray no longer than we have been dating. As long as I know that they are not true, I ignore them."

"I have to get to class; thanks for talking to me, Amanda."

The rest of the day went better. At least I have Krystin back for the moment. I'm hoping to make our relationship even better after tonight. We have a scrimmage after school in basketball practice. That should be fun. Coach Bartlett will be coaching the non-starters to see if he can mess up our defense and offense. Jim will be playing with the non-starters. I would like to guard him, but the coach will have me guarding one of the better players. I would like to settle this once and for all about who is better at basketball. Orville won't be there because the coach will not let any parents watch practice. I may get the chance to steal the ball from him or block a couple of his shots just so he knows where he stands in basketball ability. I may have to guard Cody, one of my best pals. If so, I will definitely take it easy on him. My main goal is to make Ray, Stan and Dan look good.

I remember Dr. Spear's comment, *"You don't need to be the best player, just be 2nd best."* I could be the 3rd or 4th best. According to Spear, I will still get a college scholarship. It would be nice to get a basketball scholarship also. College basketball would be fun. It would also make me more popular with the girls in case Krystin and I don't work out. It may be in my best interest to be the 2nd best.

THE BASKETBALL SCRIMMAGE

During practice, we spent about 20 minutes in a shootaround. Because of that 2nd shot of alien blood and nanobots, the goal looked like a larger bushel basket. As I shot outside on the floor from 15-20 feet out, my senses were so precise that I had to try to miss. It was like throwing a baseball into a 3ft. diameter basket that was only about 5 feet away. After 3-4 times, one could do it blindfolded. The precision was there. I could score almost anywhere on the floor if I wanted to.

Finally, I hear Bartlett blow the whistle and yell, "Let's pair up. Ray, Stan, Dan, Phil, and Nick take your shirts off. The rest of you players leave your shirts on."

When I removed my shirt, the rest of the players could see the markings on my back. However, they noticed my muscular physique was more impressive than before. Even Bartlett commented, "Phil, you are really bulking up like Ray. That extra strength from you two will come in handy during the season."

He also added, "Have you seen a doctor about your back?"

I chimed in, "Yes coach, it's nothing. I will explain it to you sometime. Let's play ball."

The coach walked out to the center court to toss up the basketball after he had discussed with the other boys what position they were playing. We gathered around the center circle with Ray and Big Al in the middle. Big Al was the center for the other squad. He was the tallest at about 6'3' but fairly heavy and couldn't jump. But he does take up space under the basket. Bartlett threw the basketball up and Ray easily got the tip and tipped the ball to me. We all hustled to our end of the floor and almost immediately, I made a perfect lob to Dan under the basket, and he scored. Cody and Ray were the other 2 guards on the other team. Nick, the sophomore was guarding Jim while I had to guard Cody. Cody passed the ball to Jim and within a few seconds, Nick stripped Jim of the ball and he passed to me which I was already ahead of Cody heading for our basket. Nick passes to me, and I make an easy lay-up. The whole afternoon was that way.

I made several nice passes to Ray, and the rest of my team, in which they all scored several times. Within 2 quarters of play in which they played 8-minute quarters, we must have scored 30 baskets to the opposing team scoring 2-3 lucky baskets. I looked over 2-3 times during the scrimmage, and I could see Bartlett with a happy smile. The scrimmage went just the way he had hoped it would go. As hard as he coached those boys to try to boggle our defense or offence, we were all over them like a bunch of birds on a worm.

As soon as practice was over, Stan came over to me and said as Dan looked on, "Phil, you need to shoot more. You are a sharpshooter. You can score at will. This evening you passed the ball when you should have been shooting."

I said, "I will shoot when we need the points. The teams that win are the teams that have all the players involved on offence."

Ray overheard us talking, "You are right on Phil. You guys just enjoy the great passes he is making to us. Phil will get his points."

"Thanks Ray, that is my philosophy." I uttered.

As practice ended, I got into the mean green machine, heading home thinking how I was going to tell Krystin about my markings and satisfy her without telling her my secret. Going down the road, I turned on the radio and it just so happened that the song (In my room by the Beach Boys) was beginning to play; *There's a world where I can go and tell my secrets to --- In my room, In my room.* What appropriate timing for me to hear that song. I have all kinds of secrets to tell and in my basement is the only place I can tell them.

I stopped at the house hurriedly to get my costume and hustled to get to Krystin's house. As I pulled into the driveway, I grabbed my Dracula costume that Krystin's Dad, John loaned me. Krystin met me at the door, and she was already dressed as a nurse. She certainly filled out that short Nurse's uniform. She had sexy black fishnet hose on under the white nurse uniform. She was already making my socks roll up and down.

When she opened the door to let me in she reasoned, "I dressed early so I could help you put your makeup on."

As soon as I entered, we passed John and Sarah sitting on the couch watching the TV show Gunsmoke. I said Hi to both of them and then thanked John again for letting me borrow his costume while we trotted upstairs to her bedroom.

Krystin asserted, "Remember what you promised."

"I know, I know, just let me get my shirt off."

I went into the bedroom, and unbuttoned my shirt and pulled it off, then turned around so Krystin could see my back. She stood there for about 30 seconds looking at the markings showing my skin with overlapping flaps.

She said bewilderedly, "Wow! What did the doctor tell you about this."

"This is what I was told. In the early development of the fetus in humans, structures do develop in the human embryo that are homologous with pharyngeal arches in common ancestors. In fish, these structures develop into gills. In humans, these structures develop into bones in the jaw and ears. He told me that on rare occasions, a human,

1 in several million, can have one of the pharyngeal arches and try to develop into gills. The task is never completed but can leave small scars. It is just a little quirk of nature. The doctor told me that nature is not perfect every time. Even though this scarring is extremely rare, more common mistakes in nature exist all the time. People born with club feet, or midgets, people born over 7 feet tall, even women born over 7 feet tall. This is just to mention a few."

Krystin added, "I could see why you went to the doctor."

"I hope this hasn't changed anything with us, Krystin."

"No Phil, I still care for you just as much and I'm sorry about believing the ugly rumors at school. I hope you will forgive me."

"Absolutely, I'm just glad I have you back with me."

"You know Phil, 2-3 girls all told me that Janene along with a couple of other girls want to jump your bones."

"I heard that too from some guys; what is this jump-your bones stuff anyway. I think I have an idea but enlighten me."

"It is another teenage way of saying someone wants to make love to you --- have sex with you."

"I thought so."

"I want to jump your bones too, but I know we have to wait and stay committed. I don't trust condoms. They have been known to fail and that could really throw a curve ball in our goals."

"You got that right. Anyhow, I want our first time to be very special. Until then, sexual torture is waiting for me when I am with you."

"I don't think you realize what you do to me. You are right. It can be misery. I can see why some couple can't cope with it and finally succumb to all the sexual tension."

"I know it is tough. Thank goodness we have enough respect for each other in which we can rely on each other to not go too far."

"You need to hurry and get your outfit on." Replied Krystin.

I began pulling my pants down, I thought she was going to leave the room, but she didn't. She stood there in that sexy nurse uniform and watched me undress completely except for my boxer shorts. Yes, she had to notice my boner. When I looked at her, she had a devilish smile on her face.

Krystin sauntered next to me and ran her fingers near my crotch area. I was flabbergasted along with the sexual tension going through the roof. My boner was swelling by the second. I thought my boner was about to protrude through my boxer shorts and be totally visible.

"Don't be embarrassed," she said. "Teenage boys get this way all the time. I like it that you have that erection. That is letting me know that you have desires for me."

I added, "You are killing me here. I'm afraid that your mom or dad will walk in on us."

"They won't. I'll leave you alone. Go ahead and get dressed, then come to the bathroom and I will help you get your makeup on."

"Ok, but no more caressing down there. You know what I'm talking about."

When I finished putting on the outfit of black pants and shirt and black cape with red interior, I met Krystin in the bathroom to put on this white makeup on my face and hands and she glued on these extra-long red fingernails that extended at least an inch beyond my normal fingernails. She had this black greasy paste that she ran through my hair. I had red coloring extending down both sides of my mouth. When I looked into the mirror, I resembled Bela Lugosi who starred in the old classic Dracula movies. I have to admit Krystin did a great job with the makeup. I looked very ghoulish.

We trotted downstairs to leave. Krystin meandered over to where her mom and dad were sitting watching the T.V. show – The Beverly Hillbillies and hugged and kissed them both. John and Sarah both complimented me on my Dracula outfit.

I replied, "Thanks John for letting me borrow the outfit. I'll get it back to you ASAP."

Krystin and I scurried out the door to the car and began a 10-minute drive to Jacob's house.

THE HALLOWEEN PARTY

As we drove down the somewhat spooky country roads, it was nearly 8 pm and darkness was setting in across the land. Some of the corn fields had been harvested while others were waiting to be harvested. Some of the farmers work late into the night in late October to harvest the corn and soybeans. They typically alternated year to year between corn and soybeans. I think the reason behind that is corn needs lots of nutrients, especially nitrogen. This makes soybeans a good crop to alternate with corn because soybeans have nodules on their roots that host bacteria that fix atmospheric nitrogen. Both sides of the road were either harvested or unharvested corn and soybean fields along with some forested areas. Most houses were ½ mile to 1 mile away from each other. We couldn't chance driving too fast because of the possibility of a deer running out in front of us. About the last 10 days in October is when deer are rutting – deer breeding season. I can tell you that deer are just as bad as we humans. If a male buck deer gets on the scent of a female deer, the male has only one thing on its mind --- to mate. They will run right out in front of your car. If you hit one going fast enough, it can really tear your car up. So, Krystin and I weren't in any hurry.

By the time we arrived at Jacob's house, it was about 8:15 pm. The temperature had dropped into the low 50's. Several cars were parked along Jacob's long driveway. We had to park about 300 feet from his house. When Krystin and I started up the driveway to the house, Bobby McGee and his band was blasting out – I Want to Hold Your Hand by The Beatles. I grabbed Krystin's hand and started to pep up our walking because I wanted to dance with Krystin soooo bad.

As she picked up her pace to keep up, I remarked, "Let's hurry and get in there. We're missing out on some good songs to dance.

"This should be a fun night." Krystin added.

I added, "I know it's going to be fun especially with you, you- sexy-thang."

"Stop it Phil, will you?"

"I'm just telling the truth."

We were just about there when someone jumped in front of us from hiding between the cars and we heard this long "Roar." It was Cody in a Werewolf mask.

Krystin stated, "Cody, you startled me."

I inquired, "Where is your girlfriend?"

"Carrie is standing behind the car watching me make a fool of myself. Come on Carrie, let's get inside and do some serious dancing."

Cody and Carrie trotted ahead of us. Krystin noted, "He just about scared my pants off me."

I began a series of "Roars jokingly to scare her pants off." Then I asked, "Are they off yet?"

Krystin punched me in my arm and said, "Shut up! Very clever. Maybe some other night, I will listen to your Roars."

I chuckled as we walked up to the front yard. I noticed 2 characters standing outside in the yard by themselves dressed up as ghosts wearing long white sheets over their heads with holes cut out of the sheets for their eyes.

I didn't know who they were but spoke, "Nice night for a Halloween party."

Their response was nothing. They just stood there silently while their eyes followed us as we walked past them and into the front door.

I told Krystin, "Those 2 dudes were strange. You stick close to me."

"Don't worry; I will."

Jacob had all the living room furniture moved up against the wall again to make the living room floor the dance floor. Suddenly, Bobby's band started playing another Beatles number – Twist and Shout. Krystin and I immediately took to the dance floor and began dancing to this peppy rock song. About halfway through the song, I looked over where other students were standing, talking and drinking who-knows-what, and there were the two slightly taller ghosts with their eyes glued on Krystin and I. When the song ended, I grabbed Krystin's hand and said, "Let's go to the kitchen and get a soft drink. Jacob keeps them in the kitchen."

"Ok. Those 2 ghosts are starting to spook me out." Asserted Krystin.

"I'm keeping my eye on them."

We slowly walked to the kitchen while at the same time I was keeping up my senses. If one whispered, I would possibly be able to hear them if no music was playing. The music was temporarily stopped, and this gave me an opportunity to listen very close. The problem was that there was a lot of chatting going on with everyone else.

Trying to decipher a conversation between two people was difficult. Just as we were entering the kitchen, I thought I heard someone say mixed in with all the other chatter, *Orville ---- gone to kitchen.* Hearing the word, Orville alarmed me. I knew we didn't have any juniors or seniors at our school with that name. When I got into a cooler and got out our 2 Cokes, we turned around to go back to the dance floor. The two ghosts were standing in the kitchen doorway. Not moving to let anyone else in or out. Krystin and I stood there for a few seconds. They made no attempt to move. Finally, I led the way holding Krystin's hand and walked toward them.

I affirmed, "Excuse me."

I was going to push them out of the way if I had to. As I approached close to them, they moved just enough so Krystin and I could pass in between them. As we proceeded, I had to brush up against them. I didn't want either one of them laying their hands on Krystin so I looked back as she walked between them. I should have just grabbed their sheets and pulled off their sheets as I was walking back to the dance floor. We walked over to Jacob and his girlfriend Angela, who came down from I.U. I thought it may be a couple of college students that Jacob got to know.

I asked Jacob, "Hey Jakeroo, who are the 2 ghosts?"

"I don't know Phil; I just had the party for any Austiana student."

"I thought they may be a couple of your college buddies."

"No! This place is not ready for college student parties."

Krystin chimed in, "They are really starting to creep me out."

"Just stick close to me you-sexy-thang. Hey, let's you and I take a little moonlight stroll around Jacob's Lake. His dad always has those pine trees around the lake lit up so nicely."

Krystin agreed, "Sounds good to me; I'd like to get away from the 2 ghosts."

We left the dance floor and the party temporarily to take a moonlight stroll. As we were walking out the back door to Jacob's house, we strolled towards the lake which was about a 3-minute walk away. I was right; Jacob's dad had several pine trees lit up with small white Christmas lights. The trees were all about the same size approximately 8-10 ft. tall. The lake appeared to be about a 6-acre lake. I could hear an occasional splash in the water from the fish jumping out of the water. The lake was filled with Bluegill, channel catfish, bass, and crappies along with some other breeds of fish. The pine trees were in a line around the lake and were planted about 15 ft. from the edge of the water and they were about 20 ft apart. It was going to be a beautiful stroll, so I thought. As Krystin and I began our stroll down the path, I looked back and couldn't believe what I saw. The 2 ghosts were following us about 100 feet back.

I alarmed Krystin, "You are not going to believe this, but the 2 boys dressed as ghosts are following us."

"Oh, damn Phil, let's get outta here."

"Hang on a second; let's stop and kiss. Turn toward me so I am facing them, and I will see what they do. Don't worry, I'm not going to let anything happen to you. See the other couple walking around the lake ahead of us. I am pretty sure that is Derek and another girl ahead of us."

We stopped to kiss when I told Krystin, "Kiss me like you mean it."

We stood there exchanging a passionate kiss that lasted for over a minute. I noticed that they had stopped also. We stood there a couple more minutes and hugged and kissed. When we started walking again, they started walking again. After we were over halfway through our stroll, I noticed 2 other couples taking a stroll behind the ghosts. At least they have no back door to run out if they are up to no good. As we ended our stroll, we went back into Jacob's house to do some more dancing. Bobby McGee and his band played some nice songs for us to dance our hearts out. They played Elvis Presley's – You're The Devil in Disguise; Hey Paula by Paul and Paula; Be My Baby by the Ronettes; Sugar Shack by the Fireballs. It was about 10:30 when the band announced that this was their final song. It was another Elvis song – I can't help falling in love.

When the song started, I put my arms around Krystin's waist while she laid her head on my shoulder with her face lying where she could hear every beat of my heart. She was a little shorter than me by about 4-5 inches so she tilted her head so her lips were almost touching mine. The words to the song began; *Wise men say, only fools rush in, but I can't help falling in love with you.* I was beginning to get that boner again and I know she could notice it. She didn't seem to mind.

As the song went on, I moved my lips close to hers and gave her an intimate kiss. Afterwards, she began kissing my neck and kept one kiss going so strong that I ended up with a hickey. When the song ended, everyone started to leave. I noticed the 2 ghosts were watching us most of the night. They began to leave also. I wanted to stay behind them to keep my eye on them. Krystin and I were slowly walking to the car. I noticed the 2 ghosts were well ahead of us and got into a car that I didn't recognize. They pulled out and left.

"Finally, they are gone." I whispered.

"They freaked me out, Phil. I think they were up to something but just didn't get the chance to accomplish it."

I added, "I love you so much; I would die first before I would let anything happen to you."

"Gee thanks. What would happen to me after you are dead."

"Well, I guess you would be on your own."

Krystin slapped me on the shoulder berating me, "The last thing in the world that I need is a dead hero."

I looked straight into her eyes, "Relax, I'm still here."

We got into the mean green machine and started down the spooky country roads to take Krystin home. As I was driving, Krystin scooted over next to me and she took my right hand and put it on her leg. I could feel the fishnet hose and my hand was up high enough to feel that they were attached to a garter belt. Yes, I was developing another boner immediately.

I began talking so I wouldn't be so sexually distracted. "Except for the 2 ghosts, I had a great time. I was with the most beautiful girl at the party in the whole school, the whole state of Indiana."

"Keep talking; flattery will get you everywhere." Krystin conceded. "None of the girls I talked to said that they didn't know who the 2 ghosts were."

"I asked Jacob; he didn't know either. They were acting like a couple of perverts."

We only had about 2 miles left to reach Krystin's house. She began kissing me on my neck again. This time she was kissing me on the right side of my neck. My hickey was on my left side, hopefully low enough that a collar shirt would hide it.

"I don't want you to stop Krystin, but I don't need 2 hickeys on me which I may have to explain to my mom. You also aroused me so that you could cause me to wreck the car."

"Sorry, I enjoy getting you aroused, but keep control of yourself so we won't wreck."

"I see your house with the porch light on."

I pulled into her driveway but not too close because of the porch light. I turned the motor on the car off. I leaned over and put my arms around her and gave her a mad, passionate kiss. She eased up and put her right leg over my lap with those sexy fishnet hose. As we were still kissing, she straddled my lap and sat on my lap facing me. I could feel her hose and I ran my hand up her leg feeling the garter belt top. I could tell she was breathing deeper and faster. So was I, mercy, she was driving me crazy. Even though I still had my pants on, my boner was poking her in the right place. She began to French kiss me as she began humping me while straddling my lap. I ran my hand under her, feeling her private area. Her panty was so wet. We both were breathing so fast and were so aroused. I began to slowly run my finger up her vagina. I figured that this was safe and no way of getting her pregnant just as long I didn't substitute my finger for my penis. I wouldn't have done that anyway because I respect her too much. She started humping harder and harder.

After a couple of minutes of fierce foreplay, I heard her say, "Oh, Oh, Oh my God." Shortly afterwards, the passionate breathing slowed down along with the rapid humping. I know we had that car rocking back and forth, synchronous with our humping each other even though we still had our clothes on. I didn't make any attempt to remove her bra even though I was kissing the exposed part of the breast. I ended up giving her a hickey on her left breast just above the bra. If her dad had been out on the porch watching, I'm sure he would have seen the car bouncing and rocking.

Krystin remarked, "I'm pretty sure I climaxed but I don't think you have yet."

My boner was still at 100%. She began slowly humping and gyrating on top of me while we were sitting just to the right of the steering wheel. She told me she wasn't going to stop until I climaxed. She continued the gyrations. Her legs were so firm. Then she began humping me, aiming her vagina right for my boner. She began humping me harder. My breathing picked back up quickly. Her heavy breathing started in also while she was humping me; she laid her head on my left shoulder while my face was buried in her hair. After about 5 minutes, she heard me yell out an intense moan.

I ravishingly moaned, "Ooooh my God. You have caused me to cream my jeans."

"That's what I wanted to do. We need a little sexual relief without actually having intercourse." She responded.

I replied, "I know it doesn't take the desire to have intercourse completely away, but it does help to relieve the tension. I'm going to have to get in the house without mom seeing me in these wet jeans. It is after 10 pm; she will already be in bed."

I guess I could tell mom that I didn't get my pants down fast enough and had a peeing accident. I have heard other boys use that story. We got out of the car, and I walked Krystin to the door. As we were approaching the door, the porch light was getting brighter. She had her head on my right shoulder while I had my arm draped over her shoulder.

I whispered, "Those sexy hose and garter belt along with your intense humping, caused me to shoot off like a rocket. Shame on you for being such a distraction, you-sexy-thang."

"You know what you did to me after fingering me the way you did. Are you an experienced nerd at this?"

"I've read some things and heard some things from boys' gossip. I know for a fact that you girls talk among yourselves regarding foreplay."

"Yes, the girls talk too. Nevertheless, it was fun with you and a big relief from built-up tension."

"You are right, Krystin. When my head hits the pillow tonight, I will probably pass out til morning."

"Yeah, me too."

I gave her another goodnight kiss and told her I would see her tomorrow morning. We were up on the porch so I didn't kiss her in a passionate way because I was afraid her mom or dad may be peeking through the curtains from inside.

"I think I love you, Phil. I have so much fun with you and I feel comfortable being with you. You don't pressure me about anything. So far, you are perfect for me."

I spoke back very softly while still holding her hand, "I love you too. I have had a crush on you for the last 2 years. That just makes my love for you even stronger. You are perfect for me too."

I let go of her hand while turning to walk back to the car. She waited to go into the house until she saw me get into the car. I started it up and turned around into the driveway and started down the spooky country road.

CHAPTER 08

ORVILLE'S RAMPAGE

I turned on the radio and as I was driving home, the song *Stand by me by Ben E. King started playing --- When the night has come, and the land is dark, and the moon is the only light we'll see. No, I won't be afraid, no I won't be afraid, just as long as you stand, stand by me.* I was thinking so much about my and Krystin's relationship while the song continued on. I was still thinking that I still haven't been honest with Krystin. I still haven't told her what really happened that cool October night after Jacob's party when I was changed from a low-confidence nerd to an assertive, positive-thinking, higher intelligence, stronger person.

I know I would have noticed the difference when this change happened so quickly to someone else. She has to be thinking about it. I know there have been other students at school that have noticed the quick change. What about Aaron? He has to be suspicious after seeing that film clip. I'm just glad I talked him out of the skeptical film segment.

I try my best to hide these extra powers, but it seems to be getting more difficult. Mainly because that extra shot enhanced everything even more. My clothes are getting tighter because of the muscle build-up. I am beginning to look more like a weightlifter. I need to buy larger, looser clothes, but money is an issue. Maybe I can talk mom into getting me a couple of loose pairs of jeans, 3-4 shirts, and 3-4 pairs of underwear. I'm going to have to do this fast or my friends will notice me more. I need to act on this topic this weekend. The guy that runs the clothing store, Mr. Gradstein has been good in the past at selling mom merchandise on credit. He knows that she will pay every month on her bill until she gets it paid off.

As I kept driving, I noticed that there were still some corn fields to be harvested. I also noticed through my rear-view mirror 2 cars were coming upon me pretty fast. I first thought that it was some of my classmates screwing around but as they got closer, I realized that wasn't the case. Someone else was behind me. My next thought was maybe the 2 ghosts. Then suddenly the first car bumped into the rear end of my car breaking my taillights. I began to speed up enough to get away from them somewhat. The faster I traveled, the faster they traveled, intending to keep up. As I came around a curve, I noticed a car ahead of me parked across the road. I had nowhere to go. I was going to be forced to stop my car. I thought that it would be best to stop my car some distance back before I reached the parked car. At least I may have some chance to get away.

So, I pulled alongside a cornfield that hadn't been harvested yet. I stopped the car suddenly, shut off the engine, grabbed my keys, opened the car door looking back at the headlights. The two cars had stopped, and I could hear car doors slamming shut. I couldn't see who it was because their headlights were on (bright – high beam). I just knew that someone or a group of people was after me. I immediately darted into the cornfield that I knew was a large 40-plus acre field. My abilities were keened up. I ran into the cornfield much faster than was expected by the people chasing me. Then I saw that they had large flashlights with them and were wearing masks. One of the guys was bashing my headlights in on the *mean green machine*. Now I'm really pissed.

I heard one person say, "He's gone into that corn field; git him." I could tell it was Orville's voice. Just as soon as I heard him, I took one quick leap into the air cruising through the air about 40 feet up and landed about 100 feet farther away from them. I took another quick leap and landed another 100 feet away from them. Then I ran several rows over to the left from my previous location in much less than a second. As I was trying to hide from them, I was rustling the corn leaves. Then I heard them shooting in my direction with rifles.

I heard Orville say, "Spread out about 10 ft. apart and sweep the field. When we find yoou boy, yoou belong to us. End of the line fer yoou."

When I heard those remarks, I lay very still in one of the rows. I had jumped sideways so fast from where I was; as they swept the field, I was at least 25 rows over. They would not be able to spot me. They were still shooting their rifles ahead of their locations as they swept.

I heard another person say, "Everyone stop, be quiet. Listen for rustling corn leaves."

They didn't hear anything; then they started moving again. Finally, they were even with me except for being about 25 rows over from where they were. They were slowly passing by me. Suddenly, in the distance ahead of them I heard leaves rustling. They started shooting. Several shots were fired. Then I heard a thump hit the ground. I was thinking someone got shot and that bullet was meant for me.

Orville yelled, "We got him."

As they worked their way up to the moving corn stalks, one of the other guys said, "Hell, we shot a damn deer."

Just as they were starting to move on, I stayed flat on the ground, turned around and quickly crawled back toward my car making sure I stayed below the corn stalk leaves not to rustle them. When I made it back to the road, I stayed low in a ditch and went to the 2 cars behind me that still had their headlights on. The first thing I did was to memorize their license plates. Orville was so stupid he left his car running. I grabbed a big rock by the road, took my shirt off and got into Orville's car. I draped my shirt over the steering wheel and began to drive his car down the road toward the car that was parked across the road. About 150 feet from the car parked across the road, I stopped Orville's car. I noticed one person was standing there with his car with what appeared to be a rifle. Having Orville's headlights on and glaring at him made it hard for him to see anything. I aimed Orville's car directly in line with the parked car crossing the road. I opened the driver's side door and stood low behind the open door so the guy standing by the car parked across the road couldn't get a clear shot at me. I laid the rock on Orville's gas feed then jumped into the driver's seat of the car. The car began speeding towards that parked car. I jumped out of the car while grabbing my shirt.

By now, the car was cruising at about 35 mph. When I looked toward the car parked across the road, the other guy ran and jumped into the ditch attempting to distance himself from the crash that was about to happen. Orville and his buddies were trying to run back out of the cornfield. Suddenly there was a loud crash. Orville's car hit the parked car going about 50 mph. The guy in the ditch was about 100 feet from me. While he was distracted by his car getting totaled, I ran the 100 ft. in about a second and surprised him. He was caught totally off guard. I grabbed his gun and quickly hit him on his ribs with the wooden stock of his rifle. I meant to hit him hard enough to break his ribs. He went down to the ground immediately. He was disabled and in excruciating pain. I pulled his mask off, and it was Willard Dodd.

I berated, "It's you, redneck No. 2." When I jumped out of the moving car, I grabbed my shirt and tucked part of it into my pants. I quickly proceeded to put my shirt back on.

Willard was no longer going to be a problem. When Orville and the 3 others made it back to the road where he thought his car was parked, Orville saw what had happened.

He yelled, "You SumBitch, I'm going to keeel yoou."

There was a thick wooded area on the other side of the road with a lot of trees and thickets. I ran into the woods with lightning speed.

As I was running to disappear again, I yelled, "Come and get me, you dumb ass."

I didn't want to kill anyone, but I'm trying to survive myself. Orville and the other 3 guys came into the woods after me. The gun that I confiscated ended up being very convenient. He had a nice strap attached to the rifle. I put my head through the strap and the rifle was hanging from my back while I took one big leap up into the air and grabbed a large branch of a tree. I knew my climbing abilities were excellent. I was about 40 feet up from the ground. Orville and his buddies were about 150 ft. away, heading my way. I figured that If I could stay quiet in that tree, their flashlights would be focused on the ground. They should walk right past me again. Sure enough, they did. I waited until they were pretty deep into the woods and began to climb down quietly. I could still see their flashlights off in the distance. As I eased out of the woods without a sound, I ran up the road to the other car that was parked behind me. I found part of a log lying alongside the road that appeared to have fallen off a log truck. It was about 6 ft. in length and about 18 inches in diameter. I got this bright idea about using that log. It must have weighed 400-500 lbs.

Nonetheless I was able to pick it up and I was holding it in front of me to be used as a battering ramp. I ran from the other side of the road holding the log upright in front of me positioned on my right shoulder, heading for the passenger's side door of the other car. I was quick enough and strong enough with enough speed to ram the door of the car with the log to cave in the door as if the car had slid into a tree. I hit the car hard enough that it slid into the ditch. I walked behind the car and memorized that license plate and tossed the log into the ditch. I was still pissed and angry over what they did to my *mean green machine*. They busted my headlights and my taillights by ramming my car. Now I want a piece of Orville. I figured the best thing for me to do was get into my car hoping it will start, and drive to the police and report that Orville and some of his friends vandalized my car. I eased up to my car and got in to start it. I looked over into the woods and saw the light from their flashlights scurrying out of the woods. They must have heard the crash of the log into the side door. My car started but I shut it off. I didn't think I would have enough time to get away. I got out of my car remembering to take my keys with me and hid behind their car in the ditch.

As soon as they came out of the woods, Willard who was already disabled yelled at them, "He has my gun."

As soon as they heard Willard's warning, they hunkered down behind the wrecked cars. They still had their masks on. There was about 200 ft. of distance between the wrecked cars and my parked car and the other car behind mine with the door bashed in.

I yelled back at them, "You want me, come and get me."

I didn't want to kill anyone, but I had to worry about myself. I eased back up to my car and retrieved my school jacket from the back seat. I found 3-4 large rocks alongside the road each weighing about 4-5 lbs. I stuffed them in my coat pocket and scurried across the road back into the woods. I did it so quickly that they didn't see me going across the road. They still thought I was behind the car. I was hoping to make an arc or semicircle of travel in the woods and make it down to where they were located while being very quiet. My night vision with all my other senses were heightened. For me, it was like looking at my surroundings just after the sun had set but with plenty of daylight. For everyone else, it was pitch dark. I slowly made it back to the edge of the woods and could see them hunkered down behind the wrecked cars. I eased up into some tall grass staying very low. I had one of them easily in my sight. I rose up very quickly and hurled a rock hard toward him with marksmanship accuracy and hit him in the lower back with the rock. He went down mumbling a painful groan. His rifle fell beside him. As soon as I threw the rock, I hunkered back down into the tall grass. They could not tell where the rock came from.

Just then, I got the break I needed. One of Orville's buddies said, "We are not hunting him; he is hunting us and picking us off one-by-one."

His other buddy remarked, "Screw this; let's get out of here while we still can."

They started running down the road as fast as they could with their rifles in their hands. I heard Orville yell at them, "Yoou come back heeer, you chicken shiiits."

I waited until they were about ¼ mile down the road and positioned myself to hit Orville with another rock. I had a rock about the size of a softball. Just as soon as he turned his back to me, I stood up from behind the bushes and hurled the rock hitting him in his lower left back probably cracking some ribs. He let out an agonizing yell. In an instant, I covered about 50 ft. in ½ second and was upon the both of them. The other guy that was on the ground had his gun lying next to him. I immediately kicked it away from him and then moved over to grab Orville's gun. I took the butt of his gun and quickly smashed it into Orville's knee.

He screamed, "Oh my knee." Both of them saw that the quickness that I moved wasn't humanly possible. I smashed Orville's other knee to make sure he wasn't going to be walking for quite some time.

He let out an excruciating yell, "Oh God, no more; please don't hurt me again."

The other guy was scared out of his wits and begging me not to hurt him. I walked over to Orville's lone buddy and pulled his mask off. I didn't recognize him. Then I walked back to Orville; I eased down close to Orville to give him a message where the other guy could not hear me and whispered, "If I have to deal with you again, I am going to kill you the next time." I jerked his mask off. "You arc lucky I am letting you live tonight. You had better let that soak in."

Where in the hell is the CIA when you need them if they are on my side like Dr. Spear said. I grabbed the two guns, and had the other gun strapped over my back, picked up the 2 rocks that I had thrown, and walked away to get into my car. On the way to the car, I stopped and hurled the two rocks that I had thrown high into the air and over the trees into the woods. They had to have landed about 200 feet from the road. I had an old blanket in the trunk of my car and used it to rub down the three guns to get rid of my fingerprints that may be on the guns. I walked back to Orville's wrecked car holding the guns in the blanket and threw all three in the back seat of his car. I had a small, short-handled broom in the trunk of my car and an old piece of cardboard along with an empty quart canning jar. I used the jar to sweep up the broken headlight pieces. All three men were laying there in menacing pain from the broken ribs and busted knees. I wasn't sure where the other 2 guys that ran were located. I'm assuming they were ½ to 1-mile down Gallagher Road.

I was nervous about them and kept my hearing keened up because of the possibility they may try to double back to where the wreck was located. I used the broom to sweep up the busted headlight pieces. I put them the quart jar. I put the busted headlight pieces in my car. I got into my car and started it up to leave. I drove past the wrecked cars and purposefully drove close to the ditch beside the pavement at a high speed to leave tire marks. I did that for a reason to have an excuse for the wreck. Then about 100 feet down the road from the wreck, I stopped my car and took the headlight pieces and scattered them in front of my car. I'm glad I thought of that to make it look like they busted my headlights where my car was currently sitting. I started my car up and I then doubled back to town on another road to the Sheriff's office. I drove slowly because my headlights were out, even though I could easily see the road in the dark. I gradually made it to the sheriff's office. It was close to 11 pm. One lone deputy was on duty. Paul Walls, Ray's dad, who is the county sheriff was not on duty. I walked in the door and began my story.

Deputy Roger Morten was sitting behind his desk. He looked up and spoke, "May I help you."

I proceeded to tell my version of what happened; "I want to report vandalism to my car and attempted assault."

The deputy stood up and glared into my eyes and said, "Are you serious."

"Yes, at least 3 guys wearing masks tried to assault me. They had guns and were even shooting at me."

The deputy came from around his desk, then pushed a button on a tape recorder and declared, "Start from the beginning."

"I was just leaving a Halloween party being held at Jacob Evans' house. I had my girlfriend with me."

"What is her name?" asked the Deputy.

"Krystin Adkins."

"Sorry, continue," replied the Deputy as he was twirling a pen between his fingers.

"When I dropped Krystin off at her house, it was about 10:15 pm. I continued on down Gallagher Road to go home." One of the fluorescent lights in the Sheriff's office was blinking on and off as I continued to tell my version. "As I was driving home, I saw car headlights approaching through the rear-view mirror. I looked back again and realized a 2nd car was approaching along with the first car. Both cars kept getting closer to my car. Then they were very close, so close that I could not see the first cars headlights. Then The first car behind me rammed my car hard enough to break my taillights out. I began speeding up to keep ahead of them. By now, they are honking their horns at me. Then I heard a gunshot. After about 2 miles of them chasing me, I looked ahead and saw a car parked across the road. They had me trapped on the road with nowhere to go."

"Then what happened?" asked the Deputy. "I need every detail." The reel on the tape recorder continued to turn.

I continued, "When I realized they had me trapped, I began speeding up faster toward the car across the road. I then gave a sudden swerve to the right and drove halfway off the road just missing the car. When I got my car back on the road, I heard a loud crash. When I looked back through my rearview mirror, I was no longer being followed. Somebody had to have been hurt. I stopped my car to go back and see if anyone was hurt. Suddenly I heard gunfire coming from one of the wrecked cars. There was another car that stopped about 200 ft. from the wreck opposite my location. I ran into the woods to hide. I heard one of the guys go up to my car and busted my headlights out. I turned to go back toward my car trying to stay low and out of sight. One person was still standing there by my car holding a rifle. I found this rock and got close enough to hurl it at him and luckily hit him in the back with the rock. He went down dropping his rifle. I know it was a stupid thing to do, but I ran out and caught him by surprise and kicked his rifle away. Then I quickly got into my car and drove off."

Suddenly Deputy Morten interrupted me, "Hang on a minute." He put the recorder on pause and proceeded over to his dispatch microphone. He spoke through the mike trying to reach the other deputy Lance Billings who was out driving about town, "Hey Billings, can you hear me?"

Another voice came through the speaker of the dispatch unit, "Yeah, what's going on."

Morten continued, "Drive out Gallagher Road and check to see if there was a car wreck out there."

"You gotta be shitting me." Billings replied. "I'm on my way out there now."

Morten walked back toward me and sat on top of the corner of his desk beside the tape recorder. He said, "Let's give him about 5-10 minutes and let him call in what he finds out there."

After about 10 minutes, the dispatch speaker came alive again. "Morten, this is Billings, and it looks like some car has broadsided another car that is sitting sideways across the road. I have 3 guys with injuries and the ambulance is on the way."

"Ok, stay in touch." Morten replied as he pushed the pause button again to start the recording. "Ok Phil, continue on with your story."

"When I got back into my car, and after they had shot at me, I got scared, and here I am telling you about it."

Morten pauses the recording again and goes back to the dispatch, "This is Morten calling Billings." There was no answer for about a minute then the dispatch speaker blurted out again, "Billings here."

Morten continued, "Did any of the injured people have any guns?"

"No guns close by to where the guys are located. But I did find three rifles strewn about in Orville Smith's car.

The rifles have been fired recently because I can smell fresh powder burns from the barrels. The guys are all outside their cars. There is one car parked on the roadside about 200 ft. from the wreck. When I approached the car, I heard the corn leaves rustling in a corn field that has not been harvested by the road. So went into the field about 100 feet and found a deer that was still alive trying to get up but couldn't. The deer had been shot by a 22 rifle. I will have to shoot the deer, but I will dig the bullet out where it had been shot. That car looks as if it slid into a tree and then into this ditch. So, he must have hit a tree earlier. Orville appears to have 2 busted knees and is complaining about his lower back. Willard Dodd is in the ditch complaining about his ribs being broken. Another guy that I don't recognize is not a local resident here in this town and also has a lot of pain in his lower back. He says he is from the town of Beddington. He said he was struck in the back by a big rock. I asked for his driver's license, and I have his name. His driver's license says Charles Denton. Orville as usual is not talking. There are several empty beer cans with a few unopened beers in all three cars. All these guys appear half-drunk. This is strange; they do not appear to have been thrown out of their cars. I know that Orville did not just walk out of the car by himself. We have a puzzle on our hands. I can smell alcohol on all three guys. I have to go; the ambulance is coming."

Morten said, "Before you sign off, be sure to give all three of those guys a breathalyzer test. When you hear Phil Marland's side of the story. This will complicate things even more. Stay in touch. Morten over and out."

Then Deputy Morten pushed the pause button again to begin the recording. Morten added, "Why would these guys want to be shooting at you?"

I had an answer, "Orville Smith and Willard Dodd both have sons in school that were hoping to be starters this year on the basketball team. I tried out for the team and beat them out from being starters. Since then both Orville and Willard have been pissed at me."

Morten added, "Is there anyone else that may help verify their hostility toward you." The tape continued to roll.

"Yes, my girlfriend Krystin Adkins was with me at Bill's Café last Friday night. Orville and Willard stopped by our booth and started giving me a tough time. They started yelling at me, then shortly afterwards, Bill Wilson, the owner of Bill's Café came over to my booth and asked them to leave. They were hostile toward Bill too. Orville started in on him telling him to get his hands off him; he was leaving."

"Anyone else that may add to the truth of your story."

"Mr. Mudd the grocery store owner and Mr. Clover has a nasty note in Orville's handwriting.

Morten declared, "This state is basketball crazy. I can see how things could get out of hand. The parents of these athletes all think their son is a superstar and no one is better than their son. I have heard from others that you have some quickness, can pass accurately, and you can shoot the lights out. I could see where Orville and Willard could be upset. I know how people are in this town regarding athletics."

I chimed in, "I know; the reason I went out for the team was to hopefully be good enough to possibly get some scholarship help for college, like Ray Walls. He has a good shot for a basketball scholarship. I started working out and bulked up and hope I can help our team win a sectional. That would increase my chances, and Ray's chances for a basketball scholarship if we were sectional winners and possibly regional winners."

Morten's eyes widened and replied, "Boy, if our team did that you would be making history around here and put us back on the map. Is there anything else you would like to add before I stop the recording?"

"Yes, one last piece of information. I memorized all three cars' license plates." I recited the license plate numbers for the recording. "I think I have told you all I know."

"Ok Phil, let me take you home since your lights are all broken. I believe there are enough stores and streetlights shining so you can drive your car down the street to Johnson's Garage. Then I will drive you home. I don't want you having a wreck because of the darkness."

I said, "Thanks Deputy, I appreciate that. Can I use your phone to call Krystin?"

"Sure, go ahead."

As I dialed Krystin's number, I was going to have to tell her the same story I told Deputy Morten along with an explanation of why I can't pick her up for school tomorrow. The phone starts ringing for about a minute.

Finally, I hear a female voice, "Hello, Adkins residence." I could tell it was not Krystin's voice. Crap, her mother has answered the phone.

"Is this Mrs. Adkins?" I asked.

"Yes, it is."

"Mrs. Adkins, this is Phil Marland and I apologize for calling so late, but I need to talk to Krystin."

"Are you Ok, Phil."

"Yes, I'm Ok, but I had an incident tonight and had some goons chasing me. They busted my headlights and taillights in my car, and I won't be able to pick Krystin up for school tomorrow. Krystin knows there are a couple of parents mad about me making the basketball team and keeping their sons from starting."

"Oh, my goodness." Replied Mrs. Adkins. "Hold on a few seconds and I'll wake her."

After a couple of minutes, "Hello Phil, are you Ok?"

"It is so good to hear your voice Krystin. I had another confrontation with Orville, Willard and 3 others that I don't even know. They were shooting at me, but they must be bad shots."

I could hear Krystin start crying, "Oh Phil, they could have hurt you or even took your life. I told you I didn't trust those two bozos. The other night at the restaurant, Orville scared me."

"I am here at the Sheriff's office filing a report of what happened. They busted my headlights and taillights out on my mean green machine. So, I won't be able to pick you up for school tomorrow."

"Mom will let me drive her car and Dad will take her to work. So, I'll drive to your house and pick you up.

"Thanks Krystin, that will keep me from having to ride the bus."

Krystin added, "How are you going to get home tonight?"

"Deputy Morten is going to let me take my car to Johnson's Garage, then take me home."

"I'm scared for you; those bums are crazy. I'll pick you up around 8 am."

"I'll tell you more tomorrow morning." I walked away from Deputy Morten where he couldn't hear me and added, "I love you. You sexy thang."

Then I hung up.

Deputy Morten followed me down to Johnson's Garage which was only a couple of blocks from the Sheriff's office. The streetlights were bright enough for me to see the road. With my enhanced vision, I could easily see the road anyway. Johnson's Garage had a drop box for car keys so I locked it up and dropped the keys into the drop box. I got into Deputy Morten's squad car, and he drove me home. As I got out of his car, I closed the car door as quietly as I could hoping not to wake mom.

By now it is almost midnight, and if my mom is awake, I know she will be frantic. I slowly unlocked the basement door and eased over to my bed. I didn't hear mom up so she must have been in bed. I set my alarm on my radio then I turned on the radio fairly low and the song 'In my room – by the Beach Boys' was just starting to play the 2nd verse, *In this world, I lock out, all my worries and my fears, In my room, In my room*. How true for me. Mom was used to hearing me play the radio low late at night. By the time the last verse came on, I was asleep. I had no idea what Wolfman Jack was playing on WINN after that.

THURSDAY

The alarm went off at 7 am and Herb Alpert and the Tijuana Brass were playing the instrumental – A Taste of Honey on the radio. A jazzy tune. This song has woken me up more than once. It seemed like the radio station WINN had a set time of 7 am to play that song. I get up thinking about what I had told Deputy Morten last night and how I was going to cover up what really happened. I was hoping I had covered all my bases, not leaving any word for doubt. I quickly do the 3 S's – shit, shower, and shave. Then I scurry upstairs. I knew what was waiting for me regarding my car, MOM, and her many questions.

As soon as I opened the door to enter the kitchen, "Where is your car, Phillip Marland?" Mom asked. When mom uses my full name in a sentence, I know she is in a tizzy.

"Isn't it out in the driveway?"

"No. Did something happen to it?"

"What makes you think something happened to it?"

"Because it is not in the driveway. Quit yanking me around Phillip, I am not in the mood this morning. Start talking."

"Well, let me start from the beginning. When I made the basketball team and became one of the starting five players, that kept a couple of boys that made the team previous years from being starters. They were mad at me along with their fathers."

"They shouldn't be mad at you if you are a better player than they are." Replied Mom.

"Every parent thinks their son is the best player. Coaches have to deal with that all the time. Anyway, to shorten this story, when I was coming home last night, their dads were chasing me in their cars. It appears they set a trap for me on Gallagher Road. I luckily swerved to miss the car that was parked sideways across the road. The car that was chasing behind me hit that other car. I stopped my car to see if anyone was hurt and someone fired a rifle at me. He was trying to shoot me."

Mom interrupted, "Oh Phil, you could have been killed. We need to call the police."

"I already filed a report last night. Deputy Morten gave me a lift home and I left the car at Johnson's Garage to be fixed. After they were shooting in my direction, I ran into the woods to disappear and hide. That is when one of the guys came up to my car and busted my taillights and headlights out."

Mom asked, "How did you get to the Sheriff's office?"

"I eased quietly back to my car by staying low in the weeds until I got close enough to see the guy standing there by my car with the rifle in his hands. I picked up a good-sized rock and hurled it at him hitting him in his lower back. He went down dropping his rifle. That is when I leaped out and kicked his rifle out of the way and got into my car and took off before the other guys knew what happened."

Mom replied, "I will see to it that they pay for your car being fixed."

"Thanks mom. I may have to go talk to Sheriff Walls about all that too. Those guys are probably in the hospital or in jail."

"Are you going to ride the bus to school?"

"No, Krystin is driving her mom's car to pick me up. So, I need to hustle and be ready when she arrives."

"Do you know when you will get your car fixed?"

While getting into the refrigerator to get milk for my cereal, I answered, "I will have to stop by Johnson's garage and talk to them. They may have to order the taillight covers unless they can get them from a junkyard. If they have to order parts, I'll be hurting for wheels to get me to work etc."

"We'll manage." Said mom.

I was gulping down my cereal and didn't get to finish the bowl before Krystin pulled up in her mom's car. I grabbed my jacket, kissed mom on the cheek and went out the door.

As soon as I got into the passenger's side of her car, Krystin leaned over and gave me a tight hug kissing me on the cheek and neck. When she leaned back to start her car, I could tell she was teary-eyed.

She said, "I just can't believe those guys."

While driving to school, I proceeded to tell Krystin the same version of the incident that I told the police. I told her that Orville wouldn't be bothering anyone for a good while with two busted knees and broken ribs.

Just before Krystin shut off her car in the school parking lot, she said, "Phil, it is easy to believe why those guys are suspicious of you, especially when it affects their boys on the basketball team."

"What do you mean, Krystin?"

"Over the weekend, you seemed to have changed into a different person mentally and physically. Especially in the physical part."

"I can't explain it. I had been working out on weights for weeks and it seemed like I was getting nowhere. Then in a matter of a few days, all my hard work started to pay off."

Krystin agreed, "I believe you, but most of the kids in school including Orville and his goons, and including me, saw a good person on the nerdish side turn into a hero on the basketball court and at school regarding the bullies. It seemed like it all happened so fast. You have no explanation, but Orville and Willie the drunk have a possible explanation, even though it is farfetched."

I added, "I know; I wish I had a better explanation. I know guys work out for several months and sometimes years to get to look like me. My physical change happened so fast. I know that I have changed from this small-framed nerd to a muscular person that is afraid of no one."

Krystin continued, "Even in the timed writings in typing, you previously had no chance of typing faster than myself and the other two .... which you refer to as the speed demons. During this same period of time, you beat us. Your exam scores are much higher in the academic classes........."

I interjected, "Krystin, I have been staying up late at nights studying. That is why my grades are improving. I want to make sure I have the best chance I can get to enter college."

"Phil, I am not doubting you, but all this change seemed to have happened so quickly and about the same time. I have not seen you play basketball yet, but your improvement seems to have been miraculous according to some of the classmates that have seen you play. Even your attitude toward the bullies has been more aggressive."

"Now, wait a minute. You know that I was sick of those guys pushing me and my friends around for at least 2 years. I finally had enough. I was just lucky that I had been working out and could take care of myself. If I hadn't been working out when Ray tripped Derek that day. I would have still stood up to him. I probably would have been beaten severely, but the confrontation still would have happened."

"I know Phil, which is one thing I admire about you. You are exercising and all trying to make things better for yourself. You are willing to pay your dues to get what you want."

Krystin didn't know about the promised scholarship to me from the CIA so I admitted to her, "If I can't get some financial help for college, I'm dead in the water. My mother cannot keep the lights on and pay for my college at the same time. I'm depending on my grades, but Basketball may help."

"The bell is about to ring so we better get into school. Remember Phil; I doubted you once about that girl. I won't doubt you again. I love you."

As we were entering the school I chimed in, "I love you, Krystin. You sexy thang."

THURSDAY AFTERNOON AT THE HOSPITAL

Paul Walls, the Sheriff, walked into the hospital to question Orville, Willard, and Charles Denton. He had his notebook with him to write down what happened and to see if their stories matched.

He walked up to the nurse's station and asked, "Is Orville Smith able to talk to me."

The nurse replied, "He is sore in the back and can't walk because of broken kneecaps from the wreck, but he should be able to talk."

"What about Willard Dodd, and this uh.... Charles Denton?" Asked Paul.

"They are all conscious and should be able to talk."

"May I have their room numbers?"

"Orville Smith is in room 117, Willard Dodd is in room 143, and Charles Denton is in room 149."

"Thank you nurse," Paul turned and decided to visit Orville Smith first. He had a battery-operated tape recorder tucked under his arm. He walked into room 117 and Orville was sitting up watching TV.

Orville mumbled, "Hello, Sheriff. I knew that you would be visiting me?"

Paul replied as he started his tape recorder, "You are correct regarding the visit. I just need to piece together what happened last night."

Orville acknowledged, "Sheriff wee had been beeer drinking and decided to have some fun with that Phil Marland as he was driving down the road and had a wreck."

"Orville, you have to quit messing with these young kids. You are going to get yourself in serious trouble. You could be sent back to prison, my friend. Furthermore, why was Willard Dodd's car parked across Gallagher Road when you hit it."

"You better be telling me the truth; if your story doesn't match up with Willard and this Charles Denton, all three of you will end up in jail."

"I have nothing else to say except that nerd Phillip Marland has kept my boy from being a starter on the team. As for last night, I don't know what happened."

"This statement is certainly not helping you from being prosecuted."

"What do you mean prosecuted?"

"I mean that Phillip said that you and your buddies were shooting at him, and one of you busted his headlights and taillights out."

As Orville stared out the hospital window he muttered, "That little blabbermouth."

"I wouldn't call him a little blabber mouth anymore, Orville. He has bulked up and I'm pretty sure he could handle your ass one-on-one easily if he needed to do so."

"I'll fight him any day of the week." Threatened Orville.

"You see, that is your problem, Orville. You don't know when to quit. Ray has talked to me about Phil; Ray is tickled to death that Phil is on the team. He tells me how Phil can thread passes to him and it makes it easier for him to score. My son feels sure that he is going to help the team possibly win a sectional at the end of the basketball season this coming Spring."

"Everybody is soooo high on this nerd. I guess we will find out how good he is tomorrow night at our first game of the season. You know we haven't beaten Scottsville in over a decade. I think those players are going to surprise Phil and kick his ...."

Paul interrupted, "Let's get back to our discussion of last night. I'm only going to ask this once. Did you shoot at Phil Marland?"

Orville vowed, "I have nothing to say. This discussion is over."

Paul added, "I have a copy of a note you wrote Phil and put it on his windshield. I'm positive it is your writing. We can have a handwriting expert testify if we have to."

"Did that nerd giive youu that note too?"

"No, the high school principal did. Orville, this crap is getting out of hand. If principal Clover notifies the welfare department and shows them that note about how you are going to beat Jim's ass, you are going to be in a lot more trouble than you are already in. They can take your kids away from you."

Orville insisted with wide-opened eyes glaring intently at Paul, "Sheriff, that boy has changed since the spaceship crash a couple of weeks ago. Willie Willis said he saw him go into that thar spaceship. Willie said there was an alien inside it. He said Phil ran out of the ship before it blew up."

"Orville, it was just a meteorite. They had specialists from IU and Cornell University studying it. There was no evidence of any alien."

"Well, those college experts don't know everything."

"You had better hope your buddies don't implicate you. I'm going to talk to them as soon as I leave your room."

As Paul turned to walk out the door, he heard Orville make one last remark, "He is an alien, he is an alien."

Paul shook his head in disbelief of Orville's remark as he walked on down to room 143 where Willard Dodd was located.

Paul's next visit was to room 143 which was the room of Willard Dodd. The Sheriff gave a couple of knocks on the door while he proceeded to come in.

"Willard, I need to talk to you to get to the bottom of what happened last night on Gallagher Road."

"What do you want to know, Sheriff?" Replied Willard.

Paul pushed the record button on the tape recorder, "I want to hear what you have to say about last night. Before you start, I have already talked to Orville, and I will be talking shortly to Charles Denton from Beddington. Your stories better match up or you all 3 could be in a turd pile of trouble."

"Orville had contacted me and wanted to make plans to get Phil trapped on this country road. He said he only wanted to scare him."

"How many were in your group?" Asked Paul.

"Orville, myself, and three of Orville's buddies from Beddington."

Paul said, "Did you know the other three?"

"I only knew Charles Denton. I was introduced to the other two that night."

The Sheriff added, "I have one question about all this; how did you know that Phil was going to be coming down that road that night?"

"Our sons told us about this Halloween party at the Evans' house. They said that Phil would likely be there with his girlfriend. We didn't tell our boys, but Orville and I came to the party ourselves dressed in white sheets draped over us with holes cut out for our eyes. We followed Phil and his girlfriend around until they left. We figured Phil would take her home and then go home himself, so he had to go down Gallagher Road himself. We followed him to her house. I drove South of her house while Orville and his buddies stayed North of her house with their car lights off waiting for Phil to leave. He finally left her house and there is where we had the trap set. As soon as I saw Phil turn South on Gallagher Road, I drove well ahead of him to get my car parked across the road."

Paul reminded, "Willard, wasn't you concerned that someone else may come down the road?"

"Orville and I talked about that and decided that the odds were in our favor of no one showing up at that time of the night."

"Then what happened?" Asked Paul.

"Once Orville caught up with Phil's car, he must have gone crazy. He hates that boy. He started shooting his rifle at him. One of his bullets landed near me because I heard it bounce off some rocks. I was asking myself, what in the hell is he doing? I hunkered down; then I saw Phil stop his car about 200 feet up the road. Orville and his friends pulled in behind him. There were two in Orville's car and two behind Orville in the other car."

Paul interrupted, "So there were three cars. What happened next?"

"Phil ran into the corn field and Orville got out and busted his taillights and headlights out. Then they took off after him in the cornfield shooting wildly. I heard one of them say (*I got him.) Then, I heard another person say, you shot a damn deer.*"

"All of you had been drinking. Am I correct in saying that?"

"Yes, we were all loaded with alcohol."

The Sheriff added, "Phil told a different story and where we found the headlight and taillight pieces matches his story. He said he swerved to miss your car and Orville being close behind him hit your car. Then Phil stopped south of the wreck and ran into the woods."

"I'm just telling you what I witnessed Sheriff, I don't want to get into any more trouble with the law. I'm done with this and done with Orville. I realize that my son is not a good basketball player, but I was just hoping that he could have a decent year playing basketball and not riding the bench."

"Orville swears that Phil is an alien. What do you think?" Asked the Sheriff.

"Phil is just another kid that just happened to bulk up and became stronger while our boys were out doing nothing to help themselves. I will have to say this When Phil surprised me getting my gun, he had to have moved super-fast to surprise me like that. He came out of nowhere."

The Sheriff spoke, "Just remember Willard, you were half drunk. So, you are saying that Orville was shooting at Phil."

"Yes. Orville hates this boy so bad because of his son that I was afraid that if he got the chance, he might kill him. I want no part of that. I was laying in the ditch and couldn't see anything else."

Paul berated, "If Orville stopped his car about 200 feet North of your car, how did the wreck happen?"

Willard continued, "The headlights of Orville's car were on, so it was hard for me to see what was going on. Phil must have gotten behind them and ran out of the cornfield. Orville must have left his car running. You know he is not the *sharpest knife in the drawer*. Maybe Phil got into Orville's car and drove it down toward mine, he stopped briefly, then I heard the car engine get louder and the car headed for my car speeding up all the time. I ran into the ditch to keep from getting hurt because I knew Orville's car was going to hit mine. Just as soon as the crash happened, I turned around and there was Phil taking my gun from me and hitting me in the ribs. He broke 2 ribs."

Paul added, "A big guy like you letting him get your gun from you. Come on!"

"Sheriff, this kid is strong-as-an-ox. After he put me on my knees, he ran into the woods with my rifle. He ran lightning fast. I don't know of anyone that can run that fast. At the same time, Orville and his three friends came out of the cornfield and ran into the woods after Marland.

I could tell Orville was pissed about his car being smashed up."

The Sheriff asked, "Did you see Phil drive the car and crash it into yours?"

"No. The headlights were on bright, and I couldn't see what was happening." Replied Willard.

"Did you see Orville and the other 3 guys come out of the cornfield?"

"No, I only saw them after the wreck occurred and saw them run into the woods after Marland."

"How many beers had you drank at that time of night?" Asked the Sheriff.

"I had drunk 4 or 5 beers." Replied Willard.

The Sheriff added, "The bottom line is that you had been drinking and not sure what happened. Your story does not match Marland's story. Our evidence matches his story. To make matters worse for the three of you, all three of you were over the alcohol limit. You were all drunk. You are definitely going to be cited for DUI and most likely assault."

Willard insisted, "Sheriff, I did not shoot my gun at that boy. I can't speak for Orville and Charles Denton. I know I heard gunfire. I know better than to do something stupid like that."

"You inferred that there was 5 of you involved. Is that right?"

"Yes."

"Where did the other two guys go? Were they in the other car that looked as if it had slid into a tree?"

"I think the other two guys got spooked and ran off."

"Did you know them?" Asked the Sheriff.

"All I know is one of them was named Dewey. I didn't know the other guy."

The Sheriff speculated, "I wonder where they could have gone being out in the country at least a mile from any residence. They would have had to have stopped somewhere to make a phone call. They could have walked back to town and used a pay phone. I'll check on that."

As the Sheriff rubbed his chin, he stopped the recorder and started out the hospital room door. He looked back at Willard and said, "Don't get any ideas about leaving town Willard, I'll come and find you and things will get really ugly for you."

The next visit was to Charles Denton's room (149). The door was halfway open. As Paul walked in, he gave a couple of taps on the door.

Charles looked up and said, "Come in."

Paul affirmed, "I'm the Sheriff of Greene County and I would like to ask you some questions regarding the incident on Gallagher Road last night." As the Sheriff pressed record on the tape recorder, he announced, "State your name."

As Charles began to speak, he had a scared look on his face. "Charles Denton."

The Sheriff began, "Tell me what happened on the night of October 31st on Gallagher Road."

"Sheriff, I was too drunk to give an accurate account of what happened."

"Tell me what you do know." Replied Paul.

"Orville had contacted me, Dewey Williams, and Claude Spicer to help him scare this boy that lived in Austiana. He told us to bring our rifles, but we wouldn't be using them."

"How do you know Orville Smith and Willard Dodd?"

"We used to go deer hunting every year during deer season and often times we would Fish a lot on the East Fork White River."

"Was this Dewey Williams and Claude Spicer with you guys that night?"

"Yes, but they got scared after the shooting started and ran off. I wish I could have run off with them. I'm sorry I ever agreed to be a part of Orville's scheme. When he gets to drinking, he goes crazy and is always wanting to confront someone. I know him well enough that I should have known that where he goes, trouble follows. Now, here I am laying in the hospital and may have to miss several days of work."

"Did you have your rifle and shoot at that boy?"

"No, Sir."

"All the rifles had been fired recently."

"I was shooting upwards into the air making sure I hit no one."

"Someone shot a deer in a cornfield. They weren't shooting up into the air."

"As I said, I was too drunk to know everything that happened. When we came out of the woods, I heard Willard yell from over in the ditch that the boy had his gun. We all hunkered down behind the wrecked cars."

"The 3rd car was yours. Did you hit a tree or something before this incident? You passenger side door is caved in."

"I don't know what happened there. I don't have a clue."

The Sheriff inquired, "Who smashed Orville's car into Willard's car? Was it Orville?"

"Orville was with us in the cornfield shooting wildly toward the boy."

"Were you positioned where you could see Orville?"

"Know, we were spread out and I only heard the gunfire."

The Sheriff insinuated, "Orville could have gone back to his car and while being under the influence of alcohol, slammed his car into Willard's car." The sheriff added, "Would you think that could be a possibility?"

"I suppose, but when we came out of the cornfield, Orville came out with us, and the wreck had already happened. That is when I heard Orville yell to that boy that he was going to kill him."

The Sheriff reminded Charles, "Phil Marland's story doesn't match your story and the evidence doesn't match your version of what happened. All of you will be charged with DUIs and Orville will be charged with attempted assault along with reckless driving."

THURSDAY AFTER SCHOOL

After the last class, Krystin and I headed to the gym. She would be at cheerleading practice while I would have my last practice before the big game Friday night with Scottsville Warriors. I wanted to concentrate on shooting the ball while moving and up in the air jump shots. When warm-ups started I wanted to make as many shots as I could in a row without drawing attention. As I was warming up with the others, I would shoot 2-3 shots making the baskets; then I would doddle around for several seconds just dribbling the ball around before I would shoot again. The intention was to space out my shooting even though I was keeping track of my shots. I made 15 baskets in a row from different spots on the floor including 3-4 20-footers. Then I purposefully missed 2-3 shots. As I was continuing to shoot at different locations on the floor, Ray Walls came over to me.

"Phil, I am going to need those good passes tomorrow night. This team we are playing is no slouch. They have one of the best guards in the state, and they have a big boy that I will have to stop. He is not as rough and rugged as I am. I think contact bothers him so if I can rough him up some without getting fouls called on me, I think I can take him out of the game."

"You and Stan are our 2 best shooters. You just concentrate on getting yourselves open and I'll get the ball to you guys. The coach has some good plays that should do that for you. Study the strategies that he has for us."

Ray added, "I really feel good about tomorrow night. I think we are ready. You had better guard their superstar tomorrow night."

I added, "If coach puts me guarding him, I'll take care of him. He won't be getting his average tomorrow night. Even if Nick guards him, I'll be helping to double-team him when I can. I hope coach just puts me on him."

Practice went well. I feel like we are ready to pull a big upset. We have the home-court advantage so most of the fans will be pulling for the Austiana Eagles.

I was expecting someone to ask about the incident after the Halloween party last night, but apparently no one knew yet. With Jim and Ron, Orville and Willard's boys on the team, something has to be said about it soon. Krystin already knows and hopefully, she hasn't said anything. Sooner or later, someone is going to ask about where the *mean green machine is*. I need to be clever in my reply.

As soon as practice was over, Krystin was already waiting for me in her car in the school parking lot. It was just beginning to get dark. By November, the days get pretty short. She was taking me home because my car was still in Johnson's Garage. I'm hoping to pick my car up by tomorrow afternoon between the end of school and the big game.

We pulled into the driveway of my house. I stirred up enough nerve to ask Krystin in even though our house was not nearly as nice as her parents' house. If she is serious about me, she should know that I may not live in the boondocks, but my standard of living is considerably less than hers.

She followed me in, and my mother was in the living room watching an old (Andy Griffith Show titled -- Citizen's Arrest.) Mother came into the kitchen, and I introduced Krystin to her.

"Mom, this is my girlfriend Krystin. Krystin, this is my mother Shirley."

Mom's eyes widened and said, "It is so nice to meet you Krystin. Phil has told me what a beautiful girl you are. At least I know he has good eyesight."

Krystin had a big smile on her face and added, "It is so nice to meet you Ms. Marland."

Janet poked her head out of her room and yelled, "Hi Krysten," then disappeared back into her room.

Mom asked, "Has he been the type of gentleman that a girl would expect him to be?"

"He has been Ms. Marland. I think a lot of him because he has goals and is planning for his future. Not every boy thinks the way he does."

"I have tried to instill that attitude in him. I want him to have a better life than we are having to live currently." Replied Mom.

I insisted, "Krystin, how about you and I go down in the basement to my humble abode."

Mom had some peanut butter cookies on the table; I grabbed 3-4 cookies in my hand. I took Krystin's hand, and we headed down the steps. We had a light switch at the top of the stairs to turn on the basement lights. I always flip the on switch as I go down the steps. If the light is not on, it is pitch black in the basement. I closed the basement door to the kitchen behind me. I also have some Christmas lights hooked up along the steps and around the walls. I leave them up all year long because most of the time unless I am studying, I turn the main lights in the basement off and leave the colorful Christmas lights on. I like the nice near-dark ambient glow of the lights. It is especially neat when I am listening to music.

Once we were in the basement, Krystin whispered, "Is your mom OK with us being down here with the door closed?"

"I don't think she minds the door being closed. If she does, she will let me know."

"Is this the first time you have had any girl down here?"

"Yeah! You are the first. I want you to be the only girl I will ever have down here. This basement ain't much, but mom has given me the OK to fix it up the way I want it."

I took a couple of steps to the light switches and turned on the Christmas lights; then I turned off the main lights. I had 5 strands of 100 lights on each strand. It was pretty dim, but we could easily see each other in the faint ambiance that was glowing from the different colored lights.

I took Krystin's hand and led her over to this old leather couch that had several rips in it that was given to me by Mr. Willoughby, my neighbor down Gallagher Road. All I had in the basement for furniture was the couch, and old wooden desk, an old worn coffee table, and a couple of folding chairs that I had picked up from the town garbage dump. I had also purchased an extended phone hook-up and had a phone on the table by my radio. I had covered most of the rips on the couch up with this old warn green bedspread that mom could no longer use. I took off my jacket and laid it on one of the folding chairs. I lay down on the old couch on my back, reached my hands up to Krystin to have her lay on top of me. She was reluctant at first to lay down probably because mom and Janet were upstairs.

I whispered, "It's Ok, no one will bother us. Anyhow, we could hear the basement door open, and we could sit up before mom or Janet saw us."

She removed her coat, threw it over the back of the couch, and said, "You know I can't stay long."

"Just a couple of minutes." I replied.

She began to lay her luscious firm body on top of me. Mercy, she felt soooo good pressed up next to me. I had my radio in the basement set on Wolfman Jack on WINN radio station. It was on a little table by the couch. I reached up over my head and turned on the radio. The slow song – You really got a hold on – by Smokey Robinson and the Miracles was slowly playing. Krystin had her head resting on my shoulder with her hair brushing my face. I grew an obvious boner that she could no doubt feel. She began a slow humping against my bulge.

After a couple of minutes, she whispered, "I have to get home."

I groaned, "Wish you could stay longer. You feel so good to me."

She whispered again while kissing my neck, "There is no use of us torturing each other."

She rose up off me as we both sat up on the couch. She asked, "Is the team ready for tomorrow night?"

"Yes, I hope so. I have put some extra time with Ray, Stan, and Dan practicing quick passes. I will be the point guard, making the most of the passes to them. I have been making quick passes which are sometimes pretty hard. They have to be ready to catch them and not bobble the passes."

"I love your innovation of basement lighting," said Krystin as we walked up the stairs to the door that entered the kitchen.

"Do you want a cookie for the road?" I asked.

"No, I don't need the extra calories," she replied.

"Guess I'll see you tomorrow morning. Are you still going to be able to pick me up?"

"Yes, I'll be here about 8 am. It is supposed to be below-freezing tomorrow morning. Could be a cold walk to school if you had to walk."

"I know, seems like cold temperatures bother me more than they used to." I walked her to her car and gave her a big hug and kiss before she got into her car to leave.

When she pulled out of the driveway, I hustled downstairs to call Dr. Spear.

A few seconds after I dialed the number, I heard "Dr. Spear's residence."

"Glad I contacted you. This is Phil Marland."

"Good to hear from you. How are things going for you, Phil?"

"Ok, I suppose. I had an incident with one of the town locals and some of his goons."

"What happened?"

"I had this guy named Orville and some of his friends try to hurt me last night. They even shot at me."

"Mercy, Phil. Why would they do something like that?"

"Orville has reason to believe that the crash a few nights ago was piloted by an alien. He believes that I went into the spacecraft after the crash. I think he has noticed my changes more than anyone else and is not buying the reasons that I give for bulking up. To complicate things, when I made the basketball team, it kept his son from getting to play as much. His son will most likely set the bench a lot. So, he is pissed at me because he thinks I'm keeping his son from playing."

"Did you display any of your special abilities?"

"Yes, but I had to act fast to keep them from shooting me."

"So, they saw you do things that most humans can't do."

"Yes, but I have an out."

"What's that?"

"They had been drinking pretty heavy. I also did some things to the location of the incident so I could tell a different story, then I went to the police."

"Who are they? Orville and who else?"

"Orville Smith and Willard Dodd are the two locals. Also involved were 3 men from Beddington, Charles Denton and I didn't know the other 2 guys or their names."

"Do you think the police believe you?" Asked Dr. Spear.

"I can't say for sure, but I think I sounded pretty convincing last night at the Sheriff's office. The Sheriff was supposed to visit those guys today in the hospital."

"You put them in the hospital!"

"I didn't want to, but they were trying to hurt me. In fact, I believe Orville would have killed me if he had the chance. This was my third run-in with him."

"What did you do to them? I hit a couple of them with big rocks breaking their ribs, and I busted a couple of their kneecaps with the butts of their rifles."

"Were your fingerprints on the rifles?"

"I wiped the rifles down before I threw them into one of their cars. It is my word against 3 drunks. By the way, where were these special agents when I needed them."

"They try not to get involved as much as possible. I don't know why they didn't follow you home that night.

They want you to live your normal life with these changes as much as possible."

"I could have used them last night."

"I'll think about this and in the meantime, let's wait and see the police explanation. Did you get hurt?"

"No, I'm Ok."

"That's good. Just be cool and let me know if something new comes up regarding this incident."

"Ok. Thanks Dr. Spear and I'm sorry about all this. I'm finding it difficult to be secretive about my changes, but I know that I have to lay low about all this."

"Yes Phil, you most certainly have to remain quiet. Have a good night and win your 1st basketball game tomorrow night."

"Thanks Dr. Spear. Bye."

As soon as I hung up the phone, I studied really quickly for my assignments for school tomorrow. Then I turned on the Christmas lights and went into a deep sleep.

CHAPTER 09

COUNTY RIVAL BASKETBALL GAME AND BANK ROBBERY

FRIDAY

The radio alarm goes off at 7 am with loud music on WINN. It seems like it is planned for the instrumental song (A Taste of Honey by Herb Alpert and Tijuana Brass) to come on almost every morning at 7 am. When the radio volume is up, those trumpets wake you up quickly. I get up and do the typical 3 Ss. My mom had purchased me some looser-fitting clothes. I'm glad she did because I still seem to continue building up in physique. I measured myself this morning and I am also a little taller. I have gone from 5'10" to 6'2". Even Ray is 6'6" now. He has grown another inch. Since the spacecraft crash, I have gained 30 pounds from 155 to 185. I must remember that I need to talk to Aaron, our film buff, about not filming me. I don't want him getting me on film again.

By 7:30, I am scurrying up the stairs to the kitchen. Mom is up fixing gravy and biscuits and frying eggs. I haven't shown mom yet, but my gill flaps must be completely formed. They are not bothering me anymore.

The marks are not very visible. They look like a couple of red scratch marks going down inside my shoulder blades.

Mom asked, "How about some gravy and biscuits?"

"Thanks mom, you make great gravy and biscuits," I said.

Janet was almost finished eating.

She looked up at me and said, "We won't have 6th period today."

"Why?" I asked.

"The school is having a pep session today, getting everyone up for the big game tonight."

"I had forgotten about the pep session with everything else going on." I remarked.

Janet added, "Guess you are too busy thinking about Krystin."

"Shut up," I growled with a deep base voice.

Mom chimed in, "Some of my co-workers are saying that the game will be a sellout. That gym only holds about 2,000 people, but that is still a lot of people. Good luck tonight, son."

"Thanks mom."

Janet had to mouth off one more time. "All eyes will be watching Phil to see how good he is since he is the new player and one of the starters. Don't let the pressure and loud noise get to you."

I boasted, "Not to worry little miss negative, I got this."

"Woo! I can't wait for the game. I hope you don't embarrass the family name."

I refuse to sit and argue with her. I just finished eating and headed toward the front door and waited on Krystin to pick me up. Johnson's Garage is supposed to have my car done after school. After a few minutes, I saw Krystin pulling into our driveway. I hustle out and get into her mom's new 1965 Ford Galaxy – 4 doors. It was a pretty red color and had all the newest gadgets.

As soon as I got in and sat down, Krystin scooted over and hugged me and started kissing me. Then she scooted back over and backed out of the driveway and began driving to school.

She asked. "Are you excited about the big game tonight?"

"Yes, I forgot about the pep session."

"I know; that is why I had to bring my cheerleading outfit with me. That gym will be packed. They always oversell tickets. People will be standing everywhere and yelling at us cheerleaders to sit down and get out of their line of sight."

"I suppose it will be a mad house, Krystin."

"You got that right. No Chemistry class today to even make the day better." Added Krystin

"I kind of hate missing Chemistry. I've grown fond of the class since I am now doing (A) work."

"Don't rub it in. I am still having to study hard just to keep a (B) average in that class."

"I told you that I could probably help you in that class. But now I have my doubts because I don't think I could keep my mind on helping you. I would be constantly thinking about ravishing your body and making mad, mad passionate love to you."

"I'll be Ok. You are just too busy anyway. If I were doing (C) work in Chemistry, I would ask for your help. Nothing wrong with a (B), especially in Chemistry."

I added, "I just want to see you get into college easily."

Krystin bubbled up saying, "This town will be dead tonight because everyone will be at the game. People in Southern Indiana are more religious about these games than they are their church."

"I know; that is probably why Orville and Willard are so upset at me being the – *Black sheep of the team.*"

"Don't you worry about that Phil. When you do good tonight, everyone will forget all about that and be welcoming you onboard. If we win this game, your name along with Ray and the others will be on everyone's tongue. You will make history. This community wants to win a sectional and maybe a regional so much they can taste it."

"I'll do my best tonight to make Ray and the others look good. I have had Ray, Stan, and Dan practice with me giving them quick passes. They needed practice in being able to catch quick faster than average passes. That will give them that extra second they need to score."

We were just a few minutes early when Krystin pulled into the school parking lot. Hopefully, Aaron is at school so I can talk to him about not filming me but concentrating on Ray, Stan, and Dan. It is Ok if he films me shooting a free throw or taking the ball out of bounds. I just don't want him to be filming me when I am guarding someone. That is when I get intense and go to work, keeping my abilities just within the believable range.

As we entered the hallway, I had to stop by my locker to pick up a couple of books. I told Krystin to go on to Geography class and I would be there as soon as I talked to Aaron. I still had a few minutes before 1st per. Started. Aaron was already in his class. Just as I was about to ask him not to film me playing basketball, I suddenly had this thought. Even though we are friends, my request may raise suspicions. Then he may film me every chance he gets during the game. There will be times I will be quicker to steal the ball or move quickly to penetrate and score. So, I decided not to say anything to him. This is just a reminder that I must know my limitations. My quickness and abilities have to be just a little better than everyone else. I turned from his doorway waving to him and went on to class.

As I walked down the hallway, nearly every student was wishing me and the team good luck tonight. Goodness, these people in Southern Indiana live this basketball stuff. I like playing, but there has to be more important things in life.

When 1st period Geography class started, Mr. Shields began the class by talking about the big game tonight and how we haven't beaten Scottsville in 13 years.

Mr. Shields said, "I am hearing by the grapevine that we have a much-improved team this year thanks to having

Phil Marland on the team." Everyone in the class looked at Stan, who was also in the class, and me. Then everyone in class including Mr. Shields began clapping and cheering.

After the cheering quieted down, I looked over at Stan again and noted, "Stan, we don't have too much pressure on us, do we?"

Then Mr. Shields told everyone to settle down and get to the business of learning about the Geography of the Soviet Union and how Communism is the wrong type of government for them; and they are the main reason for the current going Vietnam War.

One good thing which I didn't know at the time was going to come to an end on Dec. 1, 1969, 4 years later, was if you went to college, you had an automatic deferment from the draft.

For that reason of the automatic deferment, there were large numbers of high school graduating boys trying to get into college to avoid going to fight in the war.

During lunch, Ray, Stan, Dan, Nick, and myself sat and had lunch together. All of them talked about how popular we were and how it was important for us to win the game.

While eating, I looked over at the other boys and reminded them, "Remember guys how we have put extra practice in on catching the sharp passes. If you can catch my quick passes, that will give you a better chance of getting open for a good shot. Just run Bartlett's plays and I can get the ball to you."

Ray added, "We will be looking for them, Phil. We got this."

Stan chimed in, "I know Scottsville has one of the best guards in the state, but so do we. In fact, we have 2 quick guards in, Phil and Nick. No one outside Austiana knows it yet. They are going to find out tonight."

The rest of the afternoon went well. I even got the phone call from Johnson's garage to tell me that my car was ready to pick up. There is no cheerleading practice or basketball practice after school on a day of a game. So, Krystin can drop me off after school to pick up my car.

Finally, 6th period came and I headed to Chemistry class. We had barely started class when the intercom blurred out with the voice of our assistant principal, Mr. Gullon, "We need to have the cheerleaders and basketball team dismissed from class to go to the gym."

They always dismiss the cheerleaders and players about 15 minutes before the pep session begins and everyone else enters the gym. When we got there, coach Bartlett had us stay in the locker room until the gym was filled with students. I began hearing this loud cheering in the background. Then I heard Bobby McGee's band start playing (School Days by Chuck Berry). The cheering became much louder. As soon as the song was over, coach Bartlett came in.

Bartlett sternly said, "Let's go out boys; they have chairs sitting in the middle of the floor in front of the crowd for us."

We began walking out led by Ray, Stan, Dan, and myself. Everyone was standing and cheering as we approached our seats. I saw adults from town standing along the walls. I just had no idea that winning was so important. Especially winning over a team that we haven't beaten in 13 years.

When we sat down, Dan leaned over and said, "It will be louder than this tonight. It will be so loud that we won't be able to think."

I replied, "We will have to be thinking tonight Dan, or we won't pull out a victory."

Dan hit my shoulder with his and said, "You know what I mean."

I sat and looked at the crowd of 500+ students and several local adult fans and all eyes were on us. We have been put on a pedestal and I am beginning to have doubts about us as a team pulling this off. This is so out of place for a nerd like me. I have practiced every night so hard to build my basketball skills. My special abilities have paid off, but I must use them with caution. Will I get into foul trouble when I cleanly knock the ball out of a player's hands. If Ray and I get into foul trouble, we will lose the game. Guess we will find out tonight. The pep session was loud and chaotic. They announced each player's name and had us stand up. When I stood up, the whole student body gave me a standing ovation as they did with Ray. I looked over towards Krystin who was standing with the rest of the cheerleading team, and she was looking back at me with her right hand over her heart patting her heart. I think it was a special moment for her too.

As soon as the pep session was over, I met Krystin at her car and told her that she needed to drop me off at Johnson's garage to pick up my car. It has only been a couple of days, but I have missed the *green mean machine.*

Krystin pulled into the garage parking lot and gave me a big hug and a kiss. She said, "Good luck tonight. I have this feeling that we are beginning to make history for this town."

I looked at her with wide eyes open and remarked, "I hope so; I am still nervous about all this and hope I don't disappoint everyone."

"You will be great," said Krystin. She has been so good about keeping my confidence up.

I kissed her and said, "I will see you tonight."

I went into the garage and the mechanic, Randall Everitt affirmed, "The Sheriff came by and informed me that this repair bill has been taken care of by Orville's insurance. Here are your keys. By the way, good luck tonight and bring us home a victory."

I added, "You gonna be at the game tonight?"

Randall assured me, "Are you kidding, everyone in town will be at the game."

"That's what I hear. We will do our best to get a victory."

I walked away, got into my car, and drove home. I wanted to get some rest and didn't have too much time. We were told to be at the gym by 5:00 pm. That is about 30 minutes before the JV team warms up. That gave us varsity boys enough time to go out and have one last shoot-around before our game at 8:00 pm.

As soon as I arrived home, I ate a ham sandwich and a piece of mom's fresh-baked apple pie. Then laid down for about 30 minutes to give myself some rest. I told my mom to get me up at about 4:50 pm giving me just enough time to get to the gym for about 15 minutes of extra practice. As I lay there, I am thinking about how much my teammates are depending on me to make good passes to them and help them on scoring also.

I had just dozed off when my mom's voice rang in my ear. "It is time to get up, Phil."

I replied, "Thanks mom."

Mom said, "Play hard, don't get hurt, and remember, I love you regardless of the outcome. Too many people in this town take this baseball too serious."

"It's not baseball mom, it is basketball. Yes you are right, the people in this town live and breathe basketball. Thanks for having trust in me and loving me regardless. I think we can win the game. I'm ready to be a part of history for our school."

I went out the kitchen door to the car. I drove by to pick up Krystin. When she came out of her house, she looked soooo sexy in that cheerleader outfit. Seems like their skirts get shorter and shorter every year. She got into the car and leaned over and gave me a big hug.

She said, "It is going to be wild and crazy at the gym tonight. Good luck and play hard. Don't get hurt."

"I think we are ready. I just have to put the crowd and noise out of my mind so I can concentrate. Coach Bartlett has put a lot of responsibility on me playing the position of point guard. I have to get the ball to our guys so they can score."

"I know you can do it." Replied Krystin.

When we arrived at the gym, Krystin met the other Cheerleaders there and went with them. I hustled in to begin a little practice before the Junior Varsity team came out. These are the Freshmen and Sophomores that play first before the Juniors and Seniors on the Varsity play.

It was about 5:15 pm when I came out on the floor to practice shooting. The goals still looked like huge bushel baskets to me. I purposefully missed a few to look like a normal player even though I knew I could typically shoot at 90% accuracy. Ray, Stan, Nick, and Dan were out shooting. I gathered them over into a huddle.

I said, "Boys have your hands ready to catch quick sharp passes. That will give you that extra half to a whole second to be open for a good shot. Run Bartlett's plays like we have been doing in practice, and we got this."

The Junior Varsity game started at 6:00 pm and we sat in the stands until the beginning of the 4th quarter. Then we left to go get dressed for the game. It did not turn out very good for our Junior Varsity team. Scottsville beat our boys 48 to 30.

At about 7:30, the Austiana team came out on the floor. Scottsville was already out there warming up. When we came out, I looked up into the bleachers where about

2,500 screaming fans were yelling and cheering us on. I had to tell myself not to get nervous. It seemed as though that everyone was watching me. When we huddled for the starting five announcements, Bartlett told Ray that there were a couple of college recruiters in the stands. They were here to see mainly Ray and the guard for Scottsville that is supposed to be so tough. Bartlett put me guarding Scottsville's best ball player who was the good guard.

When we went out on the floor to start the game, it was the tradition that all players on the floor shook hands. Then the referee in the center of the court, holding the ball blew his whistle and threw the ball up for the jump ball. Scottsville had a tall center of about 6' 6". He was a little taller than Ray and was somewhat thin but could jump good. Ray could dunk a ball if he got a running go at the rim. I heard that this boy on Scottsville's team could jump up flat-footed and dunk a basketball. We definitely had our work cut out for us. The good thing about Ray was he was more filled out and took up more space.

They got the ball first and the ball came over to Carl, Scottsville's best player. I was guarding him, and my senses were heightened through the roof. I knew I was much quicker than him. It still looked as though he was dribbling in slow motion. As soon as he made a move, I made sure I was a little quicker. I stole the ball from him several times and either made lay-ups myself or passed it off to other teammates to score. It ended up being a miserable night for him and a great night for me and the rest of my team. We finished the game beating them 86 to 64. We had finally after 13 years, beaten Scottsville and beat them decisively. The fans in the gym were going nuts.

At the end of the game, their coach shook my hand and said, "I have never seen anyone as quick as you. I heard that you didn't even play last year. How did you develop these skills so fast?"

I commented, "I just started working out a lot over the beginning of the school year and practiced handling and dribbling the basketball. I guess it paid off for me."

Their coach replied, "It sure did. These college scouts had to be pleasantly surprised at your performance. You may be a candidate for a college scholarship."

"Thank you, sir. I hope you are right about that. I could sure use some financial help."

"You keep playing like this, and it will be coming your way. You had 10 steals, 8 rebounds, 7 assists, and 24 points. With Ray's 29 points, the two of you finished us off."

He shook my hand again and walked away. I was keeping in mind what Dr. Spear said to me. "Don't be the best, be 2nd or 3rd best. Don't draw too much attention to yourself."

I was just glad that coach Bartlett's plays worked well to get Ray open to score that many points. The team stayed out on the floor for several minutes as several of the fans came up to us to shake hands. I was still sweaty with my uniform on. Krystin came over to me and gave me a big hug. I wanted to shower and get dressed so I could take Krystin over to the Sock Hop. After home games, our school would open up the school cafeteria for about an hour for the students to go listen to music and dance. They would even have chili suppers for the adults during the Sock Hop. Students would pull their shoes off so they wouldn't scar up the cafeteria floor and go out on the cafeteria floor to dance. Every home game, we had a Sock Hop afterwards. It was a great way to relieve all the stress during the game. It also gave me a chance to hold Krystin close even though we had to be on our best behavior because there were always several adults and parents sitting at the tables eating chili while watching us dance.

Krystin and I danced for a little while, but we wanted some alone time. We left early to get that time. I drove Krystin home and as I pulled into her driveway, I shut off my car headlights before I turned off the car engine. It was still cool out, but the car was nice and warm as Krystin pulled me toward her while I helped slide my body from behind the steering wheel. She immediately straddled me with that sexy, short, white cheerleading skirt on and the cheerleading sweater with that big black (A) in the middle of the front of the sweater. This is virtually any teenager's dream to be in this situation. My life had definitely turned out for the best, thanks to those nanobot shots.

Krystin began kissing my neck while her body began gyrating on top of me. She wanted me to make her climax using my fingers again. So, I started fondling her with my fingers. Finally, I heard that familiar moan from her while my boner swelled to the limit. This time she had my pants totally wet in the crotch. I still would not unzip my pants and take this any further. I respected her too much for that. She started humping me to help me climax myself. It didn't take long to have a beautiful cheerleader straddling you and humping you until you either climaxed or died, whichever came first. We both still had this college degree thing implanted in our brains. I finally gave out a loud moan and achieved my quest instead of dying.

"Mercy, Krystin. We are punishing ourselves. But afterwards, it feels so good that it sure beats the alternative of not climaxing."

"I know Phil; We need that relief."

I said, "Evolution works well with humans. We are at the age we are supposed to be having great sex and reproducing, but society and successful living forces us to postpone what evolution had planned. I have seen too many boys and girls get caught up in that trap and a lot of times their lives are never the same and future goals are not achieved."

Krystin saw her porch light come on. Even though we were still a good distance from the porch, she was like a trained robot.

"I have to get in." She said as she had both of her hands cupped around my face.

"I understand. I have to work tomorrow at the grocery store. I will pick you up tomorrow night for a movie at the town's indoor movie house."

"What movie will we watch?" She asked.

"A Fistful of Dollars, starring Clint Eastwood. I haven't seen it yet, but Ray told me it is a good movie."

She gave me one last kiss as she opened the car door to get out and said, "I'll see you tomorrow; at what time?"

"The movie starts at seven, so about 6:30."

I started my reliable mean green machine but waited until she got into her house before I left. While driving home, I started thinking about several different things. I wish a couple of my friends had the opportunity to have that shot of nanobots flowing in their bloodstream to help repair damaged cells and even making all their cells stronger and more durable. Especially Derek Turner who is crippled from polio. Those nanobots could possibly cure his affliction. I wonder how powerful those little, microscopic bits of metal computers are regarding medicine? My body and mind are a testament to their power already. However, is this as good as it gets? Will I gradually become even stronger and faster than I currently am? Even if I don't increase my abilities anymore, I already have a huge advantage over any other normal person.

Another question that has been nagging me is: Do I need to have another shot every so often? This is why I need to stay in touch with Dr. Spear and become closer to Anokmar, the master Alien.

What will happen to me if this particular secret project between the Aliens and the CIA begins to fail and people like me start dying off? I suppose it would be *the end of the line for Phillip Marland.* Would this country's current medical discoveries be able to save us by draining our blood getting rid of the nanobots and replenishing our bodies with new blood.

I also have not told Krystin about any of this. I need to talk to Dr. Spear about that. I just need to call him tomorrow sometime and let him direct me on what to do.

He hasn't steered me wrong yet and he has been completely honest with me.

I pulled into the driveway and got out of my car. It was late and thought I would walk around to the back side of the house to the basement door. I didn't want to wake mom or my sister. As I was walking around, I looked up and saw some of those strange lights that some people had been talking about. I could tell that the way they changed direction so fast that the lights were part of an alien spaceship. None-the-less, the aliens have a good cover-up. There is a military base not too far from us. I unlocked the door trying to be quiet as the neighbor's old dog kept barking at me. Mom was used to the dog barking at night as was Janet. They know he barks at anything that moves.

After the game, I know Ray and the other starters said they were exhausted from playing so hard. I didn't feel that tired. But I knew I needed to get some rest because tomorrow was another grocery store day.

SATURDAY – WORKDAY AT THE GROCERY STORE

The grocery store opened at 9 am. I needed to be there by 8:45 am. I barely made it to work on time. As I started stocking my shelves, it seemed as though everyone who came to shop that day made a special effort to go down my aisle to congratulate me on the Friday night victory. I made friends I didn't even know I had. Ray and I along with the other 3 starters were the most popular people in town. I just can't get over how popular this basketball thing is. I have fun with it especially with my friends but come on, it is just a game. Parents even brought their kids to the store and had me pose with them while they took a picture. The 35 mm camera had become popular that still used rolls of film that had to be developed and printed. While trying to be nice to the many fans, and after posing for several photos, I was getting behind in my work. At lunch, I told Mr. Mudd my problem. He didn't seem to mind. He told me to do the best I could and said that this was one of the best Saturdays for store business in a long time.

Mr. Mudd said, "Phil, you are virtually a celebrity here and everyone is coming out to see you and talk to you. Guess what? They usually buy something before they leave."

I replied, "I understand Mr. Mudd but I am not going to get all the shelves stocked if I have to keep stopping to talk to people and pose for a picture. What kind of a picture is that anyway? Me standing there with their son or daughter with a store apron around my waist."

He chuckled and laughed, "Don't worry so much about these shelves. We'll get them stocked. Just enjoy the moment. You boys made history for the school last night."

The rest of the afternoon went about the same. I believe I posed for 30 – 40 photos. I have to admit I enjoyed being the center of attention. After work, I left in a hurry to get home to get ready to take Krystin to the movie house located around Courthouse Square. People came to this movie house from other small towns that didn't have one. After the movie, Krystin and I had to walk up the street to my car since we were late getting there. Some of the buildings had doors that were recessed 6-8 feet from the street sidewalk making a good place for someone to hide out and mug somebody. There were only a few lights on inside some of the closed stores. Even the streetlight was burned out. So, we were walking down a pretty dark street.

As we were walking by a hardware entrance, 3 rough-looking boys stepped out in front of us. They had those black motorcycle leather jackets on over white t-shirts and jeans with white socks and black shoes. All of them had their hair combed straight back. The taller one of the three stepped in front of me and I stopped. I assumed he was their leader. I had never seen these boys before, so they were not local boys. Probably from Beddington or Scottsville.

He said, "Hey man don't you have some money to give me?"

I replied, "No man, I just spent it all at the movie house. They make good popcorn. You should try it."

He replied as the other two boys looked on a few feet away, "Are you trying to be funny?"

I said, "No man, I just spent all my money."

He stepped closer to me within a foot of me, "Well since you don't have any money to give us, I guess we will just have to take the girl." He looked around and smiled at his buddies.

I stared him eye to eye as he turned back looking at me; I remarked, "That's not going to happen either. Krystin, step back behind me a few feet."

Krystin pleaded, "Why don't you boys just let us go? We just want to go home." She moved back as I requested.

One of the other boys mumbled, "Carl, maybe we better let them go."

Carl said, "Naw, we can't let a pretty girl like this go. Look at her; she's a movie star."

By now my senses are heightened and I added, "Carl, do you believe in Jesus?"

"What is that supposed to mean, punk?" Carl replied.

"If I were you, I would start praying to him right now and ask for his advice regarding this situation. I'm sure he is going to tell you to let us go or his wrath will be upon you and through me, he will work."

Carl glared at me with his face turning red, "You smart ass."

Just about then, he grabbed both sides of my jacket in the front and tried to pull me toward him. He couldn't move me. An instant later, I put my hands on top of his hands and began to press my thumbs in the soft area between his thumbs and his forefingers. My thumbs dug in deep quickly and he quickly winced and tried to pull away from me. I wouldn't let him go while my thumbs dug in deeper. The other two boys stepped a couple of feet closer. I quickly looked and said, "If you boys know what is good for you, you will walk away right now and just keep on walking."

By now, Carl is down on his knees begging me to let him go, "Please let go of me."

I added, "You should have prayed to Jesus like I suggested, and you could have prevented all this pain. When you threatened to take my girl, Jesus told me that you must be punished."

I looked at the other two boys standing a good distance away and added, "Anyone of you fellows have anything to say."

One of the boys mumbled, "No, just let go of him."

I still had my thumbs deep into the soft part of his hands between his thumbs and forefingers. I told him to stand up when he did, I quickly punched him in the face, and he fell backwards to the ground. I knew I had hit him hard. I had either broken his nose or cheekbone or both. When I walked over to him, he had begun to bleed profusely.

I knelt down to him and commented loud enough so his buddies could hear while I kept my eyes on them. "If I have to deal with you again, I am going to break several bones in your body the next time." I got Krystin and we began to walk to our car. Before I got in, I yelled at Carl's two buddies, "Come over and get your loser friend and go back to the rock that you crawled from under."

When we got into the car and pulled away, Krystin said, "Why is it Phil, I always feel safe with you?"

"I'm glad Krystin, when we are out like this, I'm here to protect you. "

She commented, "Phil, you have changed somehow. You hit him so fast I barely saw you hit him. I know he didn't see it coming. It was just like your confrontation with Ray in that school fight."

I replied, "But you did see me punch him. Right! I wanted to take him down just in case the other two decided to try something. Usually, in a fight, if you take out the leader, the others usually run."

"You sound and act like you have done this before."

"Well, I had been reading some self-defense magazines and one of the magazines had that comment in it. The answer that I need to give you is NO. I have never been in this situation before. However, I knew one thing. They were not going to take you with them tonight. I would have gone crazy if they would have tried."

"That's comforting to know."

"I need to get you home because I have to work Sunday from noon till 6 pm."

By now, it was about 11 pm at night. I always made it a special effort to have her home by midnight. I want to have the respect of Mr. and Mrs. Adkins.

I dropped Krystin off with a big goodnight kiss and I went straight home. When I made it to my bed in the basement, I crashed for the rest of the night.

MONDAY

At 7 am, the radio alarm goes off by playing Simon and Garfunkel's – The Sound of Silence. It is mid-November now and it is barely breaking daylight at 7 am. The words in the song (Hello Darkness, my old friend) were still holding true for a while. I quickly get up and do the 3 S's, then run up the stairs to get some breakfast. The smell of bacon filled the air as I approached the top of the steps. Mom was frying bacon and scrambling some eggs for Janet and I for breakfast. The smell of toast also filled the air. This was a pleasant surprise because usually, we eat cereal.

As I sat down to start eating Janet said, "I don't want to give you the big head but a lot of the people in town said that you really played good ball Friday night."

Mom added, "Yes, yesterday and Saturday both, our phone was ringing off the hook from people wanting to praise your performance."

"I did Ok. Everyone needs to remember that it was a team effort. Ray scored more points than I did."

While I was thinking about Dr. Spear's comment that I had planted in my mind --- (Don't be the best, just be one of the best.) That way, you shouldn't draw too much attention to yourself.

"I have to get to school and not be late."

I rushed out after eating a wonderful breakfast to get into the mean green machine. There was a heavy frost on the ground signaling that Thanksgiving was approaching.

I had to hustle to get to school on time after picking up Krystin. As we were heading to our first period Geography class, Ray and his girlfriend came up behind me and he blurted out into my ear, "Hey, bad boy. We worked them over last night. 1st time in 13 years. You realize that we made history at this school."

"I know, I can't go anywhere without someone reminding me of our accomplishment. Our team couldn't accomplish this without you being in the right position and being able to catch those quick passes from me." I replied.

"You played a big part too, Phil. Not only were your passes to the rest of the team on target, but you also hit some nice outside shots when we needed to score."

I added, "It was just a good team effort by all of us."

I walked into the 1st period class and had just sat down when the intercom came on. It was Mr. Clover, the principal.

"Sorry to interrupt your class Mr. Shields but I need to see Phil Marland in my office."

I'm thinking, what is this all about? I didn't know it until I came into the office; Ray had been called out of his class also. The county newspaper journalist, Mr. Finkle was there to talk to us about the game. When I went into the office, Ray's eyes lit up. He was glad to see me, and I was glad to see him. Coach Bartlett was also present.

Principal Clover said, "This is Mr. Finkle from the county newspaper, and he would like to talk to you two boys about the game."

Mr. Finkle began, "First of all, congratulations on your victory. It has been a long time coming."

Ray and I both said thanks at about the same time.

Mr. Finkle continued, "Your coach here told me that you two together scored 53 of your 86 points. That means that the rest of the team only got 33 total points. Is that right coach?"

"Yes, but I want to stress that the other boys played well also. The other team seemed to not have any answers for Ray and Phil's performance. The other boys knew that, and we capitalized on the situation during the game. The team shot over 60% from the field and hit 10 of twelve free throws."

Mr. Finkle asked, "Ray, give me your opinion about the game."

"Well, if it hadn't been for Phil's sharp passing and quick defense, I probably wouldn't have scored the 29 points Friday night. Phil has helped the other players so much. We have all worked hard on being able to catch Phil's quick, snappy passes. One thing I have noticed about Phil is his excitement when one of the other player scores." Replied Ray.

Mr. Finkle turned to me and stated, "Phil, give me your assessment of the game."

I said, "I was glad that Ray and the other boys were able to execute coach Bartlett's plays when we were on offense. I was watching for them to be in the right position and was ready to get the ball to them. Often times they would try to double-team Ray, and that left one of the other boys open for a shot. I took advantage of that. I was lucky enough to sometimes lose the person guarding me and I would score myself."

Mr. Finkle added, "Phil, some of the fans told me for your size, you had amazing jumping ability to help in rebounds. You could understand Ray getting his rebounds with his size. He is 6' 6". He dragged down 14 rebounds. You got 10 rebounds playing as a 6' 1" guard. And what can

I say about your defense? Whoever you were guarding, you was smothering them. They had no chance to do anything positive for their team. The boy you were guarding is considered one of the best guards in the state and you took him completely out of his game."

I added, "I owe everything to coach Bartlett. This is my first year of playing team basketball and the coach taught me how to play and utilize my quickness. I can't say enough about the rest of the players. They made it possible for me to utilize my finesse and quickness."

Mr. Finkle interjected, "Don't forget about your 70% field goal shooting."

"I was just lucky." I replied.

"It didn't seem like luck to me. Most of the time, the ball never touched the rim as it went through the basket." Remarked Finkle.

After a couple of minutes of taking some notes, Mr. Finkle said, "I think I have enough information to write a nice article about a victory that was a long time coming when you defeated Scottsville. In fact, it's been 13 years since you had beat that team. Thank you boys for talking to me."

Mr. Clover motioned to Ray and I and said, "You boys can get back to your classes now."

Mr. Finkle interrupted, "Wait Mr. Clover, I want to get a picture of these 2 boys."

I chimed in, "We want coach in the picture with us."

We lined up with the coach in the middle between Ray and me in front of a Big (A) painted on the wall in the Principal's office. The camera clicked, and it was done.

Ray and I both approached the office door and left. When Ray and I were walking down the hallway towards our classroom, Ray said, "Man Phil, if we play like we did Friday night every game, we will win a lot of games."

I smiled at Ray as we started down separate hallways and remarked, "We will Ray. Never fear; Marland is here."

As I continued my way back to the classroom, I was a little alarmed about the newspaper reporter's remarks about my jumping ability. I know I have to be careful, but I just wanted our team to get an early lead and stay ahead of them. After we got about 12 points ahead of them, I was willing to trade basket for basket. However, Stan and Ray hit some nice shots and we ended up beating them by 22 points. I realize that I must be careful not to draw too much attention to myself. I could have scored 40 points but that would not be good. People would be watching me like a hawk. The cameras would be on me, and you never know when someone may be filming a game. I can't have myself being filmed using extraordinary powers. I have already had one close call with my friend Aaron.

While we have had several practices and scrimmages, I have learned to control and fine-tune my abilities. As the year goes on, I should get better at it and not have to worry about being filmed while I would be making a quick move or jumping very high that someone may notice that what I did was impossible for the average human to do.

The rest of the week was great, and we had another game on Friday night beating Betterton by 25 points. I played smart, letting Ray get 30 points while I scored 25 points. This game was easier because this team wasn't very good anyway. After another 3-4 games, most of the focus will be on Ray and he deserves it. He is accomplishing this with the abilities he was born with. I have little nanobots in my bloodstream helping me.

I was bulging out of my clothes; I asked mom to get me some larger pants, underwear, and shirts. She did so that helped me to not draw much attention to my stronger physique even though Krystin has noticed my body changing. I was taller going from 5' 10" to 6' 2" in just a weekend shortly after my incident with the spaceship crash. I was hoping that I would not grow taller. 6' 2" is about right. I don't need to be any taller. As far as playing on the team, I could get any rebound I wanted within reason. I could dunk a basketball easily. I have to be careful with that move because it is extremely rare for a high school student 6' 1" or even 6' 2" to dunk a basketball.

I have also noticed that since winter has set in, the temperatures seem colder to me. I noticed that when I visited the alien site in the cave, it was much warmer inside the cave than the average temperature of a cave here in Southern Indiana. The average temperature is about 56 deg. F at this latitude. When I was inside the alien site cavern, it was well above 72 deg. F. They must be warm-blooded, and I am experiencing that also. At home, I have already thrown an extra quilt on my bed. The basement is cool, anyway.

By Thursday, the newspaper article came out. It was a nice picture on the front page of the weekly newspaper. Below was the caption reading: (Ray Walls toughness and Phil Marland's finesse along with great effort from the rest of the team, brings Austiana a decisive victory over Scottsville with a score of 86 – 64).

I knew that wasn't going to set well with Scottsville fans or the team.

SATURDAY – BEFORE THANKSGIVING

I had to get up earlier this morning to make mom's bank deposit to cover all our bills. I still had to go to work at noon. I rush up the steps from the basement to the kitchen. Mom usually gets up an hour or more before Janet and I get up.

As I walked through the door to the refrigerator for orange juice, mom said, "Phil, I have the deposit fixed up for you to take to the bank. There is $170 in the envelope. Don't lose it or we are dead-in-the-water regarding our bills."

"I'll take care of it mom."

"Be sure you do. We have electric and gas bills along with the water bill. We can't afford to have our electricity and gas shut off. This November has been colder than normal this year."

I drank my orange juice and grabbed one of mom's wonderful homemade biscuits as I headed out the door to the mean green machine. It was about 9 am when I left, and the Scranton County State Bank opens at nine.

I pulled into the parking lot of the bank located at the edge of Austiana. When I walked into the door, there were about 3 people ahead of me, one woman and appeared to be a couple of farmers in their typical overalls and flannel shirts.

While waiting for my turn, I suddenly heard some noise behind me, and there were a couple of guys standing by the front door with rifles. They had stockings over their heads to obscure their faces, and both men were carrying empty pillowcases.

The taller one said, "This is a hold-up, and we just want everyone to stay calm and no one has to get hurt." Then the taller one walked past us up to the teller carrying an empty pillowcase.

He said to the teller pointing his rifle at her, "You keep both hands above the counter. We wouldn't want you to die from pressing a burglar alarm. Fill up the pillowcase with all your money and you will live to see tomorrow."

While he was attending to the teller, the other robber yelled, "Everyone else just keep looking ahead. Don't look at me when I come by."

Since I was the last person in line, he came to me first and said, "Drop your money into this pillowcase." I noticed that the other customers were looking straight ahead. I hesitated and looked at him.

He reminded me, "What did I just say? Don't look at me. Drop your money into the pillowcase now. I still hesitated because I promised mom I would make this deposit. At the same time the taller robber up front yelled, "Is there a problem back there?"

The robber standing beside me said, "Nothing I can't handle."

My extra powers were already heightened. Suddenly in a fraction of a second, I grabbed the gun barrel of his rifle and pointed it away from me while grabbing the stock of the rifle away from him. I did it so fast that he had no chance of pulling the trigger. I quickly smashed him in the face with the butt end of the rifle stock. The other robber was about 25 feet away from me but was still looking at the bank teller. Before he hit the floor, I ran up much faster than normal past the other 3 people in front of me. They had to have noticed my super quick speed. I ran up and smashed the other robber in the back of the head just as the first robber trying to get my bank deposit was hitting the floor. I hit him so hard I knocked him out and he was bleeding while lying on the floor. I handed the teller both rifles and told her to get the bank president and give him the rifles. I also told the teller to either hit the burglar alarm if she had one or call the police. I figured that they had a getaway car and driver waiting outside the bank. So, I calmly walked out the bank door.

Sure enough, I saw a car with someone in it about 30 feet from the bank door still running. I could see the exhaust coming from his tailpipe. I calmly walked behind the car memorizing the license plate. It could have been a stolen license plate. So, I walked up along the car on the driver's side. I gave a quick glance, and I could tell he was watching me from the driver's side outside mirror. I was looking away as I approached his car door. I figured he might have it locked. I was prepared to give it a hard jerk hoping that he didn't have a gun ready to shoot me. I wanted to give him the element of surprise. I quickly jerked the door open while scanning quickly for a gun. He was so surprised his eyes opened wide. He did have a pistol laying in the passenger's seat.

I immediately said, "Uh uh. Don't even think about it. Are you waiting on your buddies?"

He said, "Who in the hell are you?"

I replied, "If you are, it's going to be a while."

He reached over to get the pistol; I moved on him so fast and grabbed him out of the car before he could grab the pistol. He also tried to step on the gas to get away causing the car to roll away from us. We were both standing on the street. By now, there were other people observing what was happening.

He tried to grab me and hit me. I quickly blocked his punch, and without moving too fast, I punched him hard in the stomach and then in the face. He went down to the ground. I yelled at the bystanders telling them to get the police here.

I bellowed loud, "This guy and a couple of others inside the bank tried to rob the bank." I was lucky assuming that this was the getaway man.

By now, I heard sirens getting louder and closer. When the police came, there were 2 cars with 2 policemen in each car. One got out and immediately handcuffed the getaway man. I went back into the bank; the two farmers and the one lady were patting me on the back. The lady remarked,

"Thank God you were here. They would have taken all my money leaving me broke."

I replied, "I know the feeling mam. I know I shouldn't have intervened, and I was risking my life possibly along with everyone else, but I just couldn't let them take my mother's hard-earned money."

I went to the front counter of the bank and pulled the stocking off the robber laying by the teller's window. To my surprise, it was Willard Dodd, Ron's Dad. I just couldn't believe that he would participate in an attempted bank robbery. I also felt so bad for Ron and his mother. I'm sure they wanted him to have no part in this. They most likely didn't even know of his attempt. Even though they didn't succeed, Willard will likely spend some time in prison.

By now the police had the other person handcuffed, the stocking off his head. I didn't recognize him. Two other policemen came over to Willard, handcuffed him and took him away.

I quickly asked the teller, whom my mother knew, if she would deposit this money for her before the day ended. I knew this bank was going to turn into a crime scene and would probably be closed for the rest of the day. The nice lady bank teller assured me that she would make the deposit. I thanked her.

She said, "I need to be thanking you. For a while, I thought this might be my last day on earth."

I added, "You don't need to be thinking me mam."

She added, "You moved so lightning fast to catch those bozos off guard. I have never in my life seen anyone move that fast. You must be some kind of Super Man like Clark Kent on the television show (SUPERMAN). To be blunt, you appeared super-human."

I asked, "I would rather you not make a big deal about this. Especially to the newspaper reporters. The less attention I get, the better off I will be."

She remarked, "Oh, you are just too modest. You are a hero."

I walked away from her toward the front door of the bank knowing that this was not going to be a good situation for me. I also knew the newspaper and radio were going to be relentless wanting every little detail. As soon as I stepped outside, I found out that news travels fast. Standing on the sidewalk in front of the bank was Mr. Finkle, the journalist.

Mr. Finkle said, "Phil, we have to quit meeting like this. Monday's report in the newspaper was: you are a basketball hero. Next week's issue, you will be a hero again by foiling an attempted bank robbery. The word that sticks in my mind is this town has some kind of Superman."

I said, "Please don't say that Mr. Finkle." He took out his notebook and began writing.

I added, "It was a really stupid thing I did. I could have been killed and possibly responsible for others in the bank being hurt badly or dying. Trust me; I regret acting on those guys."

"What was your thought when this was happening?" asked Finkle.

"I was in line to make a bank deposit for my mother. She works hard to earn the small salary she makes. I just couldn't bear to see 3 thugs rob me of my mom's hard-earned money and the other honest people involved. In hindsight, I knew that I had made a mistake. No one's life is worth the money that they would have stolen had they been successful."

"Phil, you don't know for sure, had they been successful, they may have killed you and everyone else in the bank anyhow leaving no witnesses. You may have saved everyone's life. That is the way I see it and that is the way I'm going to write it."

Within a couple of minutes, my mother pulled into a parking spot. She got out of the car and came running to me crying and gave me a big hug. Everyone standing around cheered and clapped.

Mom grabbed me by my jacket with both hands and said, "You could have been killed. What did you do and what were you thinking?"

By now, Sheriff Paul Walls is there and said, "Miss Marland, he foiled an attempted bank robbery. He is our hero."

Mr. Finkle patted my mother's back and smiled, "Miss Marland, you must be very proud of your son."

"I'm going to beat him when I get him home for doing such stupid stuff." Replied Mom.

The sheriff remarked, "Well before you take him home and bust his ass, I need to get a statement of the occurrence from him. Don't be hard on the town hero Miss Marland.

Just be thankful that he and all the others involved are Ok."

Mom spoke up, "I am sheriff, which was just the mother in me talking."

After I made my statement to the sheriff, I followed mom home. I still had to go to work that afternoon at the grocery store. When I got home, Krysten was there waiting for me. She came running to me also crying. She gave me a big kiss and a tight hug. Mom began tearing up again.

Mom said, "Phil, you have to quit putting yourself in harm's way."

Krystin declared, "You are correct Miss Marland. Last Saturday night, 3 punks confronted Phil and I as we were walking to the car from the movie. They asked for money, but Phil wouldn't give them any. Then they said that they were going to take me. Their leader was standing in front of Phil and grabbed him by his jacket. Phil immediately grabbed that punk's hands and rendered him helpless while the other two boys looked on. Then Phil punched him hard on his face. I'm telling you Miss Marland, Phil is much stronger than he looks even though he is buffed up. I am just afraid that sooner or later, fate will catch up with him."

I said, "Have faith in me, Krystin."

"Phil, you never said anything to me about that encounter." Emphasized mom with eyes wide open.

"It wasn't that big of an ordeal." I explained.

"Well, it is to me. You both could have gotten hurt." Replied mom.

Krystin added, "A month ago, Phil was this skinny nerd in school. Now, he is a hero. I having difficulty figuring all this out."

I spoke while heading into the house, "Thanks for being here Krystin but I have to get to work. I may be late getting to work already."

I didn't want any more prying about me buffing up. So, I left quickly to get into the car and get to work. When I drove into the parking lot, Mr. Mudd was standing outside the store door with a big smile on his face while 6-7 others were looking on. I was thinking to myself hoping the Lord would hear me, "Please make this go away. I don't need all this attention."

Mr. Mudd, on the other hand, loved it because it brought more people into the store. As soon as I got out of the car, Mr. Mudd commented, "Here comes our hero."

As I walked past everyone, I was forced to give several (High-Fives). I think Mr. Mudd wanted me to stop and talk to people, but I kept walking into the store to start my work. It was another busy day at the store. I had an out-of-town journalist from the Indianapolis Daily News stop by my aisle and wanted to talk. Mr. Mudd introduced him to me and asked if I would spend a few minutes talking to him.

"I'm Mr. Watson from the Indianapolis Daily News. May I talk to you for a few minutes? I got Mr. Mudd's Ok to talk to you."

"I suppose so," as I raised up from rotating and realigning cans of pineapple on the bottom shelf.

"First of all, congratulations on foiling the bank robbery. I bet those robbers didn't know they were going to have to deal with one of the fastest ball players in the state......maybe the fastest and quickest player of the state. Young man, I have reported on hundreds of basketball games in my lifetime, but the other night, you highlighted this game."

I asked, "What do you mean?"

"I couldn't help but notice how you were just a little quicker than everyone else. You jumped as if you were 6'5" or taller. Just every facet of the game, you were just a little better than anyone else. You shot about 70% from the field with half of those being out 20 ft. or more. I got a sense that there were times when you missed a shot you wanted to miss. Almost all the shots you made; the ball hardly touched the rim. Several of your shots were (swishers), the ball just going right through the net with phenomenal accuracy. You made several difficult passes that landed in your teammate's hands. You made one bad pass, and with all your passes made with such accuracy, it appeared to me again that you wanted to make the bad pass. The shots you missed and the bad pass you made happened when your team was already ahead by more than 20 points. It is easy for me to think that you were actually holding back. It was almost like you didn't want people to realize how good you are at this sport."

After hearing all this, I am thinking, "This guy is on to me. I haven't been secretive enough about my heightened abilities. How do I get out of this?"

I pointed out to him, "I had a lucky night on the shooting. The rest of the team deserves all the credit. We worked hard on the plays that we ran in practice. When I made the passes, I knew my teammates were going to be in the right place at the right time. For some of those passes, I anticipated my teammates were going to be in position by the time the ball got there. That gave them an extra second or two to either shoot or pass whatever they needed to do. Honestly, I think you are reading too much into this."

"Maybe so, but everyone has to admit that your performance has been .... I guess the right word would be – remarkable. I don't think you had a lucky night shooting. I checked your stats. You average 66% field goal shooting. Several people are going to be watching you from now on including several college scouts." Watson replied.

"I'm not the leading scorer on the team. Ray Walls is the best player on the team. These college scouts need to be watching him."

"I'm no dummy about this game of basketball. A lot of Ray's points have been easy points because YOU have set him up to score so nicely. Even then, your shooting percentage is better than his. I'm not saying that he is not a good player. He is very good. You make him a better player....... beyond good."

"Thanks Mr. Watson; I'll take that as a compliment."

"Thank you for talking with me Phil; I appreciate it. However, there seems to be something about you that I just can't put my finger on."

"I assure you Mr. Watson, I'm just an ordinary athlete with some quickness and finesse and I try using it to the best of my abilities."

As he is walking away from me my mind starts racing. "Uh Oh! I must do a better job of masking my abilities. I wish I hadn't gone out for the team. I just want to impress Krystin. Also, by going out for the team I made a new friend in Ray and turned him into a better person getting him away from the bully attitude."

Some good has come out of all this. I have grown to really like the other 4 starters on the team. Furthermore, if I was not playing on the team, I don't think they would stand out in the news as much.

As soon as I get home tonight, I'm going to call Dr. Spear and see if I can visit him. I would love to visit Anokmar, the head alien at the secret site. Maybe Spear will take me there again.

The rest of the day, the grocery store had more than usual numbers of people coming in, and they all made sure they came down my aisle. I was busy talking to them and thanking them for their compliments. The discussions went back and forth between basketball and the bank robbery attempt. Everyone was treating me like some kind of hero. In my situation, this is not good.

Finally, the day ended, and I drove home. I need to make up some kind of excuse as to why I may be seeing her later tonight. We had planned on getting a pizza and watching some TV, hoping her parents would go to bed early to get some alone time. As soon as I got home, I dialed Krystin's phone number. After a couple of rings, she answered.

"Hello."

"Hey Krystin, it's me. I still want to see you tonight and get pizza but,".......here goes the lie, "I had a college scout stop by and wants to meet with me tonight. He is from Balle State University. I shouldn't be long and as soon as I get rid of him, I'll be over."

"I understand Phil, good luck with your meeting."

"Personally, I feel as though he is wasting my time. I'm more interested in engineering like Prudroo or Rose Hileman. I hope I'm not too late tonight."

"Ok. Call me when you are ready to stop by."

"Will do. I love you, you sexy thang."

"Stop it. I love you too."

CHAPTER 10

A SECOND VISIT WITH ANOKMAR

My next quick phone call was to Dr. Spear hoping he was home and I could contact him. The phone rings 3 times. Finally, I heard "Dr. Spear speaking."

"Hello Dr. Spear, this is Phil Marland."

"Hey, Phil how are you? Congratulations on the big victory in basketball."

"Thanks, but I need to talk to you about that. When could I drive over to talk to you?"

"Tomorrow evening would be good. I don't have any commitments Sunday evening."

"That would be great. What would be the best time for you?"

"How about 7 pm tomorrow night?"

"I don't get off work until 6 pm, but I will get there as soon as I am able. I may be a little late but only by 10-15 minutes. Would that be Ok with you?"

"Yes, I will take that as around 7 to 7:15 pm."

"Thank you Dr Spear. I would love to have another visit with Anokmar. Would that be possible?"

"I'm not sure; we will have to see. I will try to contact him and see if another visit is possible."

"I will see you tomorrow night."

Dr. Spear added before hanging up, "If you have to cancel, call me as soon as possible."

The phone clicks and all I hear is a busy signal.

As soon as I hung up the phone, I dialed Krystin's number. After a couple of rings I hear, "Hello, this is Adkins residents."

"Hey Krystin, it's Phil. The guy from Ball State had to cancel tonight and is coming tomorrow night." I thought it would be good to carry the little white lie over to tomorrow night and already have my butt covered.

Krystin replied, "Great, I didn't think I would see you at all tonight. Why don't you just come on over to the house?"

"That is why I called; I just wanted to make sure you were still home. I still need to shower and clean up but it shouldn't be long."

"Good; I'll see you in a few minutes." Krystin blurted.

A quick shower, clean clothes, and some Old Spice cologne, I was quickly out of the house, in the car, and on my way.

I pulled into the driveway and the time was about 7:30 pm. Krystin was waiting for me on her porch. She was wearing a short tight dress which easily showed off her beautiful body.

I spoke while gawking at her, "I can't believe your dad or mom let you wear that sexy dress."

"Neither one of them like for me too. Mom is more tolerant than dad. This is a good way for me to set boundaries with dad, so he won't be so protective."

"Maybe so, but don't take me wrong, I love you in that outfit; I would not want you to wear that outfit if you were my daughter. I think you do that just to push his buttons."

"Yes I do, but I trust you 100%, Phil. I would not wear this dress in front of just anyone."

"I appreciate your trust Krystin, but I don't want you to piss off your dad. He may take it out on me."

"No, after I told them what happened the other night after the movies, mom and dad really like you and they feel secure about my safety when I am with you. Oh! By the way, they will still be up for a while. So, let's go in and watch some TV, and you can do some socializing with both of them."

"This sounds like fun." I replied.

"Don't be a fuddy-duddy." She said while tickling me on the ribs.

When we entered, her parents both went on and on about the big game and the bank robbery. After a few minutes of them making me a hero, I finally had the chance to speak and stay with my story that it was a stupid thing to do. They were both sitting on the couch with Mrs. Adkin's head resting on Mr. Adkin's shoulder.

I looked at them and stated, "I'm glad that things turned out the way it did regarding the attempted robbery. However, I'm still upset with myself because in hindsight, I thought it was a stupid thing to do to not only jeopardize my life but others in the bank. When I reacted, I didn't know the outcome. I just didn't want them to take my mother's money that she worked so hard to get. I could have gotten us all shot and killed."

Mr. Adkins replied, "You shouldn't be hard on yourself Phil; I may have reacted in a similar way, especially if Sarah or Krystin had been with me. The good thing is..... everything turned out Ok. So, just enjoy and revel in the outcome you wanted."

While we were talking, Krystin had gone to the kitchen to heat up a pizza. She came out with pizza, plates, and 4 Pepsi Colas. It was time to watch a Saturday night movie that was made in 1951, – The Day the Earth Stood Still. I had seen it before, and it was about a spaceship landing on earth with an alien named Klaatu and a powerful large robot named Gort. I remember the famous words to control Gort to keep him from going on a rampage – Klaatu Barada Nikto. Oh! How this movie was bringing reality home to me.

After the movie was over, John asked, "Phil, do you think there are aliens out there in the universe somewhere?"

I replied, "As far as I know, scientists today don't know how large our universe is. I have a hard time fathoming the idea that we are the only life forms in the universe. Scientists know that our Milky Way Galaxy is made up of millions of stars along with our sun. There are millions of other galaxies out there with millions of stars. I think somewhere there are other forms of life in the universe. The distance is so vast."

"I see your reasoning." Said John.

Krystin gently commented, "Since the 1947 Roswell, New Mexico incident, there has been an increase of UFO sightings. Now currently in 1965, sightings are still making the news along with alien abductions. In 1961, there was a report of an alien abduction in New Hampshire by Betty and Barney Hill."

I spoke up saying, "I know it is easy to think that these people that have been subjected to abductions are a little wacky with too much imagination. But think about it. If you were an alien on another planet. Wouldn't you want to be secretive as possible and not be discovered?"

John added, "After watching that movie, it is just something to think about. Goodness, it is 10 o'clock. No wonder I'm tired and ready for bed. Are you two staying in or going out."

"We are just going to stay in and watch some TV." Said Krystin. "If that is Ok with you and mother."

"That is fine." Said John. "Just don't be up too late, Krystin."

"We won't dad. Good night."

As soon as they went upstairs, Krystin dowsed all the lights. The only light was a bluish hue coming from the TV. I could see the bluish light reflecting off Krystin's face.

Krystin immediately straddled me and whispered, "I'm not wearing any panties."

I said, "Krystin, we have talked about this. We keep our clothes on and I keep things tucked away; there shouldn't be any problems."

She added, "You still keep you-know-what tucked away, use your fingers, and we will still be Ok. I think you know what I want you to do to release my sexual tension."

"Yes, you have trained me well."

The next hour was pretty intense for both of us, and Krystin received what she had planned, the release of sexual tension.

It was about 11:45 pm as I was heading back to the car. I was looking forward to seeing Dr. Spear tomorrow evening. The rest of the night, I had difficulty sleeping because I had all these questions on my mind. Should I tell Krystin about me and my encounter? What will happen after college when we do finally have sex? If Krystin and I finally marry, how is my offspring going to be affected? Will she be affected in some way?

SUNDAY EVENING

Work at the grocery store was a busy day, especially down my aisle. I am beginning to feel like I'm some sort of freak show with people wanting to stop by and talk about the big basketball victory or the bank robbery incident. If the public only knew the truth.

While driving home to get ready for my visit with Dr. Spear, I was still hashing out what I wanted to ask him, especially everything regarding Krystin and myself. When I finally got home, mom could tell I was in a hurry.

"What is all this rush about?" Asked mom.

"I have to go meet a friend and we are going to work on some schoolwork." I replied, hoping that the story would satisfy her curiosity.

"I was hoping you would be in tonight to spend some time with your favorite mother and your favorite sister."

As I stood in front of her, holding a couple of schoolbooks tucked under my arm, "I would like to mom, but I need to get this stuff finished. You understand I need to keep my grades high for college entry and to score high on the ACT or SAT exams."

My story seemed to pacify her, "Well Ok, just be careful and don't be late getting home. Remember, I want you home by midnight."

Most of the time if I am later than midnight, she is usually in bed and in a deep sleep. I was probably going to be late tonight if I was to visit Anokmar. The drive to Jasperville would be about 30 minutes.

I gave mom a kiss while possibly lying again. "I'll be home by midnight." I ran out the door of the house and quickly got into the mean green machine.

After about 30 minutes of driving as it was already getting dark, I arrived at Dr. Spear's house. I went up to his door and rang the doorbell.

He opened the door and spoke, "Come in Phil; it is good to see you."

"Good to see you also, Dr. Spear."

"I wanted to talk to you about your heroic actions at the bank Saturday morning." Dr. Spear remarked with raised eyebrows.

I interrupted him, "I know, I know. I shouldn't have done what I did. You have to understand Dr. Spear, what it is like to be poor. I just couldn't let those thugs take my mother's hard-earned money."

Spear said, "I understand why you took those actions, but you must also understand that your secrecy is of utmost importance not only to you but to the rest of us. Just be patient and you won't have to worry about money anymore. You will have enough to take care of you and your mom. You just needed to let them get away and let the police handle the matter."

I added, "Trust me, I know that now. I have had to cover myself continuously since then. I have told everyone that it was a stupid thing to do, and I could have been hurt or killed and maybe others in the bank."

"That was a good way to direct your story, Phil."

I said, "I have some other disturbing news. That afternoon at work, I had this sportswriter, Mr. Watson, interview me about the big victory."

Spear interjected, "This is not good. I know this guy and he is very observant and is handy with a camera and filming techniques. You need to avoid people like him. I'm beginning to think if this basketball thing was a good idea. Unfortunately, you can't just quit now."

"I was hoping that I could quit, but then I would draw more attention to myself. Also, I just don't want to let down the other teammates."

"I don't think you will have to Phil; you may need to play poorly a couple of games to help with masking your abilities.

I added, "This Mr. Watson made a comment to me that there was something about me that he can't put his finger on. He said that he got the sense that I missed a shot at the goal in basketball only when I wanted to miss. I'm afraid he is too close to knowing that I am different."

"This is the type of person where secrecy is a must. There is an old saying – Don't mess with the man that buys his ink by the barrels." Spear quoted.

"You got that right. I was hoping for a chance to visit Anokmar again."

Spear reached for his coat and said, "It is good timing for us. Let's drive over to the cavern again."

We walked out the door and got into Dr. Spear's car. As we began our drive, I started with the questions.

"Dr. Spear, what type of propulsion do they use in order to travel light years in just a few weeks?"

"Well Phil, it is clear for you to see that their technology is hundreds of years ahead of us. They somehow use water with some other substances as their fuel and some type of fission as they break down the molecules. This releases a huge amount of energy. Our scientists are obviously very interested, but they will not show us their secrets."

"Why won't they show us?"

"Think about it. We are in a cold war with the Soviet Union. We are at war in Vietnam, which is an old man's war, but a young man's battle. They are afraid to let us or anyone else get their hands on that kind of massive energy. If we do, the aliens are pretty sure that we would not use that energy for purposeful things. We would use it to destroy things and people. Since they are so advanced, we are smart enough not to try to steal their secrets. Even if we did, it would take years to build an arsenal. They would have already wiped us off the earth."

"Wow man, that is something to think about."

"Our CIA is just trying to get the little advancements that they are willing to give us to maybe have an advantage over the Soviet Union and China, our biggest threat. Who knows, the Soviets and Chinese may be trying to do the same thing. You know this is not the only alien location in the world. They have several cells -- (where aliens reside) around the world."

"Are the other cells as adamant about remaining incognito as this one at our location?"

"Yes, but it is difficult for them to remain disguised everywhere without cooperation from others. So, they are very selective on where they establish a cell."

"I can see where they would be very hesitant in their selection of a location."

"The aliens don't want to destroy us. They want to live in harmony on the earth with such bountiful natural resources. Their big concern is that we humans may force them to destroy us. Can you imagine the panic in the world if we humans realized that an alien society was already living among us? Imagine the hostility that would also be occurring. Humans would probably start attacking the aliens. Trust me; the aliens will fight if they have to. With their advanced technology, they would easily win. Our nuclear bombs are dwarfed in size compared to their destructive forces. They have weapons of nuclear destruction, but their weapons are of nuclear fission in nature. Remember, they travel through space light years in just a few days. We can't even get out of our own solar system."

"Yeah. You are right about these guys. They could take us down any time they wanted. Thank goodness they are a peaceful society."

"Now you see why they want to remain secretive with respect to humans in general. You and I are caught in the middle since we are part of their experimental research regarding merging their cells with ours and the use of the nanobots in our bloodstream."

We finally came to the small gravel road that led into the woods where the cave entrance was located. There were still 2 military guards standing by the roadside at the edge of the woods. As far as I could tell, the military guards didn't even know what they were guarding because all this was so top secret.

As we drove on into the woods, I asked, "Dr. Spear, how were you chosen to be part of this experiment?"

"I had a close friend that was a 5-star General in the military that was heading this secretive program. He offered me the opportunity to be a part of this program. They want well-educated people for this program. He told me that I could possibly live an extra hundred years with all these extra powers that you and I have. He also told me that he trusted me to keep my mouth shut and be quiet about everything. He said that if I became a part of this alien blood-merging experiment, and I panicked and started talking, I would be eliminated. He let me know that there would be no place that I could hide. When we took the shots, a small number of the nanobots were programmed to send out a tiny signal to the aliens. They know our whereabouts at all times."

Spear added, "You being a part of this Phil was a chance happening. You just happened to be there when Anokmar's brother crashed the spacecraft. When you showed compassion to his brother as he was dying, and then you received the shot of alien blood along with nanobots, Anokmar made the decision to take a chance on you hoping you would be secretive. You were secretive thank goodness because of your fear of our own scientists and our government. That was a legitimate reason. If you or I fell into the wrong hands, all hell could break loose."

We finally came to the cave opening that was set in an elevated area of limestone rocks. Above the rocks was a thick patch of forest and brush hiding the landing and departure area above the cave. As we came into the cave area again, it was warmer than the average temperature of caves around this region. The aliens must be somewhat warm-blooded. That explains the reason that I feel chilled or cold as compared to the average person. Anokmar met up with us quickly and acted as if he was glad to see us. He bellowed out some strange sounds. They sounded like someone possibly choking. Then the interpreter box deciphered the sounds into English.

"Welcome back." Anokmar stated. "Glad to see the both of you again. Both of you are so important to our research regarding our experiment."

I replied, "Thank you Anokmar; I am glad to be back here to visit with you. Also, I am so sorry about the loss of your brother." Had to wait 3-4 seconds for the interpreter box to start making strange sounds so Anokmar could understand what I was saying.

Anokmar stated, "Thank you, Phil. I appreciate everything you tried to do for Elingock before he died. How can I help you this evening?"

I began asking, "I have several questions to ask you. First of all, I feel lucky that things turned out for me, and I also feel lucky to be part of this experiment. You don't have to worry; my lips are buttoned tight. However, I have to ask, what should I say to my girlfriend? We have become very close and maybe someday marry."

Anokmar answered, "You are not going to change physically much more than you already have, but you will still have those extra powers that you need to keep hidden as much as possible to avoid suspicion. Your DNA has changed some because of the nanobots and our blood being inside you. You are most likely going to age much less than those around you. Someday, you and your mate may have children. If you do, some of your DNA will be transferred to them. They may not have the intensity of the extra powers, but their abilities will definitely be beyond most humans. So, some of those abilities will be transferred to your offspring. That may be the proper time to tell your mate everything that has happened. You will need to swear her to secrecy because her safety along with her offspring could be in jeopardy. Animals will do amazing things to protect their young. Humans are just another form of animal. For your offspring to have an extended lifetime, they will need a shot of the nanobots. Maybe your mate may want to be part of our program. It would be nice to have an entire family involved for us to observe. What would really be interesting to us is what would happen if your mate had the shot of our blood and the nanobots before gestation? We think the nanobots and the alien blood would be transferred to the fetus through her bloodstream. We think that their powers would be as strong as your powers because your mate would also have these powers. Their physical appearance would be like your physical appearance which makes it easy for you to blend in with everyone else. The nanobots are programmed to change certain DNA but the changes avoid having major physical changes like our beautiful scaly skin. We have already observed this in another family living in the Amazon rainforest and another family of aborigines in the Australian Outback."

I answered, "That sounds great, but I don't want my spouse beating me up all the time."

Anokmar made some strange sounds again and it was interpreted by the box as laughing sounds. He began again, "I think it would be Ok to tell her everything if, deep down in your heart you know that she will keep quiet. Just keep in mind that we will be watching very closely. Give me a couple of days to decide if I give you the OK to tell her."

"You have given me a lot to think about." Dr. Spear stood watching intently saying nothing.

"Anokmar said, "If she gets the blood and nanobots shot, she will become more intelligent, have extra strength, sense of smell will be much stronger, hearing will be enhanced 10-fold, her vision will be greatly enhanced, especially night vision. The nanobots will give her a much longer life span because they repair damaged cells and replace old cells with new ones. She will be just like you. Will she be willing to keep those abilities secretive?"

Dr. Spear spoke, "I think Anokmar has laid this situation on the line for you, Phil. You have a lot to think about. Give Anokmar some time to decide. Don't hesitate to talk to me or Anokmar if you need to do so."

I thanked Anokmar by us grabbing each other's right arms grasping just below the elbows. It was their way of greeting and departing. As I started to walk toward the cave entrance door, I watched a large, elongated spaceship; I assumed it was one of their spaceships, center itself in the center of the large platform in the center of the cavern. The platform holding the vehicle began rising toward the roof while the metallic roof began to split and pull back on both sides of the cavern. I could see stars and even the moon was positioned to be observed as the roof continued to pull back exposing the platform and the craft. I went outside while Dr. Spear and Anokmar were still talking among themselves. I heard a hissing noise and watched the spaceship lift up above the cavern, then watched it disappear into the darkness of the sky extremely fast. Within 1-2 seconds, it had to have been traveling 1,000 miles per hour to have disappeared so fast.

After witnessing that event, I told myself, "We definitely don't want to piss these guys off."

Just after the lift-off, Dr. Spear came out and we got into our car to leave the sight. The military didn't stare at Dr. Spear as we were leaving, but they sure were staring me down.

On the way back to Spear's house where I had left my car, I asked Dr. Spear, "Put yourself in my shoes; you have this beautiful girl that is in love with you. You are in love with her and would like to spend the rest of your life with her. Would you tell her about your changes?"

"That is a tough one because remember, if you tell her about yourself, you may also be putting her life in danger if she decides to talk."

"Does your wife know about you?"

"Yes, she does. I took that chance and stressed how important it was to keep it secretive. Later on, after a couple of years, she finally decided to get the shot of alien blood and the nanobots herself. We got Anokmar's approval. Our kids had already been born before I became a part of the program."

"So, neither your son nor daughter has special abilities."

Suddenly, while driving down the country road, a deer ran out in front of us. Spear swerved and barely missed the deer. After he got the car straightened up he acknowledged, "You're correct about my kids. That deer was a close call. I need to slow down. The deer are thick out here. I'm sorry when I get to talking, I tend to speed up driving."

"Have you kept everything secret from your children?"

"Yes, we have. They know nothing and will never know anything. I might add that this is hard to do, to keep secrets from the ones you love so dearly. It is also difficult not making them a part of this program knowing that there is a chance they could have the opportunity to live another 100+ years."

"What is going to happen in the future when they get older while noticing that you and your wife's aging is barely happening?"

"You are asking good questions, and I currently don't have an answer for that yet. I have been giving that circumstance a lot of thought because it is most likely going to happen. You are going to be faced with the same situation regarding your mother and especially your sister.

You will also be faced with Krystin getting older while she watches you stay youthful."

"Man, that is a tough one to think about."

"We will also most likely have to move from the community and establish in a new place and have fake ID's after 30-40 years. Everyone around you will notice your slow aging. But the CIA will help us with all that."

"You are insinuating that we will have to give up our family and old friends never to see them again and move to another place and establish new friends in a new location."

"You are exactly right. Unless something drastic happens to us, we may have to repeat this 2-3 times in our lifetime. Anokmar has a lot of evidence that we may easily live 200 years or maybe more."

"Think about this Dr. Spear; I'm not sure that I want to live that long. That's enough time that history may become very ugly. We may witness a drastic global warming of the earth. We may even witness the earth become like the planet Venus with a runaway greenhouse effect."

"On the opposite side of that, we need to think positive. Along with the aliens' help, maybe the earth will be saved."

"What about the possibility of a third world war?"

"If that happens, the aliens will take over and turn the countries involved into total rubble. There will be no winners. Everyone would have lost the battle. This is what would happen in a worldwide nuclear war anyway. The only difference is the earth may be saved from all the radiation that would have occurred, killing off several more millions of people along with the millions killed during the world war. Either way, millions of innocent lives would be lost."

"You are right. We need to be positive. Currently for me, life has never been better. I really should be thankful that Anokmar decided not to eliminate me that night of his brother's death."

"Showing compassion saved you from death. Thanks to Anokmar, you have been given a new outlook on life with all kinds of advantages over other people your age." Spear looked at me with a raised eyebrow, "You have to feel good about that."

"You got that right, I do."

I asked Dr. Spear to turn on the overhead light in the car and looked at my watch. It was after 11 pm.

"It is approaching midnight. It is later than I thought."

"We'll be back home shortly." Said Spear while giving a big yawn.

As soon as his yawn ended, I continued with another question. "Do you think Anokmar would agree to let Krystin be a part of this program?"

"They don't want a lot of people involved yet; they want to see how things go during the next 50-60 years. He still may be Ok with it because they don't have that many couples or pairs that could give offspring. This is a relatively new area for the aliens. I would get his Ok first."

"Would you be willing to help me get his, Ok?

"I have a direct line to him through an interpreter box. I will ask him for you. I think you would be a good candidate to have a spouse in the program. Give me a couple of days to contact him."

"I don't want to be aging slowly while I watch Krystin grow old in front of my very eyes. I will wait for your answer before I break the news to Krystin.... That is if I get to break the news to her. Has your wife visited the site?"

"No, Anokmar doesn't want anyone to be aware of the site and know that the CIA is part of everything."

"I understand. How can I convince her all this is real."

"If we get Anokmar's Ok, tell her every detail of what happened that October night. Swear her to secrecy. Then just do a few of your tricks while she watches. But do this with just you and her. Jump up on a 10-foot tree limb or something. Run at your normal speed instead of human speed. She should get the message."

"Yeah! That's the way I need to do this providing Anokmar's Approval."

"Don't forget Phil to tell her how important it is to keep secret about this. She is to tell no one. Tell her that her life and your life could be at stake. If she gets the shots, she needs to be secretive about her powers also. Use them only in an emergency and try to mask them as much as possible."

"You had me convinced a while back about being secretive after my visit to the alien cell site."

"Krystin probably doesn't need to know about the alien cell site. I would not tell her about that, and I would say that Anokmar will not want you tell her about the site. I won't say anything to her until I hear from you and Anokmar. It would just be difficult to explain how our offspring could do these special feats to Krystin. I would also be afraid that she may take them to see some specialist and he may detect the alien blood. Then the research would begin except it wouldn't be the CIA; it would be the public medical facilities."

Spear added, "This brings up another point Phil for you to think about."

"What do you mean?"

"Until they mature enough to understand their situation, you will need to home-bound them in education. Most states including Indiana doesn't allow that to happen. There are private schools, most of them are Catholic, but you would still have the same problem mixing your offspring in with other students. This is a situation where the CIA would help you to achieve this without too much notice from the general public. This is like the old cliché -- a catch 22."

"What is meant by Catch—22?"

"You probably haven't read the novel by Joseph Heller (Catch—22) written in 1961, four years ago. It is a satire on war and bureaucracy. The phrase itself has generally been adopted as meaning-- a paradoxical situation from which an individual cannot escape because of contradictory rules or limitations. This is the sort of situation you may be in if you have offspring. In this case, it may work out better if Krystin was part of this program."

"I see what you are meaning Dr. Spear. It is similar to a no-win scenario."

"That is one way to think about it, Phil. **Having young offspring and teaching them to be secretive about their powers can be a problematic situation.**"

Just then, Dr. Spear's driveway and my car were visible in the headlights as he turned into his drive and slowly approached his house. As we both got out of the car, I said, "I will wait on your reply regarding Krystin."

I got into the mean green machine, started it up and headed home. It is early December, and the nights are getting cold now. By the time I got home, I could tell that clouds were rolling in because I could not see any stars as I walked to the house. The more involved I get in this program; the more complicated things seem to become. Other than that, I am thankful to be alive. The Lord must have been with me when Anokmar's brother wanted me to live. Otherwise, as the mafia often says, I would have been whacked.

CHAPTER 11
KRYSTIN HEARS THE TRUTH ABOUT THE INCIDENT

MONDAY

The alarm clock goes off as the radio blasts out a song by a band that played instrumental guitar songs; The Ventures were playing one of their hits – (Walk, Don't Run). The music was loud, but it helped me to wake up. Even though it's morning, it is still dark outside. This time of year, it is not daylight until I am walking into school. Just as soon as the instrumental finished on the radio, the local radio station began a news alert announcing school closures within the region. The weatherman on the radio stated that our area had received a 7-inch snowfall overnight. I listened intently to the different schools that would be closed for the day. I hadn't heard our school's name yet. It pisses me off because our Superintendent is always one of the last to call off school for Austiana. Our school does heavy school bussing and other neighboring schools that have several bus routes are the first to cancel school in inclement weather.

While waiting, I went to the back door of the basement and flipped on the outside light. Sure enough, we had powdery snow covering everything and it was still snowing. By the time I walked back to the radio, they had announced that Austiana schools would be closed today. That excited me because it virtually gives me a free day. Just then, our phone rang, and mom picked up the phone to answer.

"Hello!"

"May I speak to Phil Marland?"

"Yes, hang on; I'll get him to answer."

She yells, "Phil, it's for you."

I picked up the basement phone and immediately said, "You can hang up the kitchen phone mom."

As soon as I heard a clicking sound from the other phone hanging up, I muttered softly, "Hello!"

"Phil, this is Dr. Spear."

"How are you Dr. Spear? I didn't expect to be hearing from you so soon."

"I know; I'm as surprised as you are. I received the message this morning that you are waiting for. You have been given the Ok to proceed with the topic that we talked about. Just remember how important it is that she understands the urgency of being secret."

"Thanks Dr. Spear. It seems like it is perfect timing. School has been canceled today because of snow and I have a free day. I am going over to her house today. Hopefully, her parents will be working, and it will be just her and myself."

"That will be good. We have about 9 inches of snow on the ground here. We are about 20 miles farther north from Austiana. When you tell her, it has to be just you and her."

"It will be. Thanks again for calling; I really appreciate it."

"You are welcome. Good luck, and I hope this goes well for you. Goodbye."

As soon as he hung up his phone, I hung up quickly only to pick it back up to dial Krystin. It seemed like it was taking forever to connect with these rotary phones.

Finally, I heard, "Hello, Adkins residence."

"Krystin?"

"Yeah, I'm here."

"Would it be Ok if I came over this morning since school is called off?"

"I would like that, but I have some of the cheerleaders coming over later today, this afternoon."

"That would be Ok. I won't be too long. I have something important to tell you."

"Is everything Ok?"

"Yes, everything is fine with you and me. I have something else I need to talk to you about."

"Now you have me worried."

"Don't worry; I do enough of that for the both of us."

I heard a chuckle transmit through the phone. Krystin replied, "How about 10 am this morning?"

"That is perfect. It will see you then."

I quickly do the 3 S's – (Shit, Shower, and Shave) and head upstairs to grab a quick bite to eat. I poured a bowl of cereal and as I was eating, I told mom, "There is no school today because of the snow."

"I didn't think there would be. Unfortunately, I am not so lucky. I still have to get to work. What are you going to do today?"

"I just talked to Krystin, and we are going to spend the morning together. I should be home by early afternoon. Does Janet know about no school today?"

"I haven't awakened her yet. I will tell her before I leave for work. She will be thrilled and will probably sleep in."

"Mom, make her at least do something around the house. Have her clean something. She is lazy."

"Aw hush. Just maybe I should have you do the laundry or something."

After that correlation, I knew I needed to shut up. I finished my cereal and began heading back down into the basement. It was only a few minutes after 8. I have to dress warmer down in the basement because the temperature is about 7-8 degrees cooler than the rest of the house. Having the alien blood magnifies the problem. I tend to be cold-natured now. I typically wear a sweatshirt down here in the basement. However, I like it down here because of privacy. I laid down on the old torn couch and turned the radio back on, listening to WINN rock station and Wolf Man Jack until about 9:30 am.

At 9:30, I headed upstairs. Janet had just woken up and was in the kitchen fixing her some toast and jelly. I said, "I'm going to Krystin's house to do some extra studying."

Janet replied, "Yeah! I bet you two are going to study. I bet you two will be studying Biology."

"Quit being such a smart ass, you little twerp."

I put my heavy coat on and went out to get into the mean green machine. It was going to take a little longer because of the heavy snowfall. They do not snow plow these country roads. Usually, a few cars have gone down the road and have left some easy tracks to follow. Even though Krystin only lives about 3 miles from my house, it will still be slow driving. I don't have the best tires on this car either so good traction is a little tricky. After about 15 minutes, I arrive and pull into the driveway of Krystin's house. I only had tennis shoes on, so my feet and socks were going to likely get damp walking up to the door. I knocked on the door and she answered the door.

"Come in Phil; I am always happy to see you."

As soon as I entered the house, she gave me a firm hug and a long kiss. I returned another long kiss to her while hugging her firmly. Her body felt so good to me; I immediately started to get an erection. I noticed that she had their nice fireplace burning in their living room. She was not looking too sexy with sweatshirt and grey sweatpants on, but I'm sure she was comfortable.

I asked, "Could we sit by the fireplace so I could dry my socks and shoes."

"Sure, let's put a couple of couch cushions on the floor to sit on."

"Did you carry in the wood for the fireplace?"

"No, Dad carried in the wood. But I could have done it. He knows I like it when the fireplace is going. He knew I would be off today. He is just too good to me."

"If I had a daughter such as you, I would treat her like a princess."

"What did you want to tell me? I am still worried."

"Please! Don't be. What I have to tell you is extremely important and must be kept a total secret. You cannot tell anyone, not even your parents."

"Phil, what did you do?"

"I did not purposefully do anything. I just happened to be in the wrong place at the right time, or right place at the wrong time. I'm not sure which expression fits the best."

"I'm listening."

"Ok, this is going to take a while. Here it goes. Do you remember the night of the party a few days before Halloween at Jacob's house?"

"Yes, I do. That was our first dance."

"Yeah! I was so nervous that night around you I could not think straight. Well, when I was going home, I was traveling down the road toward my house when I saw this big fireball crash in this corn field just as I was passing by."

"Yes, the meteorite."

"It was not a meteorite. It was an alien spacecraft that crashed."

"Phil, they had government officials and scientists there at that crash site. They concluded it was a meteorite."

"I know Krystin, but the whole thing was a government-CIA cover-up."

"If this is true, how do you know?"

"I thought it was a plane crash and I went into the wreckage to help someone that may have been hurt but still alive. Much of the debris was still burning."

"You risked your life to do that?"

"I know; it was a spontaneous response. I know that I probably shouldn't have done it, but I felt that need to help if I could."

"So, you went into the crash with debris still burning?"

"Yes, I did. Hold my hand while I tell you the rest of this story because what happened next was amazing. Swear to me that you will never ever tell anyone about this, especially some of your gossiping cheerleader friends. Swear to me on your honor."

"I swear I will say nothing."

"Once I got into the now smoldering craft, a few places were still burning but it was mostly thick smoke. I had a light that was attached to a headband in my car and had brought it with me. I had the light strapped around my head. There were misshapen metal pieces all in front of me with bars and metal tubes crisscrossing in front of me so moving farther into the craft was slow. All the metal was still hot to the touch. Breathing the unusual greyish smoke was getting to me."

"Phil, I am having a hard time believing this but continue."

I looked her directly in the eyes while I threw my hands up into the air, "Krystin, why would I lie to you? What I am telling you is the absolute truth. Please understand, and secrecy is necessary because my life and yours after I tell you is at stake."

"What, our lives are at stake?"

"As long as you say nothing to anyone, we will both be Ok. You will understand after I have finished telling you the rest of my story. Anyhow I am not lying to you."

"Now you have my curiosity up, Phil."

"Back to my story, or let me rephrase that, my true story. I was looking at some of the pieces of metal and noticed an unusual, strange writing on the metal. Nothing even close to writing in English. I first thought it was a plane from another country that had crashed. But nothing looked like the fuselage of a plane. This all looked totally different. Suddenly I heard a moaning sound behind a partially collapsed wall. I pulled back the wall away from the moaning sound I had heard. I looked around and there it was, an alien that had the appearance of a giant lizard with a human-like scaly head. He extended his hand out to me as he looked at me in agony. He had a metal pipe that had penetrated all the way through his right side. He was bleeding badly. His blood was similar to ours except it was a deeper reddish-bluish color.

I took off my jacket and put it around the back of his head. Then I held his hand. Somehow I knew he was dying. Then he grabbed my wrist and squeezed tighter. I tried to pull away, but he was too strong. Then he took his other hand and had a syringe in it with a large needle sticking out. The alien lunged his other hand toward me with the syringe and stabbed me in the right leg."

"Oh Phil, why did he do that?"

"It hurt like hell at the time. I finally broke his grip. It almost felt as though once he stabbed me with that syringe, his grip let go."

"What did you do then?" Krystin asked.

"I backed up a safe distance from him. My thigh was throbbing. Then I saw him reach for some sort of device that was near him."

"What kind of device?"

"I wasn't sure at the time, but I saw several odd, shaped lights come on and off, flashing red, blue, orange, green, etc. Suddenly I saw the lights gradually begin to go off. He took his hand and waved toward me and appeared to have put some type of smile on his face. I think he was waving to me to leave and get out. I quickly assumed the little flashing box was some type of detonating device. He waved his hand in a faster motion toward me. I think he was telling me to get out and hurry. My thigh was still throbbing. I crawled away from him and finally got on my feet and began running out of the crash. Once I got outside,

I kept running toward my car which was still about 800+ feet from me."

"Did you make it back to the car?"

"No; while still trying to get back to the car, I heard this loud high pitch hissing sound. Next came a deep muffled sound and I was thrown to the ground by a shock wave of the atmosphere. I saw corn stubble and branches go flying past me toward the crash site while I was being pulled back toward the site myself. Dirt was getting into my hair, eyes, and even my mouth. Suddenly, the pulling stopped and there was total silence. I looked toward the site while still laying in the trench the spacecraft had made. I saw a plume of white smoke roll up into the air."

"Were you still in pain?"

"Yes, it was excruciating. I started praying to God that whatever that alien put into my body that wouldn't hurt or change me."

"Oh Phil, that had to be a scary moment for you."

"You got that right. I was so fearful that I would turn into one of those ugly things if I didn't die first. When I finally made it to the car and drove home, I was so afraid to tell mom or anyone else so I just went home and quickly got into bed. After I pulled my pants off, I turned on my basement light to see the damage on my thigh."

"How bad was it, Phil?"

"I could tell I had a big bruise where the syringe went in, but I also saw bulges of my skin raising up and down and appearing to move. I hadn't stopped crying since I had gotten into the car and was still crying after arriving home.

I was afraid to tell anyone. First of all, no one would believe me. Secondly, if someone believed me and our CIA found out that I had encountered an alien, I figured my life here would be over. They would have me in some secret lab prying and probing me for the rest of my life."

"Oh mercy, I never thought about what the CIA may do to you. Phil, you poor soul. What happened next?"

"I prayed and cried myself to sleep, hoping that God would let me wake up in the morning and still be Phillip Marland."

"Well, it looks as if your wish came true."

"Not entirely. When I woke up the next morning, I reluctantly creeped to the bathroom to look at myself in the bathroom mirror. I was dreading this because I was so afraid that I would see me with leathery scaly skin beginning to grow along with me changing other body features. To my surprise, I looked the same except I was a couple of inches taller."

"You know Phil; I noticed you at school that morning; you seemed to me to be a little taller and a little more muscular. What else happened?"

"What I didn't know is that my senses were changing fast. I could see much better. I could hear someone talking that may be 50 feet away from me. My sense of smell was better. I also felt great other than the thigh being a little sore. I looked down at my thigh and the bruising had healed overnight. I found out later, after a couple of days that I was becoming much stronger and very fast at running and other physical activities. Once I found out the news that they concluded it was a meteorite, I thought this is the perfect setup for me not to let the CIA find out."

"Phil, I have to stop you here. That is a neat story. You should author a book someday, but I think you had a bad dream."

I threw up my hands in frustration and said, "Was me fighting Ray in my dream? If so, you were in the dream also because you saw it happen. You knew me before all this happened; I was a school nerd that was being picked on by the bullies."

"You told me that you had been working out. Obviously, that changed your physique, which I like very much. You got strong enough to defend yourself and me, just like the other night after the movies with those three thugs."

"I lied; I was not lifting weights and all that other stuff. My body was changing because of that shot. After a few days, I found out much more about the shot."

"What did you find out?"

"I am not saying another word until I can convince you that I am not lying to you. Let us go out in your backyard. Maybe I can show you something that will convince you."

My socks were dry, and my feet were toasty by now. I put my shoes on and we went out into her backyard. I noticed that she had a good size backyard that was fenced in. She also had a nice back porch where her father had his fireplace wood stacked. The end of the yard was about 200 ft. in length, surrounded by a chain link fence.

I looked around the yard then asked, "How long do you think it will take me to run out and touch the fence and get back here on your back porch?"

"At least 15 seconds. Dad said that Bob Hayes in last year's Olympics 100-meter dash was 10.06 seconds which was a world record. A hundred meters is about 320 feet. Going out to that fence and back is longer than 320 feet. Are any of your neighbor's home? I can't let anyone else see this."

"No, they all work."

"Hold my watch, and when the second-hand gets on the 12, say go. Remember, I am running in 7 inches of snow."

Krystin raised her hand and said, "Get ready, set, ... go."

"I took off running at my top speed, hit the fence and ran back to the porch."

When I jumped on the porch, her eyes were wide open with her jaw dropped, "Phil, that only took you 4 seconds. That was amazing."

Then I ran out to a big oak tree standing in her yard. The lowest limb was about 8 feet up from the ground. The next limb up was about 12 feet off the ground. I jumped up and planted my feet on the limb that was about 12 feet off the ground. I walked back to the porch. Her eyes were still wide open while she was shaking her head as if motioning – no, you didn't do that.

"How did you do that?"

"Have you seen any human do anything like you just saw?"

"No. You have made a believer out of me. Let's get inside."

I didn't know at the time that one of her neighbors was home and was sort of a busybody. Krystin's neighbor heard us talking and she was looking out her kitchen window. She saw everything.

As soon as we were inside, Krystin added, "Phil, I looked up and all I saw was a blur with the snow tracks from your feet extending away from me like a fast line in the snow being drawn. What was in that shot?"

"It is a combination of their alien blood and some microscopic robots that they call nanobots. It is my understanding that the alien blood cells are larger and can hold more oxygen. Along with that, the blood cells are changing certain DNA, especially those that are related to the senses and strength for muscles."

"Wow! Do you have more to tell me?"

"Lots more. Remember Krystin, you say nothing about this to anyone. I got the opportunity to visit an alien hideout not too far from here. That is why people around here keep saying they are seeing strange lights. When I visited the site with a special Doctor friend of mine, who is also like me. He has alien blood and nanobots in him. I talked to the head alien by using a special interpreter box that they had built; it just so happened that the alien that died at the crash was his brother. He told me that his brother gave me the shot because he wanted me to live and have advantages over others. He did that because I showed compassion to him while he was dying. This alien cell or hideout was watching all this happen.

The head alien whose name is Anokmar, said that most likely, I would have been killed that night along with everything in the crash imploding into cinders. Since I showed his brother compassion, He decided to let me live. The CIA is in on all this. That secret site is heavily guarded by the CIA. No one can get close without special permission. The aliens are doing research, and this is all a project put on by the aliens. They chose special intelligent people to be a part of this project in which my doctor friend had been chosen. Not only can we live longer, but once our blood gets thoroughly mixed, they can draw some of our blood and the aliens live longer. They average about 100 years, but they can also live 200+ years. The aliens have a stake in this too. So, I wasn't chosen for this project. That is what I meant by saying I was at the wrong place at the right time or the right place at the wrong time. Had I not shown care and compassion for the dying alien. You wouldn't be talking to now."

"Where is this hideout?"

"I can't tell you right now, but maybe someday you will get to visit."

"I want to tell mom and dad so much about all this."

"No! No! Krystin, you can't. You and I will be eliminated…. killed. You have to trust me on this. If you say anything, we will both be history. I wouldn't have told you except I am planning on spending the rest of my life with you. One thing the nanobots does is extend our life expectancy. Today, life expectancy is about 70 years, longer than that for women but shorter than that for men. With that shot, which I have had a 2nd shot now, my life expectancy will be nearly 200 years. I just didn't want to marry you and watch you grow old much faster than me. I couldn't bear to see that happen. I want us to grow old together, which 150 – 200 years would be nice for us to be together that long, especially if we are keeping our health. I love you too much to give you up."

"Wow Phil, I don't know what to say. After watching you perform those miraculous stunts, I have to believe you."

During my fight with Ray, I punched him 3 times and no one saw it except Aaron. Everyone just saw Ray fall backwards."

"How did Aaron see you hit him? Is he half alien?"

"No, he didn't see me hit him that day, but he was filming it with his super 8 mm camera. He noticed my arms were in a blur on 1 frame of the film. He called me and had me come over to his house that night. The super 8 mm cameras shoot 18 frames/second. So basically, I hit Ray 3 times in 1/18 of a second. He knew I had to hit him because he saw the big goose egg on Ray's forehead. His curiosity overcame him. He watched the film frame by frame during the fight later that night. Luckily, I talked him into cutting out that part of the film and splicing the rest back. He gave it to me. He can't put his finger on things, but he knows I am different. However, he likes the idea of me protecting him and his friends from those other assholes. I don't think he would say anything. If he did, he couldn't prove it. Anyhow, him and I are tight with each other."

"Was that the day that you and Ray had become friends?"

"Yes, coach Bartlett saw me play basketball that morning in P.E. class. When my senses get heightened, it is like watching everyone else in slow motion. Same thing on the basketball floor. I was playing against Stan and Dan, the next best basketball players on the team behind Ray. During the scrimmage, I was careful not to be too noticeable with my abilities. I just jumped a little higher and was a little quicker, was stronger, and Bartlett watched me virtually pick them apart during the scrimmage. Coach called me over afterwards and talked me into going out for the team.

After the fight, Bartlett came into the principal's office because of Ray. Boy, did he ever ream out Ray. He scorned him for running around with those losers. He told Ray that those losers couldn't help him. He told him directly that me and my friends were the ones he needed to hang with, and he would have a lot better chance of getting a basketball scholarship. To make a long story short, Ray and I shook hands and we have been friends since that day."

Krystin interjected, "So that is why we beat Scottsville so bad. It is because of you."

"Yes, for the most part. We are going to win a lot of games this year. This brings up another topic to think about."

"What do you mean?"

"My doctor friend warned me about drawing too much attention to myself. He told me not to be the best player on the team. He told me to be 2nd best or even 3rd best, but not the best. I can use my extra abilities, but I have to do it very carefully. When we start winning ball games, we will eventually start having TV cameras on us. I can't ever do in public what I showed you today. I already have a newspaper reporter on to me regarding my abilities. He told me that when I missed shots, I was trying to miss. When I made a bad pass, I was purposefully making the bad pass. That is why I never outscore Ray. I only make points if we need them. When we play a weak team, I will probably get a few points if I know that Ray and the others can win the game easily. Something else has happened also that you would be thrilled about."

"What might that be?"

"Notice how my grades have shot up dramatically. I'm almost a 4.0 student. Your intelligence increases phenomenally. I can read much faster and remember almost everything I read. Now you would like that."

"Oh, I know I would."

"Your cheerleading skills will be superior. However, again you would not want to be the best and most acrobatic on the team even though you know you could do it."

"I think I could do what you are doing and mask my abilities from everyone else."

"There is one drawback to all this. My doctor friend told me that because of me aging much slower, I would have to move and just disappear from my current life. I'm not looking forward to that, especially with my sister. If you choose to do this, you will be in the same situation. With our parents up somewhat up in age, maybe we could get 30 years with them. Sooner or later, we would just have to disappear, move to another town with a different identity."

"How could we do that?"

"The CIA will help us do that because we would be part of this very secret alien-human project."

"Phil, I have a tough decision to make whether to do this or not. There are certainly several positive advantages to doing so, but there are some other values that, in time, I would have to give up."

"Yes, I'm in the same boat as one would say. The difference is that you have a choice; I didn't. I was a victim of circumstance."

"Yeah, you were. I know one thing Phil; I have grown to love you dearly. The heaviest thing on my mind is being with you and watching myself gradually grow old at a much faster pace and having to give up my parents before their time on earth is done. In this case, I'm glad I don't have any brothers or sisters. I have a couple of aunts, but I don't see them often. I need a couple of days to process all this in my mind."

"Ok. Please! For God's sake, don't say anything to anyone, especially your parents."

WEDNESDAY

Tuesday went by fast with nothing major happening as I eagerly waited for Krystin's response. The school day went normal, and basketball practice went well. The other boys are getting used to my quick, snappy passes.

The next day began, and as soon as I picked Krystin up for school. We were traveling down the country road toward town in my mean green machine. Krystin asked me to stop the car. I pulled off on the side of the road. She looked up and down the road and noticed no one coming. It was just breaking daylight on this cool November morning.

She remarked, "Show me your strength one more time."

I said, "Get out of the car and stand by the car."

I began walking away from the car approximately 200 feet. I turned and spoke loud enough so she could hear me, "Cover your mouth and say something just slightly above a whisper. Don't tell me what you said."

Krystin covered her mouth and spoke very softly saying, "We need to get to school, or we will be tardy."

After a few seconds, I began walking back to her and responded, "This is the comment you made. "We need to get to school, or we will be tardy."

"Phil, that is amazing; I was just barely above a whisper."

Then I stood in front of the car and reached under the middle of the front bumper; I lifted the entire front end of the car up into the air while the car was resting on its rear wheels.

I remarked, "That is it. I'm not showing you any more stunts. You have seen enough. Let's get to school."

As soon as we were in the car, Krystin affirmed, "I want the shots. I want to spend the rest of my life with you, and I want us to be together for that 200+ years."

I responded, "I just want you to understand that this move creates other problems for us such as having to pull up roots and disappear, how we are going to raise our children while they have those special powers."

"I understand, Phil. I want us to deal with these problems together."

"Ok, I'll contact Dr. Spear who is also like me regarding the alien blood and the nanobots. He is my main contact. I'll call him this evening and we will get instructions on what to do. Krystin, I'm glad that you decided to do this. These nanobots are effective in preventing one from getting cancer. I don't think I could live with myself in the future if you had developed cancer all over this beautiful body and I knew that the cancer could likely have been prevented."

Later that night, I called Dr. Spear. I told him that Krystin wanted to be a part of the project and we wanted to do this together. While talking to him, Dr. Spear cautioned using that deep magnificent voice, "Have you made her aware that while alleviating herself of several everyday problems, she will be taking on an entirely new array of new problems."

"Yes sir, we are both aware and we both hope to have you and Anokmar as our mentors. We will be heading off to college next fall. We will hopefully go to the same university."

"I would be honored to be your and Krystin's mentor. In fact, I think it will be important for both of you to stay in close contact with me. I can't speak for Anokmar. He is a busy alien, but I feel certain that he would be in favor. They just about have the numbers of humans want for this project and they will not want any more. As you get more experience with your conditions, the better you will be able to handle things. I will contact Anokmar and get his OK. You should be hearing from me in about a day or two."

"Thank you, Dr. Spear. You have already been such a blessing to me. How can I repay you?"

"The both of you, just k-e-e-p quiet. If you don't hear from me in a couple of evenings, call me.

"Is about 10 pm a good time to call?"

"Yes, this is a good time."

"Ok. Keep those grades up. Bye for now."

"Bye, Dr. Spear."

I hung up the phone and began thinking about the adjustments that were ahead for Krystin and myself for the rest of the school year.

THURSDAY NIGHT AROUND 10 PM

I had been going over to Krystin's house almost every night. I told Krystin that I needed to be home by around

9:30 until we got the important phone call. Luckily, I received the call I had been waiting for the next night. The phone rings, I yell upstairs from the basement, "I got it. I've been expecting a call."

As I pick up the phone and answer with a soft voice, "Hello!"

"Phil, this is Spear here. I talked to Anokmar; it took some convincing, but he is on board with this. Could you and Krystin be at my office Saturday night at 7 pm? I know you have a game tomorrow night."

"We will be there. In fact, it will be perfect. We will both tell our parents that we are going out to eat and then to the movie theater in town."

"Good. I want to observe her for a couple of hours to make sure she doesn't have any serious reactions. That has happened on a few rare occasions."

"Do you think she could have a problem?"

"No. It is more precautionary. The chances are probably less than 1 out of a thousand. It is extremely rare. In this area, no one has had any reactions. Don't alarm yourself."

"See you Saturday night at 7 pm. Thanks again Dr. Spear."

"You are welcome, Phil. I can see us becoming good friends for a very long time. You know what I mean by a very long time. See you Saturday night."

Just as soon as I hung up, I dialed Krystin.

Her phone rang and she sounded eager, "Hello! This is Krystin."

I responded, "This is Phil, and everything is a go. We need to have an excuse to be together Saturday night. We are to meet Dr. Spear at 7 pm, so we will need to tell our parents that we are going out to eat and then to the movie theater in town. I will pick you up about 6 pm. It is about a ½ hour drive to get to Jasperville."

"Ok. I'll tell my parents that you are picking me up at 6 pm."

"He probably would have liked to meet with us on Friday, but he knew we had a basketball game and did not want to draw attention by you missing your cheerleading and me missing playing basketball at the same time. This should work perfect."

"I am glad you got the call, Phil. Looks like we have a busy weekend."

"Yeah! I'll see you tomorrow morning, you sexy thang.

The Friday school day went well. We won our basketball game Friday night by 28 points. Ray, Stan, Dan, and Nick all played well. I didn't score very often. I only got 11 points. I did look out in the crowd and saw Mr. Watson, the Indianapolis Daily News sportswriter. I felt as though it was good timing for him to observe me. I knew that he was watching me more than anyone else. I did make some great passes but didn't shoot as much, didn't get many rebounds either except for when the ball just landed in my hands. Some of the boys on my team, after the game told me that we could have beaten them by 40 points if I had taken a few more shots. I reminded them that we had won with ease.

All my teammates want to defeat every team by a large margin. I only want to win by just a few points. I don't have the luxury of telling them that our team could win nearly every night by 35-40 points if I wanted that to happen. So, most of the time I only stand out more if we are playing a good team and I need to score more points to get the victory.

After the game, we had another sock-hop dance. Krystin and I enjoyed dancing together, especially the slow dance songs when I had the opportunity to embrace her beautiful body.

SATURDAY EVENING WITH A VISIT TO DR. SPEAR

Krystin and I had told our parents that we were going out to eat and go to the movies. Instead, we would be on our way to see Dr. Spear. I picked Krystin up at her house and we were on our way to Jasperville. The drive took about 30 minutes.

I pulled into his driveway, and we proceeded to his front door. Krystin moaned, "I am very nervous, Phil."

"You have a right to be; you are about to change your entire life. However, we have a friend in Dr. Spear. He is just a super nice guy, and he will help give us direction."

"I hope you are right."

"He has been extremely helpful to me. Doing this with you will make this all worthwhile."

We walked up to the front porch, which was neatly painted white. The temperature was hovering around 40 degrees F. and I could see my breath fog up from the warm air from my body condensing as it mixed with the colder air. I rang the doorbell. Dr. Spear must have been waiting for us because he opened the door within a few seconds.

Dr. Spear said, "Please come in."

We walked into his house and I added, "Thank you Dr. Spear; I would like you to meet my girlfriend. This is Krystin Adkins."

Spear reached out his hand toward Krystin to give a friendly handshake, "It is a pleasure to meet you, Krystin. I have heard so much about you from Phil."

Krystin stated, "It is a pleasure to meet you Dr. Spear. Phil had been telling me how thankful he was to have met you."

I chimed in, "Dr. Spear, tell Krystin how old you are."

"I'm 67 years old."

"Can you believe that Krystin, he doesn't look a day over thirty."

"Phil is right Dr. Spear. I am amazed." Krystin replied.

Spear suggested, "Come into my office where we can discuss things in detail."

We all three entered his office and after entering, he closed the door."

Spear began his speech to Krystin, "I am assuming that Phil has told you everything that has happened regarding his alien encounter and all."

"Yes, he has," said Krystin.

"Since you have agreed to become part of this project, I want to stress to you that everything he has told you is true and has happened. After tonight, you will be entering a world of secrecy. I can't begin to explain to you how important it is to be very secret about this. Both of your lives could be in jeopardy if you decide to talk to the wrong people. I'm sure that Phil has told you that the general public is who you need to be aware of. The CIA will be your friend. Most of the CIA members don't even know about the aliens. They just do what they are told to do."

"Phil has made me aware of how important it is to keep quiet."

"Good." Replied Spear. "So, you are ready to take the plunge, pardon the pun."

Krystin nodded yes. Dr. Spear went into a special room that was locked and nearly hidden to retrieve the syringe. When he returned, he said, "Hold Phil's hand because this is more painful than your typical shot."

Krystin reached for my hand and began to squeeze it.

"You will be sore for a day or two but then you will see the soreness disappear quickly once the nanobots and the oxygen-rich blood take over. Other scratches and scrapes will heal up quickly for you. You will appreciate that."

Krystin affirmed, "I hope so Dr. Spear. I still can't believe that you are 67 years old."

As Spear began to give her the shot, she squeezed my hand tighter. I heard her mumble a long moan as the needle penetrated her thigh.

Spear remarked to her, "Don't be alarmed if you see the slight bulging of your skin and the bulge appears to be moving around slightly. That is just the nanobots beginning to enter your bloodstream and spread out through your body."

After a few minutes, she acknowledged that it wasn't hurting as bad now. We hung around and talked with Spear for another hour.

During that time, I asked, "Dr. Spear do you think that there would be a chance for Krystin to visit Anokmar?"

"Possibly, in the near future. For now, let's make sure she is Ok with this transfusion."

Krystin asked, "How do the nanobots work regarding our bodies?"

Spear explained, "They are made to repair damaged cells and they even carry a chemical with them that is DNA-rich to even regenerate aging cells. This is especially true regarding all the organs of the body. You will need to get a new shot about every 5 years. Even the nanobots gradually wear out and when they do, they know to go to your large intestine where they are expelled with the rest of the nutrient waste of your body."

I asked, "Are the aliens' body makeup similar to ours such as a heart, bones, lungs, and all?"

Spear added, "Their makeup is similar to ours except for their outer reptile-like skin. As you know Phil, they are taller than us on average. Most of them average about 7 feet tall. They can move very fast when they need to move fast."

Krystin inquired, "Will Phil and I get taller?"

"You may grow 2-3 inches taller but that should be it except for the gill slits that will develop down your shoulder blades. I do want to make you aware Krystin that because of your enhanced hearing, you may hear people who you think are your friends talk about you and sometimes just say nasty things about you. That has happened to me. You just have to let that kind of stuff roll off your back."

I chimed in, "I have experienced that too, Krystin. Your hearing will be greatly enhanced. You will be able to hear your friends whisper down the hallway at school. It will be just like I showed you before we came over here."

Spear added, "After a couple of days, you will know who your real friends are, and you will know the friends that you will no longer want to associate with."

After a few more minutes had passed, Dr. Spear told us that he thought it was safe for Krystin to go home and get a good night's rest.

He concluded, "Your thigh will be sore tomorrow, but you should be feeling much better by tomorrow night. In fact, you may feel the best you have ever been in your life. This shot is a game changer."

We finally left and I took Krystin straight home. I didn't spend much time with her. I told her that I wanted her to get plenty of rest. This stage of our lives together was now set. In a few months when we graduate, Krystin and I will be ready for the college experience.

The rest of the school year went well for both of us. In fact, it was almost perfect. The only drawback was with our basketball team. We made it to the state finals with only 4 teams left that would play in the afternoon. The winners would play for the championship later that night. Our school had never made it to the state finals in basketball. We lost our afternoon game. Ray fouled out early in the 4th quarter. I purposefully committed a couple of fouls to foul out of the game. The team that we were playing was very good, but I knew that the rest of our team without Ray and myself was not going to be able to keep up. It was a good time to lose and get that reporter off my back that had kept watching me closely during the basketball season.

With my grades I received the valedictorian award, and my friend Aaron received the salutatorian award. We both gave speeches at our class graduation. Krystin and I both received academic scholarships for Prudroo University. Ray got a basketball scholarship at a university not too far from Prudroo. I also received a basketball scholarship at Prudroo. This was going to help me tremendously financially. Mom's worries about money regarding me were over.

The rest of the summer was great. I still worked at the grocery store to earn extra spending money for the 1st year of college. This fall, Krystin and I will be attending Prudroo University. I made sure I stayed in close contact with Dr. Spear. Our college years will be another story in our lives.

THE END